Death on Night Train

By Hugh Morrison

MONTPELIER PUBLISHING

© Hugh Morrison 2022, 2024

All rights reserved. No part of this publication may be reproduced, stored in a retrieval system, or transmitted, in any form or by any means without the prior written permission of the publisher, nor be otherwise circulated in any form of binding or cover other than that in which it is published and without a similar condition including this condition being imposed on the subsequent purchaser.

Published in Great Britain by Montpelier Publishing.
Set in Palatino Linotype 10.5 point
Cover image by Miguna Studio
ISBN: 9798848946048

  Follow Montpelier Publishing on Facebook

Chapter One

The old man was running for his life. He had heard the expression many times before, but it was only now that he realised what it actually meant. He was driven by a primal terror, like a hunted animal.

'Running' in his case was perhaps an overstatement; at nearly eighty years of age, the man's movement was a combination of a jog, trot, brisk walk and limp, which was all he could manage even with the aid of the adrenaline coursing its way through his body. The terrain did not help; it was a treacherous mixture of peat bog, gorse, rocks and muddy soil that gave way under his feet with every second step.

He paused momentarily to catch his breath and clutched at his chest; even the fear of imminent death could not overcome his body's need for more oxygen. Tall and slim, with gnarled features and a shock of white hair beneath his tweed cap, the man ordinarily would have appeared in ruddy good health for his age. But now, his face had a gaunt and hollow look, and his body was crooked and sagging under the immense strain put upon it.

Glancing behind him, he saw the first signs of the bruised, purple dawn beyond the ridge of mountains. Light, at last. It would make it easier to get away, as he could move more quickly across the moorland without the risk of catching his foot in a root and breaking his neck.

He smiled grimly. Why should he worry about that when certain death awaited him if he tarried? He swallowed and his stomach lurched with fear as he saw the twinkling lights of battery torches a hundred yards behind him. It was time to move.

He took up again his lurching, limping pace across the heather to where the valley opened up before him and he saw, with a faint hope, what he had come this way to find.

The railway line curved in a large loop around the foot of the mountains ahead, the metal only just starting to reflect the first light of the dawn. He could see the squat shape of the small station with its short platform; a light gleamed in the window. His heart leaped as he saw in the distance a cloud of smoke and a small line of yellow lights from behind its carriage windows – the night train!

Barely able to catch his breath, he clutched at his heart again and renewed his pace. He could hear the yelping of the dog behind him now; it must have caught his scent. There was a chance – a slim chance.

This was almost hopeless, he thought, but if a drowning man clutches at straws, he may also clutch at a cloud of steam and smoke. He could see the train in its entirety now, rattling slowly along the line. He knew from travelling on it himself that this was the time when the stewards would be knocking gently on the doors of the sleeper compartments, with trays of tea and buttered toast for the awakening passengers. Despite his mortal terror his stomach rumbled at the thought. Preposterous notion! He might be dead in a few moments and now was no time to think of food.

If he could make it to the station when the train stopped, he would be safe. There would be people on the train – perhaps even English people – and it would not be possible to prevent him reaching safety. With renewed hope, he increased his limping pace to something approaching a run. Suddenly there was a sharp whistle and a pinging sound followed by a rumbling crash. Splinters of rock from the boulder next to him stung his cheek. They were shooting at him! He hurled himself to the ground for cover, pain searing through every part of his aged body.

Surely, he thought, that would attract attention from the station? No, he realised in despair. In this part of the world nobody would pay any attention to the sound of shots from a pair of men with a dog; shooting was the area's main attraction. The people on the train would not know the quarry on this particular shoot was a man rather than a grouse.

The moor turned dark, as if a light had been turned off, and the man saw that a heavy black cloud had concealed the first light of the morning sun. He took his chance and with the last of his energy, jogged in the direction of the gravel road which led to the station, now just two hundred yards away. He heard another booming explosion and felt his legs give way underneath him, then all went black.

A well-dressed man – too well-dressed, it might be said, for a morning's grouse shooting – surveyed the moorland with his binoculars and turned to the man beside him, also well dressed but with a slightly more rustic appearance.

He was about to fire again on their quarry, but something stopped him. As the sun appeared from behind its thick blanket of cloud again, the blueish dawn light flooded the valley and he saw the night train at the little station decamping its passengers. It was the usual collection of wealthy city folk arriving for the shooting, braying orders at the hapless porter and getting into a large shooting-brake which had pulled up next to the platform. The man could almost make out their voices from here. He raised his rifle and adjusted the weapon's telescopic sight, but his companion stayed him with his arm. It was too risky to fire again, he conceded. Besides, he thought, it may not even be necessary.

He remembered with distaste the area of boggy ground that they had encountered on their arrival at the station, where his immaculate patent-leather boots and dove-grey spats had been ruined. The old man must have tumbled headlong into it, and even if he had not been shot, he would not last long there, someone of his age and condition. He may even simply have dropped dead with exhaustion, he thought with a smile. No need to even waste a bullet.

A brief investigation with the dog, he decided, would confirm his suspicions and the body could be hidden for retrieval later. Even if alive, he could not possibly run any further. If by some miracle he was able to attract attention from the shooting parties, the well-dressed man would use his rehearsed cover story; a doctor in pursuit of an elderly and sadly confused patient.

But for the moment, he decided, they must blend in as best as they could with the shooting parties, now laughing and talking of breakfast and milling around the road by the station. After fifteen minutes or so, the last of the passengers had left, their various vehicles dispersing to the hotels and hunting lodges three miles away on the other side of the valley. The elderly porter, the sole attendant at the little halt, disappeared back into his cosy-looking office where the curtains were drawn, to snooze away the hour or so before the next train arrived.

Following his companion, the well-dressed man trudged back and forth across the boggy land between the railway line and the road. He cursed as he looked down at the filth on his recently cleaned boots.

'He cannot have got away,' said the well-dressed man, with the voice of someone that might have come from anywhere or nowhere. It was an accent that would not have sounded out of place in high-ceilinged apartments on continental boulevards, nor in the skyscraper offices of American financiers, nor perhaps even the houses of newly-enobled baronets in the Home Counties. But it did sound out of place in this ancient, windswept moorland where the only other noises were of distant bird song and the sighing of the wind in the heather.

There was a growl and then a yelp from the dog which had been let off its lead by the other man.

'Has he found something?' asked the well-dressed man.

The companion merely shrugged, and two men picked their way carefully into a circle of large, craggy rocks surrounding a tarry-smelling bog, infested with weeds and midges despite summer having long since departed.

The dog barked again, and the companion pointed to the bog. Floating on the top of the brown, peaty liquid were a man's tweed cap and one filthy shoe, which as they watched, sank slowly into the oozing darkness.

The dark haired woman with features that might be described as 'handsome' or 'well-preserved' looked at the little piece of paper in front of her.

'What on earth does it mean?' enquired the woman –

Marion Shaw – as she looked at the recently delivered telegram. It sat on the silver tray that the maid, Hettie, had brought in to the breakfast room after the Post Office boy had been sent away on his bicycle with no tip and an admonition not to be so flirtatious at the door of a vicarage.

'Read it again to me, my dear,' said the Reverend Lucian Shaw, incumbent of the adjacent All Saint's Church, and shepherd of the little flock inhabiting the village of Lower Addenham, Suffolk. His iron-grey hair and aquiline features, similar to that of his better-known clerical contemporary Dean Inge of St Paul's Cathedral, were illuminated softly by the morning light streaming through the sash windows of the little Georgian house.

Mrs Shaw held the telegram at a legible distance and read out its contents once more. '"Uncle James gravely ill stop. Come at once stop."' Is it some sort of joke?'

'My dear,' said Shaw, dabbing the last of his breakfast crumbs away from his mouth with his napkin, 'at this moment I think I shall utilise Occam's Razor.'

'But you've already shaved this morning,' said his wife in a puzzled voice.

Shaw chuckled. 'I am sure you really know to what I refer,' he said.

'Not really. Something theological, I should imagine.' His wife tossed the remains of a sausage from her plate to Fraser, their little West Highland Terrier, who jumped at the morsel from his basket in the corner of the room.

'The writer William of Ockham,' explained Shaw, 'stated that when faced with competing hypotheses one should choose that with the fewest assumptions. In this case, the assumption ought to be that the telegram is genuine.'

'It's far too early for philosophising, Lucian,' said Mrs Shaw briskly. 'But why on earth should he be gravely ill?

This is the uncle I'm thinking of, isn't it? Colonel James Shaw, your dear departed father's younger brother. He wrote us that long letter a month or two ago and sounded perfectly hale and hearty.'

'Quite so,' said Shaw. 'But a lot can change in two months. The man must be at least eighty by now, and "The days of our years are three score and ten" as the Psalmist says.'

'Is he really that old?' said Mrs Shaw with a sharp intake of breath. 'I remember him as a sort of late middle aged person in fine fettle. He was the one we stayed with that summer just before the war, wasn't he? When the children were small.'

'Yes, but that was nearly twenty years ago.'

'I suppose so,' said Mrs Shaw wistfully. 'What are you going to do?'

'Do?'

'About the telegram?'

'Go to him, of course.'

'But it's hundreds of miles away.'

'We are not living in the age of Dr Johnson, my dear,' said Shaw. 'Scotland is no longer traversable only by military road. There is a perfectly good train service.'

Shaw stood up and crossed to the sideboard where the copy of Bradshaw's train timetable was kept. He leafed through the pages and then stabbed his finger at a line of print.

'The *Flying Caledonian* leaves King's Cross this evening at 19.25 and will arrive in Inverness tomorrow morning. I recall that there is a halt before the terminus – Inver-something else, ah yes, here it is, Inverbrodie – which is not too far from Uncle James' house. If I leave shortly I shall be able to join the train in London this evening without too much difficulty.'

'All the way to London?' said Mrs Shaw. 'Doesn't it stop anywhere in the Midlands, so that you can cut across?'

'Hmm,' mused Shaw, running his finger along the page of the timetable. 'It does stop at Peterborough, but that means I will have to change at Norwich and then Cambridge. It will be quicker to go into London and out again, I fear.'

'It's an awfully long journey Lucian,' said his wife. 'And think of the cost. It's a sleeper train and will cost a fortune, assuming you can even get a berth.'

'"Store ye not up treasure on earth,"' quoted Shaw. 'What is money for if not to help others? Uncle James has nobody else – he never married so has no children.'

'Didn't he have a brother?' asked Mrs Shaw. 'I'm sure you mentioned another uncle at some stage.'

'Uncle George, yes,' said Shaw, 'but he died out in India some years ago if you recall, just before he was to retire. His son is Cousin Bertram, also in the Indian Civil Service. He writes to me from time to time from New Delhi.'

'Oh yes, of course,' sighed Mrs Shaw. 'Well *he's* not likely to come, is he? Oh dear, I suppose needs must. But oughtn't you to at least telephone first? What if he's got better?'

'I think it highly unlikely that Uncle James is on the telephone,' said Shaw, 'or even that it would be possible to put a trunk call through to him if he were. I shall investigate.'

Shaw disappeared into the hallway and after a few minutes conversation on the telephone, he returned. 'It is as I expected,' he said. 'The operator says there is no subscriber of the name of Colonel James Shaw in Inverbrodie.'

Mrs Shaw sighed again. 'I shall get Hettie to help pack your things. How long will you be?'

'It does rather depend, my dear,' said Shaw. 'If it is as grave as the telegram implies, then a couple of days at most. It is Monday today so I shall have plenty of time before I need to return for Sunday's service. I can work on my sermon on the train just as easily as in my study.'

'What about morning and evening prayer, and your parish visiting?' asked his wife.

'I have no urgent visiting now that poor Mrs Smy has departed, may she rest in peace,' replied Shaw briskly, 'and Mrs Dixon, despite her monumental proportions, is not expecting for at least a fortnight I am told, so no churching nor baptism will be required this week. Laithwaite can attend to the other duties.'

'Poor Mr Laithwaite,' said Mrs Shaw. 'You do rather treat your curate like the hired hand, you know.'

'Nonsense, my dear,' chided Shaw. 'Laithwaite was saying only the other day he wished for more responsibility. I do not believe I have called on him to assist in my absence at short notice since…since that unpleasant business* a year or two ago.'

Mrs Shaw shivered slightly at her husband's allusion. 'Let's not talk about that, dear. I'll get your things ready. If we hurry you can make the ten o'clock train to Ipswich.'

By early afternoon Shaw had arrived in London. He realised he had quite some time before the night train left, and as the train from Suffolk pulled slowly into Liverpool Street Station he felt a little guilty. Should he have taken a cross country route, changing several times at obscure

*See *A Third Class Murder*.

junctions in order to arrive in Scotland sooner? After all, he was needed at the bedside of a dying relative.

No, he decided. A dash by branch lines would only have shortened his journey by an hour or two, and might have risked all sorts of delays. The London to Inverness service he knew was fast, reliable and modern and would enable him to get a good night's sleep into the bargain.

Shaw stopped at the booking office to purchase a ticket for the Inverness night train, and then descended into the bowels of the London Underground, through echoing tiled passageways smelling faintly of Jeyes' Fluid, and took a tube train to Piccadilly Circus. From there he walked via a back street to his club, feeling something of a country bumpkin in his heavy tweeds and with his old army rucksack on his back.

The Clerical and Medical Club, on the outermost fringes of what could legitimately be called Clubland, was really a glorified Victorian townhouse catering for clergyman and doctors without the necessary influence (or financial means) to join the Athenaeum. Shaw occasionally stayed here on the rare occasions he was required at formal events at Church House.

He had a simple, rather stodgy luncheon, pleasantly surprised at the recognition he received from the elderly waiter, and then settled down in a heavily worn leather armchair in the sepulchral gloom of the smoking room where fires, announced a small notice by the chimney piece, were not customarily lit until after six pm.

He took out his pipe, a rustic briar chosen to fit in more with the Highlands of Scotland than a London drawing-room, filled it with Three Nuns tobacco and sat back to puff on it reflectively. He then took out Uncle James' letter from his waistcoat pocket.

He had found the missive after some searching in his

desk just before he left the vicarage, and had brought it with him partly to serve as a form of introduction should there be any obstructive doctors, or hired nurses and the like at Uncle James' bedside. He had had sufficient experience of visiting the sick to know that was a distinct possibility.

He had also brought it to see if there had been any mention of illness or infirmity that he should have known about. It was a long letter, containing quite a lot of local details of activities on Uncle James' land and much mention of his favourite hobby, bird watching.

There was nothing to suggest he was suffering from any kind of malady. But then, thought Shaw, Uncle James had never been the type to complain about, or even mention, illness. He was a quiet, self-contained man who, after a long career in the army, had retired to Scotland for the peace, solitude and low property prices.

Shaw tried to remember the last time they had met; he realised it had been almost a year ago. It had been a reunion of a few members of his old school at Rules' restaurant, and having found out that his uncle had intended to be in London on some sort of business, he extended the invitation to him also. Uncle James had attended the school many years earlier and so was a little left out, there being none of his contemporaries there, but he was still able to regale the company with amusing stories of the school in the eighteen-sixties.

Shaw sighed, and replaced the letter in his pocket, then looked at his watch. He disliked trying to kill time, and decided that Choral Evensong at Westminster Abbey, followed by a lengthy walk through London's parks, would see him through nicely to the time of his train's departure.

Harry Moffat glanced around the concourse at King's Cross station furtively, and turned up the collar of his grubby raincoat, partly to keep out the damp autumn chill and partly as a form of disguise. A smallish, dark-haired man with a nondescript, clean-shaven face and anonymous, slightly shabby clothing, he nonetheless felt conspicuous.

He wished he had a scarf to help conceal his features, but he had not brought one with him when he had come from Inverness. He assumed that it would be warmer in London, but it was not. If anything it was colder, or at least the fog and the damp seemed more penetrating somehow, mixed with the smoke from a million coal fires which hung listlessly in the air above the grimy streets.

He looked at a little shop on the concourse which displayed scarves, gloves and the like but baulked at the price tickets: ten shillings for a scarf, and that was only artificial silk! No thank you, he thought; it was not something he could claim on expenses anyway.

He tutted again at the price tags; London was an awfully dear place, he reflected. The English just did not seem to have any care of what they spent, tossing down florins and half-crowns on the bars of public houses as if they were mere farthings and ha'pennies.

Not that he spent much time in such places; he did not approve of that sort of thing, except in moderation, and anyway, strong drink was something else he could not claim on expenses. A barmaid in one public house had laughed in his face when he had asked for a receipt for his half of bitter, people had stared, and since then he had given up the idea of trying to claim the money back from his client.

His client…Moffat suddenly came out of his fiscal reverie and glanced around again nervously. There was somebody following him, he was sure of it. A tall man, or at least one above average height, in a well-cut overcoat with a white silk scarf, appeared in the corner of his vision by a newspaper kiosk, but when he turned to look, the man was gone.

He swallowed nervously. Out of my depth, he thought to himself. This was supposed to be a straightforward case. A lot of nonsense, really; he was only doing it to humour the client who seemed to think everyone was out to get him, but he was willing to pay handsomely. After some enquiries in London, however, Moffat had started to wonder if the man might have a point after all. If what he had found out was true, it could mean…

He took a deep breath. Don't be silly Harry, he thought to himself. This isn't one of those detective stories or the talking pictures. There must be thousands of men above average height in London, wearing well-cut overcoats and white silk scarves. And thousands of private investigators making thousands of enquiries into thousands of cases. As if anyone should notice this one in particular! Just because they had sent him away with a flea in his ear did not mean they wanted to hurt him.

To be on the safe side, however, he decided to warn his employer. A telephone call would be next to impossible so he dropped into the late-opening post office on the concourse and sent a brief telegram (he shuddered at the cost) asking his employer to meet him at Inverbrodie station the next morning. That way he could break the news of what he had found right away before…before anything could happen.

He had remembered his training from his time as a corporal with the military police in British Mandatory Palestine after the war. How to tail suspects in the maze-like alleys of Jerusalem without being spotted, and how to shake off anyone trying to do the same to him.

It was unlikely anyone could have tailed him with all the dodging and back-tracking he had done across the two cities of London and Westminster that afternoon. He was probably just letting his imagination run away with him. Was the telegram too much? Well, he thought, as he stepped back on to the concourse, it was done now.

Moffat looked at his wrist-watch and realised it was nearly time to board his train. He began walking towards the relevant platform, and then frowned as he thought he saw the flash of a white silk scarf under a blackened brick archway at the barrier of the same platform, fifty yards ahead.

There was a piercing whistle and a roar of escaping steam as a nearby train departed, and the archway was covered momentarily by clouds of vapour illuminated by a dim electric light. When he looked again, the clouds had cleared but there was nobody there.

Chapter Two

Shaw had not travelled by sleeper train for some years and had forgotten just how cosy and comfortable they were. He felt a twinge of guilt at the expense of going first class, but at least this meant he would have an undisturbed night; in third class he would have to share a compartment.

A short, stout steward whose spherical torso in its white jacket had the appearance of a large billiard ball, showed him to his compartment amid the bustle and noise that surrounds the imminent departure of any major train service.

'Here's your temporary abode, sir,' said the steward, in 'posh-cockney' tones, as he slid open the door.

After some hesitation Shaw sidled into the confined space; the steward, despite his proportions, did not seem to have any difficulty entering. The compartment consisted of two tiny rooms, with a sliding door between them; on one side was a sitting room with two armchairs and a basin; on the other, a tiny bedroom with a single bed.

'Bed's not made up yet but I'll be in later to put on the sheets and blankets,' said the steward. 'This here's the washbasin.' He lifted the top of a small table to reveal a little sink and tap, like something made for a child to play with, complete with some tiny bars of green soap.

He replaced the lid and then pointed to a small switch

by the door. 'This here's the light and this is the electronical buzzer, if you needs anything just press that and I'll come, assumin' I'm not attendin' to some other gentleman at the time. Shower compartment and lavatory at the end of the carriage. Oh and by the way, my name's Loake. Like the shoe-makers. No relation, s'far as I know.'

'How do you do, Mr Loake?' said the cleric. 'My name is Shaw, Reverend Shaw.'

The steward raised a finger. 'Pleased to meet yer, but no mister required with me sir, it's just Loake. Even to the wife. Always has been and I daresay always will be.'

'Quite so,' said Shaw. 'You mentioned "beds",' he continued, as he placed his rucksack under the seats. 'Am I to assume I will be sharing the compartment?'

'Bless me no sir, you're in first class. You'd only have to share with another gentleman if you was in third class. And it would be another *gentleman*, mark you, not a lady; we don't go in for that sort of thing in our sleepers unlike in some countries I could mention, so they tell me. No, you won't be disturbed, though the dining car might be a bit busy, as we've got a lot going up for the shooting this week. Although I'm assumin' you're not a sportin' gent, sir?'

'Not often,' replied Shaw.

'On church business in Inverness, then, I suppose?' probed Loake. 'Only I thought the 'ighland brigade didn't hold with us on matters of religion.'

'A family visit,' said Shaw, 'and I shall be alighting at Inverbrodie, not Inverness.'

'Right-oh, sir. Glad you mentioned it, as I'll give you an earlier knock. She doesn't stop for long at that little place so you'll needs be ready to jump off by seven or so.'

'Thank you,' said Shaw. 'You must have a long night of work.'

'Oh, that don't bother me sir,' said Loake, grinning as he plumped up the cushions on the seats and flicked imaginary dust from the little curtains by the window. 'There's six of us at home, the better half and her ma plus the three kiddies – and another on the way. All in a little Peabody Buildin's flat. It's far more quiet and comfy for me on here!'

There was the shrill sound of a whistle and the noise of banging doors outside on the platform. Loake straightened himself up, as far as that was possible for a man of such globular stature, and moved to the door.

'Bless me sir, here's me rattlin' on about the happy home when I've got other gentlemen and ladies to attend to. We're off in a couple of minutes so I'll say cheer-oh for now. First service in the dining car's at eight pm.'

'Thank you,' said Shaw. He fumbled in his pocket for a coin.

'Oh no thank you sir,' said Loake, 'that won't be required...just yet. You can leave me something when you get orf, if you like.' He looked around furtively and lowered his voice. 'But a word to the wise, if you can't find me, put it in the washbasin out of sight. No offence intended, but some of them passengers of the Scotch persuasion sees a shilling...or even 'alf a crown, p'raps... and then "do those things which they ought not to have done", if you know what I mean. Which as a man of the clorth I'm sure you do.'

Loake wobbled out of the compartment and slid the door shut. Shaw smiled and shook his head. The man reminded him of his old Cambridge bedder – he had forgotten the fellow's name now – or Craddock, the batman that had served him and the other chaplains at the front during the war. Always fussing around with a constant stream of chatter. Harmless really, thought Shaw, but he wondered how those men with their own valets put up with it. How did they have peace enough to think? Perhaps they did not, he reflected, glad it was a problem he was unlikely ever to have to contend with.

He sat down on the seat nearest the window. There was a clanking of metal bumpers and a lurch, and then with a hiss of steam the train began to slide out of the station past soot-blackened brick walls into the autumnal London night.

The Reverend Callum McKechnie of Inverbrodie parish church was worried. Perhaps worried was not the right word, as it was not really one in his lexicon; 'concerned' might be more accurate.

He finished cleaning and oiling his hunting rifle and replaced it next to his shotgun in the steel gun cabinet in the corner of his study.

A somewhat intimidating-looking man with a rugby prop's physique and a bristling red moustache, he paused to poke the logs in the little fireplace into life again. He then crossed to the window and gazed out into the last of the gloaming.

From the leaded windows of the little manse, he saw the final embers of the autumnal sunset behind the Benmurie Braes to the west, the brooding range of hills which circled the valley of Inverbrodie. Then they blinked out, and all was dark.

He sighed and drew the curtains, crossing to an ancient wooden cabinet from which he took a bottle of whisky produced by a still so small and local that it bore only a handwritten label, and poured himself a glass.

He drank reflectively, and mulled over the events of the day in the few moments he knew he had to himself before his wife, Jean, would come in to announce supper.

He had trained as a minister rather late in life. After something of a dissolute youth as a private soldier in the peacetime army, his had been one of the first regiments to cross to France as part of the British Expeditionary Force in 1914.

He had felt at his most alive in those heady few weeks when entire divisions had advanced at dizzying speeds across Flanders, and cavalry with fluttering standards and gleaming sabres had galloped across golden fields in the late summer haze, as if it were all some elaborate medieval pageant.

Then had come the winter, and the war had ground to a muddy stalemate. As he rose through the ranks to that of warrant officer, he gained a reputation for fearlessness, leading regular raiding parties into enemy trenches, but even that was not enough to prevent disillusionment setting in.

By 1917 when he received a battlefield commission and led his company 'over the top' for the first time, all enthusiasm for the war had gone. It was then that he was hit by a shell blast and trodden into the ground by hundreds of kilted Scotsmen who had not realised he had been partially buried by the explosion.

By some miracle he had survived, temporarily blinded but managing to breath and drink rainwater through a crack in the mud, and after three days, the rain had softened the soil enough for him to dig himself out (the Christian symbolism was not lost on him), by which time most of his company were dead.

Lying there in the darkness and the mud he had had, he now realised, something of a religious conversion; he was convinced it was the Lord's doing and also He who had sent the nurse, later his wife, that looked after him behind the lines for months afterwards, talking to him softly and reasonably about faith in a way he had never heard anyone speak before.

By the time he had sufficiently recovered from his injuries and regained his sight, the war was over, and he had lost any lingering appetite for soldiering. Instead, he married Jean and threw himself into religious studies. Within a few years, he had been ordained in the Church of Scotland and was now minister to the handful of folk who attended his little grey church in the centre of Inverbrodie.

Most stayed away; like many Scottish towns the churches had split over the centuries through numerous schisms and there were at least four other churches and chapels in the local area, all with their own dwindling congregations.

Some of the nearby gentry disliked McKechnie for his humble social origins ('jumped up NCO' as one landowner called him) and his brusque refusal to cow-tow to social niceties; some of the more dogmatic locals disliked him because of what they called his 'worldly ways' which included taking a glass of beer from time to time in the local public house, the Benmurie Inn.

He also loved grouse shooting and deer stalking, and was known to even gamble on horse racing from time to time. In short, he was too common for the gentry and too gentry for the common; the all-too-familiar story of the man promoted beyond his social status.

He shook himself out of his reverie. No sense brooding on the past, he thought. Here he was, and here the Lord had chosen fit to send him, and to have regrets, he always said, was to think oneself a better judge of matters than the Lord Himself.

Back to his concerns. One of the few local people that he got on well with, counted as a friend, almost, was old Colonel Shaw up at Auchentorrin Lodge. The Englishman did not seem to put on the airs and graces of some of the larger landowners, who looked down their noses at everyone and anyway, spent most of their time in Edinburgh or London, nor did he seem to have any of the drab puritanism of some of the villagers.

Being English, he ought to have been more at home in the 'pisky', the Scottish Episcopal Church, closer in doctrine and ritual to the Church of England, but he had told McKechnie that, having no car, he had no easy way to travel the five miles to the nearest branch of that denomination. Instead, McKechnie would have to put up with him if he were willing.

Put up with him he did, although the man only attended services sporadically. Apparently Colonel Shaw had not got on with the previous minister ('dreadful Calvinist bore' was his dry judgement) and had more or less given up going to church, but when they had met by chance in the high street, McKechnie had readily accepted the offer of a glass of beer at the Benmurie Inn and the two men hit it off straight away.

It was not only their military background that they had in common, but the Colonel, a keen bird-watcher, had liked McKechnie's conservative attitude to the shooting, impressed that he only killed birds for his table rather than for sport.

The man was lonely, suspected McKechnie, though he tried not to show it. He wondered why someone who seemed more suited to a villa in Henley-on-Thames should end his days in this rugged, rocky place. He said it was because of the peace and quiet, but McKechnie wondered secretly if it reminded him of South Africa's high veldt; the

Boer War having been the last campaign the Colonel had served in before he retired.

He looked at the crumpled, hastily pencilled note, barely legible, that he had found pushed through his letterbox that morning. 'Send urgent telegram Rev Shaw Lr Addenham Suffolk: Uncle James gravely ill come at once.'

McKechnie sighed deeply as he looked back on the events of the day. He had found the note when he had come down in the morning, and had immediately dressed, jumped into his little Austin Seven and hurtled along the unmade road to Auchentorrin Lodge.

Colonel Shaw's squat, tumble-down house, held together largely by ivy and brambles, overlooked around 70 acres of moorland on the side of the low hill which led down to the bottom of the valley. It had cost him very little, he confided in McKechnie with a smile. The house was almost a ruin and the treacherous rocky and boggy ground made it poor land for grouse shooting, especially for parties of wealthy city folk unused to walking in rough terrain. But for simply watching the birds, he added, it was perfect.

Why on earth, thought McKechnie as he brought his little car to a skidding halt on the weedy carriage turn in front of the house, should someone want him to send a telegram, instead of doing it himself?

And why had whoever it was not banged on the door of the manse until he had got an answer? He had not even heard Shaw was ill apart from some old trouble with his leg a while back, and that was hardly likely to put him on his deathbed.

He banged on the door with the rusty knocker, and felt the timbers shake slightly. There was no sound from inside the house. He realised he had never been inside, having only met the Colonel either in church or the pub. He could not recall any mention of servants, and wondered if the man was lying insensible inside with nobody to help him.

He knocked on the door again, harder this time, and the door opened a crack. A woman's face appeared; it was in early middle age and one which bore more than a hint of cosmetics; not quite the face he would have expected for a housekeeper.

'What...do you want?' enquired the woman. Her accent was certainly not of the Highlands, but McKechnie could not quite think what it was. It was not foreign, exactly, but nor was it English.

'I've come to see the Colonel,' said McKechnie. 'I don't believe we've met before. I'm Reverend McKechnie, from the manse. I got a message saying he was very ill.'

'Message?' asked the woman suspiciously. 'What message? Who gave it to you?'

McKechnie was about to describe the note that had been pushed through his door asking him to send a telegram, but something stopped him. Was it all some elaborate practical joke, he suddenly wondered? Some of the local boys were known to practice the sport of ringing the manse's doorbell and running away...was this perhaps a more sophisticated version?

'Aye, well not to mind,' said McKechnie brightly. 'Is the Colonel at home? I'd like a wee word with him.'

'He is not to be disturbed,' said the woman curtly.

'So he *is* ill, then?'

'He is sleeping...and...ill, yes. If there is nothing else...'

The door began to close but McKechnie placed a large, ginger-haired hand against it and impeded its movement.

'You'll be kind enough to tell him I called, Mrs...?'

'He is not to be disturbed.'

McKechnie stepped back from the door as it slammed shut. He knocked again, but this time no answer came. He got into his car and drove out onto the road, then stopped a little way further along the valley from where he could see the house, its windows reflecting the grey clouds in the sky above.

He watched as a man in a homburg hat and a heavy overcoat, dressed more for the city than the country, appeared from over the brow of the hill and walked towards the house. He was leading a dog, which he locked in an outhouse, and then without pausing to knock, he let himself in through the back door of the house.

Who was he? A relative of the Colonel, he assumed, though it seemed odd to be out shooting if his host was lying in bed, perhaps seriously ill. McKechnie drummed his fingers on the little car's steering wheel and paused for a moment in thought. What to do?

He had realised, in that dark time trapped underground in the war, that physical and mental struggle over a problem usually achieved very little. The answer was always to be still, and wait for the light. 'Be still, and know that I am God,' he had said to himself under his breath, then he had driven rapidly to the post office to send the telegram.

He was brought back to the present moment by his wife entering the room.

'Supper time, Callum,' she said brightly, then stopped short. 'A penny for your thoughts. You're looking awfully broody. Is it about Colonel Shaw?'

'Aye,' said McKechnie, as he got up from his chair. 'Perhaps I should have tried to telephone his nephew again before I got them to send that telegram.'

'But they said at the post office it could take hours to put a trunk call through that far,' replied his wife. 'And just think of the cost. You told me yourself. If the poor Colonel really is taken badly, his nephew will want to come quickly, probably by the night train. You were right to send the telegram. Better safe than sorry. He'll maybe be on his way even now.'

'Aye, but if I've brought him on a fool's errand, I'll regret it,' said McKechnie, shaking his head. 'And if the Colonel really hasn't got long, I'd like to see him. Both as his minister, and his friend.'

'You said his nephew's a minister – a vicar, I suppose they call him – so you'll not need to worry about your pastoral duty when he comes. And that housekeeper, whoever she is, will hardly be able to turn away the Colonel's kinfolk.'

'Och, you're right as always, Jeanie,' said McKechnie, realising he had a considerable amount of visiting to do that week with other members of his congregation. It would not be right for him to practice favouritism and spend too much time on just one of them.

'I'll look out for this nephew,' he continued, 'and I'll call again in a day or so.'

'That's right dear,' said Mrs McKechnie. 'Let's trust the Good Lord will not take the poor man any earlier than He has to.'

'Amen,' replied her husband. 'And let's hope also that housekeeper lets me in next time.'

The *Flying Caledonian* began to pick up speed as it finally broke free of the gravitational pull of London, past wide, empty arterial roads and half-built housing estates. Soon it was racing through the desolate Hertfordshire farmlands, sparks flying from its cab as the fireman hurled another shovel-load of coal into the fire-box. Its whistle gave a long, piercing shriek as it raced across a lonely level crossing, where the small headlamp of a solitary bicycle glimmered, its rider waiting patiently for the enormous, deafening train to roar past.

Inside the train, Moffat checked the lock on his compartment door again, glad that the chattering steward had finally left him in peace. He winced when he thought of the extra cost of travelling first class instead of third, but he was anxious not to be disturbed.

He yawned. It had been a tiring day, and it was only nervous energy that was now keeping him awake. It felt as if he had tramped across half of London, calling at various records offices and other institutions to find what he was looking for. He knew, from asking an old military police contact now working as a fraud investigator for a bank, that something was rum about this firm he had been asked to look into. 'Due diligence', he had once heard an American client call it. In the end he had found out what he needed to know – or at least, most of it – by chance.

He had actually called at the head office of the firm again; he had tried before on a previous occasion but had been given the bum's rush by the stocky commissionaire who manned the door. This time, he waited until the fellow went on his lunch break and marched in, bold as brass, asking to see the director. The man who had sent the 'cease and desist' letter to him previously, containing all sorts of veiled threats which had served only to make Moffat more determined not to give up.

The man's secretary, who dropped her nail-file in surprise at this unexpected intrusion, demanded that he leave the building, and when he refused, she stalked off in search of assistance.

Moffat had seized the opportunity and glanced quickly at some papers on her desk, and his heart skipped a beat as he saw a letter lying on a sheet of carbon on top of a folder headed 'letters for signature'. He grabbed it and stuffed it into his pocket, then turned to go. Just as he left, the door to an inner office opened and he fancied he saw someone catch sight of him, but he could not be sure. He had walked calmly out of the office just as the secretary and the commissionaire appeared in the lobby.

'Sorry to have troubled you,' he called gaily. 'Wrong office!'

There was no reply they could give to that. Seeing a police constable on point duty on the street outside, he thought it prudent to walk calmly and slowly away rather than attract unwanted attention by running or hailing a cab. Had that been a mistake, he wondered? If he *was* being followed, it would have been better for him to have fled in a taxi, and hang the expense.

He took the letter out of his jacket pocket and placed it on the top of the washbasin lid, where he smoothed it out. The letter, on the company's notepaper, read:

> To all concerned parties:
> Reference: sale and development of property.
> All is in place and ready to proceed. Kindly inform all relevant staff to carry out agreed plans.

Nothing out of the ordinary there, thought Moffat, although it was a little vague. Rather too vague, one might think, especially if the letter was to appear as evidence in a court of law. Whoever dictated that knew he ought not to reveal too much. But what had caught his eye were the names typed at the foot of the letter belonging to the persons who would be sent a carbon copy, or 'CC':

CC: Mr Keller, Mr McVitie, Miss Petrescu.

He had a pretty shrewd idea who those people were – at least two of them, anyway, and that was enough to know he had done 'due diligence'. His client needed to be informed of this. He looked at the letter again. He knew who the people named might be, but did 'they' know *he* knew? Did 'they' even know he had taken the letter?

He folded the letter and replaced it in his pocket, then breathed in deeply. He realised he was getting jumpy again. Even if he had been followed, what were they going to do? Demand the letter at gunpoint? He had read it by now, so it did not matter if they wanted it back anyway. They were welcome to it.

He chuckled, and felt his stomach rumble. Realising he had not eaten all day, he decided it would do no harm to pay a visit to the dining car, especially, he thought, as he still had a portion of his daily expenses left to spend.

Somewhere between Stevenage and Peterborough, Shaw entered the dining car, clutching the side of the doorway as the train swayed slightly over a set of points. Another white-coated steward, this one with a cloth over his arm like a *sommelier*, showed him to a little table, one of the few ones left unoccupied.

Despite its diminutive size, the table was complete with a white linen cloth and a small vase of flowers which was fixed in some way to the table through the cloth; a little curved lamp illuminated the setting. He peeped through the closed curtains to see nothing but blackness, broken only by the occasional glimpse of a lighted window in some distant farmhouse.

Shaw perused the dog-eared menu. The choice of fare

was, understandably, somewhat limited considering the surroundings, and he decided on roast beef with two veg. and gravy, with a glass of wine described as 'Empire Burgundy.'

He looked up from the menu to see a smallish man in a shabby raincoat standing in front of him.

'You'll not mind if I sit here?' asked the man. 'The steward said it's the only one free just now.'

'Not at all,' said Shaw. 'It is rather crowded.'

'Aye,' said the man. 'The one that showed me to my room, my compartment, I mean, said the sleeping cars are not awfully crowded the night, but the restaurant's used by the other passengers as well, so he said best get in early.'

The man plonked himself on the chair in front of Shaw and picked up the menu.

'Awfully dear…' he said under his breath as he examined the card, then looked around somewhat furtively.

'Are you sure you don't mind me sitting here?' he asked again.

'As I said, not at all,' replied Shaw. 'I take it by your accent you are going north of the border?'

'Oh yes,' replied the man, and looked furtively around the carriage again. The man seemed nervous. Shaw was used to the occasional approach by strangers on trains or in omnibuses, people who saw his clerical collar and felt the need to unburden themselves to him in some way. He did not object, considering it a part of his vocation, and wondered if the man was going to do something similar. But, he thought, there did only seem to be one seat free in the carriage, so perhaps the man was just being sociable.

'May I take your orders, gents?' said the steward, who hovered next to the table. Shaw smiled slightly at the man's manner, a sort of scaled-down grandeur which matched the attempt of the railway company to produce a scaled-down luxury hotel on wheels.

Shaw gave his order and the man nodded. 'I'll have the same,' he said, then asked 'do you not have any beer? This card here just says "wine list".'

The steward raised an eyebrow. Shaw sensed that the man had made a scaled-down *faux pas,* and had offended the standards of the narrow little restaurant.

'Beers is served only at the bar, sir,' sniffed the steward. 'Two carriages down, standin' only. Apre-teefs, wines and spirits in the dining car. I recommend the orstralian Bordeaux if you've a thirst to quench. Sold by the glarse…or bottle.'

'Aye, well,' replied the man, squinting at the prices. 'How many glasses are in a bottle?'

The steward sighed again and his eyes moved ever so slightly heavenward. 'Happroximately six glasses in a bottle, sir, give or take.'

Shaw saw the Scotsman's lips move imperceptibly, and he fancied the man was working out in his head whether to buy a glass or the whole bottle.

'Shall I come back in a few minutes, sir?' asked the steward. 'Only there *are* other tables to…'

'No need!' exclaimed the man. 'I'll take the whole bottle of the Australian…stuff. For cash.'

The steward sighed for a final time and noted the orders down on his pad.

By the time they had passed Retford, the two men had finished their meal, which Shaw had found decidedly enjoyable; he had always preferred hearty plain English food to anything which resembled *'haute cuisine'*; it reminded him too much of his years in France, away from home in the midst of war. Even the colonial wine was not too bad, he thought, as he drained the last of the glass and lifted the curtain to look out of the window.

It was hard to see much but in the occasional shafts of moonlight he could make out the changing landscape. Somewhere around Newark or Lincoln the scenery, as far as he could make out, had begun to change from the softness of the southern counties with their rolling hayfields and thatched cottages to a more northerly land of tussocky moorlands and stone houses.

It was always difficult to say, he thought, where the south of England ended and the north began; the area known as the Midlands seemed to exist more in the west than the east, and on this side of the country there seemed more of a sudden change. Nottinghamshire, he decided, was really a county of the north rather than the Midlands.

The man in the raincoat opposite revealed little of himself, and the conversation was confined to small talk about the weather and the train journey. Other than finding out that Shaw's compartment was next to his, the man did not much seem interested in Shaw and did not enquire after his business nor destination; in fact he seemed somewhat pre-occupied and as the evening wore on he was looking more and more furtive.

'Well, minister,' he said, after carefully counting out some coins for his bill, 'I'll be saying goodnight.' He rose to go, and Shaw half-rose.

'I wish you *bon voyage*,' said Shaw. 'And a good night. Let us hope we are not shunted about too much.'

'Aye…aye…' said the man, whose gaze seemed distracted by something at the far end of the dining car. Then he turned back to the clergyman and fixed him with a steely, although slightly inebriated gaze.

'You did say C32 was your compartment?' he asked.

Shaw was taken aback slightly by the man's insistent

tone. Did he, he wondered, wish to have some sort of private talk, to unburden himself in a way he was unable to in public? Shaw frowned. The man had drunk most of a bottle of wine and he did not much look forward to an alcohol-fuelled spiritual discussion late at night.

'That is correct,' said Shaw. After some hesitation he added 'You are welcome to knock, if you would like to continue our conversation.'

The train lurched slightly and Shaw deftly caught the half-empty wine glass in front of him before it toppled over. When he looked up, the man had gone.

Moffat staggered slightly as he left the dining car and entered the next carriage, feeling his way along the narrow corridor to his compartment. He knew now that he was not imagining things. He *had* been followed from that office in London.

He had done his best to keep calm when he had spotted the tall man in the white silk scarf at the other end of the dining car.

He knew he must not let on that he had been seen, and had seized the chance to sit next to the minister so that the man watching him should have no reason to approach him.

So far so good. There was only so much one man could do; he could not be watched the whole time. Or so he thought. When he had left the dining car, he had seen the man with the white scarf get up and follow him.

Then, just before he had got to his compartment, he saw another man at the far end of the corridor, idly leaning against the window and puffing on a cigarette, his hat pulled down over his eyes and his mackintosh collar pulled up.

It was the hat that did it. There was nothing unusual about the man's appearance other than a slightly swarthy complexion and a day's worth of stubble on his face, but the hat was of a type one did not often see in the British Isles; it had a fancy braided band and a colourful feather above the ribbon. The sort of hat American gangsters wore in the pictures.

Moffat swallowed. *There were two of them*. He realised they had used an old, but effective trick; they had each taken turns to follow him so that he never noticed the same one person behind him. He cursed himself; he had even used the method himself with another military policeman when following an Arab in Jaffa.

He remembered that hat; he had seen it out of the corner of his eye on the Underground platform, when he had felt someone brush past him just as the train roared in. Had they tried to…? He shuddered at the thought of how far they might go to get what they wanted, and forced himself to stay calm. He made himself appear drunker than he was, staggering theatrically and softening his gaze so that the man at the end of the corridor might not realise he had even seen him.

As he opened the door of his compartment he turned to his right and saw the white-scarved man coming towards him. A pincer movement! He entered the compartment quickly and locked the door behind him. Thank the Lord it could be locked, he thought. He was pretty sure the stewards were the only ones who could open the door from the outside, using a special key.

He breathed deeply and wished he could have another drink. After satisfying himself that his luggage had not been disturbed, he sat down to think. The steward had made up the little bed, and the soft blankets and crisp sheets looked highly inviting. He shook his head as if to rid himself of the thought. Go to sleep now, he thought, and he might never wake up. They might be able to procure a key from somewhere, or even force the lock.

He willed himself to stay awake and a plan began to form in his mind. He practiced a certain manoeuvre on the floor of the tiny compartment, trying to make it look natural; he repeated the movement until he was satisfied. He smiled. He might, he thought, just get the better of them yet.

Chapter Three

The man with the white scarf, who, though he had been known by several names in several countries, at this current juncture answered to the name of Lewin. He smiled as he saw Moffat scuttle into his compartment. Trapped like a rat. The other man, Tench, walked towards him and they had a quiet conversation in the little vestibule by the lavatories at the end of the corridor.

Lewin smiled wolfishly. Moffat had led them a merry dance across London but he was certain he had not been out of their sight the whole time; Tench had even been able to watch him when he went into the post office. He had not sent a letter; a telegram, yes, but how much could he realistically reveal in that?

Once they had seen him boarding the train, he had quickly found a telephone kiosk and left a message with his employer that he, Lewin, would be arriving at Inverbrodie the next morning. There was no way the man could get out of this now.

'Keep an eye on him from this end,' said Lewin, 'and I'll do the same at the other. Make it look natural, as if you've stepped out for a breath of air.' His accent was difficult to place, it had something of the Irish gentry about it, but yet, there was a contrasting hint of something harder to place; an accent suggestive of palm-lined boulevards under a shimmering occidental sun.

'He could be there hours. Think he'll try anything soon?' said Tench, whose vocal inflections were clearly rooted in Glasgow's East End.

'Doncaster's the next stop,' said Lewin. 'I expect that's when he'll make a run for it. So keep sharp.'

'Any chance of a sit-down, Mr Lew…'

He was cut off sharply. 'I told you not to use my name. And no, you may not have a "sit down". You are not to let this man out of your sight, understand?'

'He's already out of my sight.'

'Don't answer me back. You know very well what I mean.'

Tench sighed and lit another Capstan cigarette from the stub of the last one, which he flicked out of the partially open window of the door next to them; the red spark hovered for an instant before it disappeared into the howling black void outside. They returned to their respective posts at the end of the carriage to wait.

They did not have to wait long. As expected, Moffat made his move at Doncaster. It was fortunate, thought Lewin, that nobody was getting on or off the sleeping carriage; as the train hissed to a halt in the arc-lit station there was a fair amount of activity at the farther end of the train where the seated passengers travelled, but at this end it was quiet.

Moffat almost collided with Lewin as he turned round the corner into the vestibule, making for the door. Lewin stepped back and blocked it.

'Terribly sorry,' said Lewin suavely, 'but this door appears to be locked.'

Moffat dodged Lewin and turned back round into the corridor. Lewin watched as the man ran, then appeared to trip, sprawling in front of the door of the compartment next to his own. A moment later he got up and saw Tench at the other end of the corridor; he turned and hobbled back in the direction from which he had come, trying to make for the door into the next carriage. Lewin deftly blocked that exit also.

'I'm afraid that one's out of commission also.'

'Out of my way,' breathed Moffat. 'I'm warning you.'

The detective reached up to pull the communication cord but Lewin expertly caught the man's wrist and twisted his arm behind his back. By this time Tench had blundered along the narrow corridor and grabbed Moffat's other arm.

'Help!' shouted Moffat in a cracked voice, but he was drowned out by the blast of the guard's whistle and the sound of slamming doors.

Lewin forced a gloved hand over Moffat's mouth. 'Get on with it man, before someone comes,' he hissed at Tench, who fumbled with a syringe which he then plunged inexpertly into Moffat's exposed neck. The man's eyes bulged and a few seconds later, he slumped forward, unconscious.

Lewin took out a hip flask from his coat pocket and rapidly sprinkled its contents over Moffat's face and collar. He replaced the flask in his pocket just as the train jerked away from the station. The door from the other carriage opened and two figures entered.

Not a moment too soon, thought Lewin, as he saw the fat steward he had spoken to earlier. He recalled the man's name correctly – Loake. He was struggling with some cases as a haughty looking woman with the air of a wealthy widow followed on behind him.

''Scuse me gents,' said Loake, trying to accommodate his bulk and the cases in the narrow vestibule.

'We'll get out of your way,' said Lewin politely, as he supported Moffat on his arm. His head slumped forward and Lewin felt perspiration break out under his hat-band as he struggled to support the man's dead weight.

'Is he all right, sir?' asked Loake, looking with concern at Moffat.

'Quite all right,' said Lewin with a smile. 'Poor chap's just had a drop too much.'

'Cor, he smells like a blooming distillery,' noted Loake with a look of distaste. 'I saw him in the dining car talking to that parson. Proper toper, he was. Him I mean, not the cleric. The Scotch gets like that, I've noticed. They seems to be either tee-total or slaves to the drink and nothing in-between. Funny that. You never seem to meet a Scotchman who drinks respectable and knows 'ow to 'old it, like an Englishman does. Friend of yours, is he?'

'A business acquaintance,' corrected Lewin. 'We shall get him to his compartment so that you may let this lady through.'

The lady in question looked disdainfully at the three men as she passed by; Lewin awkwardly raised his hat while struggling to hold on to Moffat. Tench just touched the brim of his hat momentarily, and gave the woman a cool appraising glance, turning away when he saw nothing of interest in her appearance.

Lewin and Tench dragged Moffat to his compartment, following closely behind the disdainful lady and Loake as he struggled with her bags. Tench bundled Moffat inside and Lewin called out to the steward before he passed through into the next sleeping carriage.

'This gentleman is going all the way to Inverness. Be a good chap and see he's not disturbed until the last minute, won't you? He won't want breakfast in his condition.'

'Oh I don't know that I can guarantee that sir…' began Loake.

Lewin reached out past the woman to push a ten shilling

note into the steward's top pocket. 'I'm sure you'll find a way, he'll need all the rest he can get. There's a good chap.'

'I'll do my best sir,' he said, taking out the note and beaming at it. He looked up and began to speak, but Lewin stepped quickly into the compartment and slammed the door. He grunted as he pushed Moffat on to the bed.

'I'll search his clothing and you start on his luggage,' he said, *sotto voce.* 'Then we'll both search the compartment as well if we have to.'

After rummaging through Moffat's pockets he stopped and placed two fingers at the man's neck, a look of concern crossing his face. He turned to Tench, who was rifling through the detective's battered suitcase.

'How much did you give him?'

'The whole lot, like I was told,'

'Show me the syringe.'

Tench produced the sinister little glass vial from his pocket and held it gingerly upwards for examination.

'You blasted idiot,' said Lewin. 'You've used the whole lot.'

'You told me to put the whole lot in,' protested Tench.

'I said put the whole lot in the *syringe*, not in *him*! I said depress the plunger half way only, enough to knock him out and do it again if we needed to later.'

'So?'

'So,' hissed Lewin, his voice seething with anger; his hint of a foreign accent stronger now. 'You've killed him, that's what "so"'.

Tench looked down at the motionless form of Moffat and shrugged. Lewin remembered the man already had at least one murder under his belt – as did he – which would explain his nonchalance. But this, he reflected, could cause problems later. And problems were something Lewin could do without.

'What do we do then?' asked Tench. 'Bundle him out the door? Make it look like he did it when he was drunk. Fell out the train, or something.'

'Don't be ridiculous,' said Lewin, who was thinking fast. 'We got away with being seen once, we might not be so lucky next time. No, leave him here. The stuff's supposed to be untraceable. We'll just have to hope when the law finds him they'll think it's natural causes.'

'But what if someone comes in here and finds him? Say that fat party, the one who never stops talking?'

'We'll be long gone by the time the steward comes in here tomorrow. Just find that letter.'

Some time later, the train stopped at York, and the two men slipped out unnoticed onto the dark, almost deserted platform, then disappeared into the back streets of that medieval city. They may have got away with the problem of murder, thought Lewin; it was not even murder but manslaughter, legally speaking, but they had not managed to find the letter, and that was most definitely a problem.

After reciting Evening Prayer to himself from his pocket prayer book, Shaw had visited the little immaculately maintained lavatory at the end of the carriage then returned to his compartment. He undressed, brushed his teeth at the little basin and got into bed. He had not been able to sleep for a while; the surroundings, though comfortable, were unfamiliar and the train seemed to make strange noises when one least expected it.

At Doncaster there had been a loud thud outside his door; someone dropping a case, he assumed; then he had dozed off and awoken again at another station, where there was a clanking of chains and a violent crash as some carriage was either added or taken away from the train.

He thought he heard a low voice from the compartment next door, and wondered for a moment if the man Moffat was talking in his sleep; he listened intently but then could hear nothing more. He pulled the curtain aside and on the dimly lit platform he could just make out a name on a sign: York.

A station with a frontier feeling, Shaw reflected; where the first northern railway had ended in the time of Charles Dickens, and the passengers had had to continue to Scotland by stage coach. It was here the north really started in earnest. The rolling farmland of south Yorkshire, still seemed vaguely southern, unlike the real north of grim, smoky industrial cities separated by endless expanses of bleak moorland.

As the train pulled out of the station he wondered if he could catch a glimpse of the Minster, but all he could see were the monotonous backs of grimy terraced houses, a few dim lights burning here and there.

He replaced the curtain and lay back down in bed. Apart from half-waking as doors slammed at Edinburgh Waverley station, he slept soundly through the night, as the train rushed ever onward to its final northern terminus.

A gentle tapping roused him from his slumber. 'Hettie?' he murmured sleepily, wondering why his domestic servant should be knocking on his door in the middle of the night. Then suddenly he realised where he was. 'Come in,' he said.

He heard movement behind the sliding partition, and the clinking of china and cutlery. 'Good morning sir, it's Loake 'ere,' came a voice.

'Good morning, Loake,' said Shaw, as he became fully

awake and sat up. The curtains were still drawn and the room was dark. 'Where are we?'

'Just parst Aviemore, sir,' called out the steward. 'Then it's Carrbridge and then Inverbrodie's your stop. I've woken you and the other few gents getting orf there first, as the other passengers are all for Inverness. Are you decent sir?'

Shaw could not for a moment work out what the man meant but then realised he was referring to his state of dress.

'Yes, quite so,' he called out. 'You may open the door.'

'Right-oh sir,' called out Loake. 'Oh, you've drorped a letter on the floor. I nearly trod on it. Shall I put it with your things, sir?'

'Letter?' asked Shaw. Then he realised he must have dropped Uncle James' letter the previous night. 'Yes, put it in my rucksack, please,' he called out.

After a moment's pause, Loake pulled the partition back and, with a beaming smile, placed a tray of tea and buttered toast on Shaw's lap.

'Pardon me for not pouring, sir, only I 'as to get on,' he said.

'That is quite all right, thank you. I can manage.'

'Right you are sir. Anything else you need?'

'Would you open the curtains, please?'

'Very good sir.'

The attendant pulled back the curtains and then left Shaw in peace. He would have liked to have knelt in prayer but with the tea tray on his lap it was awkward, so he prayed *in situ* then began eating his breakfast. His jaw dropped slightly when he looked up from his tray to see the majestic Highland mountains rising up in the distance beyond miles of moorland. How different, he thought, the early morning light was here to the foggy dusk of London.

For a moment a dark shape darted alongside the railway line, keeping pace for an instant then falling back. It was a stag! Shaw's heart leaped and he spoke out loud the first line of the Benedicite: 'O all ye works of the Lord, bless ye the Lord, praise him, and magnify him for ever!'

After finishing his breakfast Shaw visited the lavatory again; he considered the shower bath, but time was short and he never much liked shower baths at the best of times; on a moving train the experience, he decided, might be rather unsatisfactory.

He made do with a quick wash and shave in his compartment, marvelling at the ingenuity that had enabled him to travel hundreds of miles with all the comforts of home to hand including hot water and electric lighting to brighten the shadows of the Highland dawn.

As the train pulled into the little halt at Inverbrodie, he concealed a florin under the soap in the little basin, mindful of Loake's warning about light-fingered passengers, and stepped off the train; Loake was nowhere to be seen. He shrugged his rucksack on to his shoulder and strode out past the little station hut where a small group of London shooters were waiting. The train whistled and then in a cloud of steam was gone.

As its noise died away, Shaw gazed around him at the towering mountains and the purple-tinged moorland, breathing in the air that was so clear and sharp that it almost hurt the lungs. He had not been here for 18 years but time seemed to have no meaning in this barren, empty place.

He did not remember the elderly porter who was wheeling trunks out on to the road, but it might well have been the same one who had been here all those years ago. The only thing that reminded him it was 1931 and not 1913 was the sleek, modern shooting brake that pulled up in front of the station to collect the wealthy Londoners who had been disgorged from the train. It had been a horse-drawn wagon before the war, of course; now long gone, he assumed, like so many other relics of that *antebellum* era.

Shaw paused outside the station to get his bearings. As he did so, another car, a large one, possibly a Bentley, thought Shaw, pulled up by the little hut. A man dressed in well-cut tweeds stepped out of the vehicle and hailed the porter.

'Good morning Sir John!' said the porter, touching his cap.

'Good morning Angus,' replied the man heartily in an accent that was pure Etonian.

The conversation was then drowned out by the noise of the shooting brake's engine. Doors slammed and there was good natured shouting from the small party of London shooting gents as they boarded the estate car. Cries of ''Scuse us, padre!' and 'don't spare the horses, James!' went up and Shaw stepped back to let the vehicle pass.

Once it had gone Shaw then heard the tail-end of the conversation between the Bentley driver and the porter.

'Nobody of that description did get off, sir, I dinnae think,' said the railway employee in a thick Highland brogue.

'Ah well, never mind,' said Sir John. 'Thanks anyway Angus. Must dash. Good day to you.'

'And a guid day to you, sir. And the best o' luck in the general election. We've a sair need fer somebody to look efter the working man. I hope you can help us, though I'm still no' convinced you're the right man, all the same.'

'I'd love to stay and convince you,' replied Sir John, 'but I must dash. Keep an eye on the newspapers – in a few days I think you'll be getting all the proof you need of why I'm the man to vote for. Cheerio!'

The man got into the Bentley and Shaw turned away to look at the countryside around him. He remembered it all now; the gravel road leading up the hill towards Uncle James' house a mile or so distant; he fancied he could just make out its roof on the brow of the hill. They had walked here most mornings on their holiday, he and his uncle, while Marion had stayed at the house with their children Henry and Felicity, too young then to walk. How things had changed with *them*, he thought.

A bird – a sparrowhawk, thought Shaw – swooped low in front of him and he recalled his uncle's love of bird-watching. He began to walk up the hill briskly, mindful of the reason for his visit, and hoped he was not too late.

A few moments later he heard the sound of a large, powerful engine and a crunch of gravel as a car slowed down beside him on the road. He turned to see the Bentley, with its driver grinning at him through the open window.

'I say, would you like a lift?' said the man cheerfully. 'I'd feel terrible letting you walk with all the spare room in this old bus.'

Shaw looked at the man. His moonish face was neither young nor old, but bore the unmistakeable signs of wealth and good living. Clean shaven and slightly rotund, with the reddish glow of someone used to outdoor life, but a life of pleasure rather than hardship .

Shaw hesitated slightly; it was not far to his uncle's house and he felt the need of exercise after the confines of the train. Nevertheless he did not wish to reject a kindness and so he climbed into the car and with a crunch of gears they set off.

'She's a beauty, isn't she?' said the man, tapping the steering wheel with a gloved hand.

'Indeed,' said Shaw. 'A Bentley?'

'That's right,' said the man proudly. 'Grafton coupe. Four-and-a-half-litre engine. She'll outrun anything on the road.'

'A most impressive machine,' replied Shaw.

'Can't help noticing strangers in this part of the world,' said the man. 'And a clergyman at that. Which lot are you from? Not a Roman or an Episcopal – not one of their churches anywhere near here. A Covenanter or one of the Free Reformed, perhaps? Don't tell me, let me guess. A Covenanter, I'd say – the Free Reformed don't wear clerical collars. And you can't be an Old Disrupter, because I can see a pipe sticking out of your top pocket, and their lot never touch tobacco.'

Shaw wondered briefly what the man was talking about, and then remembered the numerous schisms in the Scottish churches.

'The Church of England,' he replied simply.

There was another clash of gears and the man struggled slightly with the steering wheel as the car bumped over a badly mended section of road.

'Good Lord,' he said. 'We don't get many of your sort here. On some sort of…what do you call it…ecumenical visit?'

'A family visit,' replied Shaw. 'You seem well informed on the various Scottish denominations.'

'Have to be,' said the man. 'Standing for Parliament. One has to understand all the factions or one's liable to put one's foot in it and that would never do. By the way, my name's Debayle-Bradley. Sir John Debayle-Bradley to give you the full moniker. Bit of a mouthful. At school I was just called Deb. How do you do?'

He extended a leather-gloved hand across the steering wheel, which Shaw shook as he proffered his own name.

'How do you do? Lucian Shaw.'

'Shaw…Shaw…' said Sir John thoughtfully. 'You're not connected to Freddie Shaw at the Bank of England, are you?'

Shaw was familiar with the habit of the British aristocracy – or those aspiring to it – of assuming everyone of the same surname was somehow related.

'Not that I know of,' said Shaw. 'You are a native of these parts, I assume?'

'Oh, I'm from all over the place,' said Sir John, 'but one of the ancestral homes is up the road. Spent most of my life in sunnier climes but since I became a Justice of the Peace I've been spending more time up here and now that I'm standing for Parliament I'll be up here a lot more.'

'I take it,' said Shaw, 'your surname is Franco-Scottish? From the days of the "auld alliance" between France and Scotland?'

Sir John laughed heartily and slapped his hand on the steering wheel. 'Dammit man, that's good! The disguise is working!'

'Disguise?' asked Shaw in confusion.

'The Auld Alliance thing. There's not a drop of French blood in my people. Debayle's a *Swiss* name. That's the maternal line. All very confusing and we have to keep the hyphen due to some law of primogeniture or other which I don't quite understand. But if people think it's an old Franco-Scottish name, so much the better. Tradition's important round here.'

'You are standing for Parliament in the forthcoming General Election?' asked Shaw.

'Yes. Not long to go now.'

'You represent the Conservative interest, I assume?'

Sir John laughed. 'No, Labour! That's caused an outrage at the golf club as you can imagine. Some of those old fossils will never speak to me again. But if you ask me the old party loyalties have had their day. We need actions, not factions. Somebody needs to stand up for the interests of capital *and* labour, and create employment, or the Bolsheviks will be in charge before long.

'The Tories won't do it and the Liberals are a busted flush. And, make no mistake, should I be elected, I intend…oh dash it all, I'm not even elected yet and here's me banging on as if I'm in the House already. Order, order!'

There was silence for a moment and then Shaw saw the squat shape of his uncle's house appear in the distance. 'Thank you for the lift, Sir John,' he said. 'Would you leave me outside that house up ahead, please?'

Sir John looked puzzled. 'But that's the old Colonel's place. I assumed you were going into the village.'

'That is my destination. Auchentorrin Lodge. The owner, Colonel Shaw, is my uncle.'

'Of course!' cried Sir John. 'And there's me banging on about a silly young banker like Freddie Shaw. I'd forgotten there was a Shaw right under my nose. I always just think of him as "the old Colonel". I hope you haven't picked a bad time to visit – only I heard he wasn't well.'

The car stopped outside Auchentorrin Lodge. Shaw picked up his rucksack from between his feet and turned to face Sir John.

'I received a telegram yesterday telling me that my uncle is gravely ill. I know no more than that.'

Sir John frowned. 'A telegram? I say, I'm sorry to hear that. It sounds serious. Don't know your uncle well but we're all on nodding acquaintance around here more or less. Look here, I shan't intrude, but if you need anything, you will look me up, won't you? I'm at Balnacurin House on the other side of the valley. Telephone me if you need anything – day or night.'

'That is most kind. Good day to you,' said Shaw. He took Sir John's proffered calling-card and stepped out of the car onto the weed-covered gravel drive. For a moment he thought he saw someone looking out of one of the bedroom windows. Sir John's Bentley disappeared in a cloud of blue exhaust smoke, momentarily distracting him, and when he looked again, the windows showed nothing but the reflected sky.

'Come *along* now sir!' said Loake as he knocked again at the door of Moffat's compartment. What the devil was the man doing, thought the steward. The train had pulled into Inverness ten minutes ago and this was the third time he had knocked.

Spark-out, presumably, after the amount of booze the fellow had packed away the previous night. Loake just hoped the man had not been sick in the wash hand basin as well. He wouldn't put it past some of these Scotch fellows to do a thing like that.

He looked at his watch and knocked again, louder this time. He only had a few minutes before he was due on the morning train back to London and if he missed that his wife would give him the third degree. She already suspected he had a fancy woman.

Loake looked down at his waistline and laughed grimly. A fancy woman – the very thought of it! He shook his head and took out the pass key from the chain on his waistcoat and put it into the lock.

Loake felt the man had forfeited his right to a polite term of address, and so when he spoke again, it was in a far more familiar tone.

'I'm coming in now matey, so I just hope you're decent.'

He stepped inside the compartment and opened the partition door into the little bedroom. Moffat was slumped face down on edge of the mattress, fully dressed, one leg hanging off the bed.

''asn't even taken 'is shoes orf,' said Loake under his breath with distaste. He shook the man's arm and then recoiled as he felt it; hard, unyielding, more like wood than flesh. The shaking motion was sufficient to dislodge the man from the bed and he fell heavily on to the floor. Loake inhaled sharply as the man's ashen face became visible, his glassy eyes staring sightlessly through the window at the blackened arches of Inverness station.

'I have already told the other one, that Colonel Shaw is very ill and must not be disturbed.'

Shaw was looking upon an attractive, but stern-looking woman of around forty years of age wearing a dress which had something of the sick-room about it but which was not quite the uniform of a nurse.

The clergyman smiled and removed his cap. He decided to try again. After ringing the bell of his uncle's house there had been no reply for a few moments but eventually the woman had answered, opening the door guardedly.

'Other one?' asked Shaw. 'I am afraid I do not understand. I am Colonel Shaw's nephew,' he said solemnly. 'Reverend Lucian Shaw. I received a telegram stating that he was seriously ill.'

'I already told the other priest, the one who called before, that the Colonel is not to be disturbed. Please go.'

'Madam,' insisted Shaw, 'I have travelled all the way

from Suffolk. I would appreciate the courtesy of at least being satisfied as to my uncle's condition. If not, I shall have to make enquiries with the local doctor.'

'Wait,' said the woman curtly, and he heard the sound of the chain being applied to the door. He heard low conversation, and then the door opened widely. Shaw saw a sleek man in immaculate morning dress standing before him. He had smooth, shining hair and wore a large *pince-nez* on his hooked nose, giving his face the look of a well-fed bird of prey.

'I apologise for Miss Graham's evasive tactics,' he said, with an accent that Shaw could not quite place. 'She is rather protective of our patient. Won't you come in, Reverend? It is Reverend, your title?'

'Mr Shaw is sufficient, thank you,' said the clergyman. He rarely took an instant dislike to people, but there was something about this man he instinctively did not trust. What was he doing in his uncle's house, he wondered. He did not have to wait long for an answer.

'Forgive me, you must be wondering who on earth I am,' said the man, as he showed Shaw into the drawing room. 'My name is Keller. I am a surgeon, based at the Royal Edinburgh Infirmary, and your uncle's personal physician. Miss Graham is my medical assistant.'

'Then it was you, I assume, who sent the telegram?' asked Shaw.

Keller paused briefly before replying. 'Telegram?'

'The one stating my uncle was gravely ill,' prompted Shaw.

'Ah yes…' replied the doctor slowly. 'You will forgive me for the brevity of that communication, but your uncle was insistent that I did not go into detail. He was concerned that if you believed him to be within mere hours of death you might not think it worthwhile to come.'

'I see,' said Shaw, looking around at the dark, cluttered drawing room with its oil paintings of Highland scenes and its stuffed animal heads on the walls. It was exactly as he had remembered it. 'Perhaps, Doctor Keller, you would be kind enough to allow me to see my uncle, since he is so gravely ill.'

'It is I now who must correct you with the use of titles, Mr Shaw,' said Keller jocularly. 'As a fellow of the Royal College of Surgeons, my title is mister also.'

'Quite so,' said Shaw. He was beginning to become impatient with the man's manner. 'Once more, if you would be so kind as to show me to my uncle's room, *Mr* Keller…'

Keller raised a hand. 'Out of the question, Mr Shaw. Your uncle is resting.'

'Forgive me,' said Shaw firmly, 'but I was led to believe in your telegram that my uncle was at the point of death. Are you now saying he is not?'

'A surgeon, Mr Shaw, is somewhat like a priest, in that he cannot always give definite answers, though he might well like to.'

'Meaning?'

'Meaning, my dear sir, that your uncle is seriously ill and, as the saying has it, the prognosis is "touch and go".'

'What is his ailment?'

'A tumour of the throat. He engaged me as a specialist, knowing his local physician would not be able to help. I gave my prognosis, which was that he had but a few weeks to live. Accordingly he dismissed his previous housekeeper and I was able to provide Miss Graham's services in that regard.'

'And why may I not see him?'

'I have performed a surgical procedure on the tumour. If it is successful, he may well survive, perhaps even a few more years. If it fails, he will die very soon. But I cannot risk sepsis – contamination – at this juncture, and must insist he is left in isolation, at least until tomorrow morning. To allow you to see him now could well be the fatal blow.'

'Would it not be better for him to be in hospital?'

Keller shook his head. 'It would be dangerous to move him. Besides, I do not hold with the modern idea of hospitals as temples of universal healing. The risk of infection is great in such places. Better to perform surgery, where possible, in the patient's home. That may be a somewhat antiquated view, but it is one to which I hold firmly.'

'Very well,' said Shaw. 'I shall wait until tomorrow morning. I trust you will not object if I remain here until that time?'

Keller shook his head again. 'If it were up to me, Mr Shaw, you would be most welcome, but I regret to say I am not the master of this house, and nor is your uncle.'

'What on earth do you mean?' asked Shaw.

'Colonel Shaw, knowing the end was likely near, gave power of attorney to his solicitor. I cannot allow a stranger to remain in this house without his consent.'

'I am his next of kin,' said Shaw firmly.

'I sympathise, Mr Shaw, but as I said, it is out of my hands. I am told the Benmurie Inn is comfortable, and it is within walking distance. Rest assured I will send word to you the moment your uncle is able to receive you.'

Shaw felt a brief flash of anger. He had experienced something of the sort before when visiting the sick in hospitals, and he tried to remind himself that such obstruction, whilst tedious, was generally done in the best interest of the patient. It would not, he thought, to antagonise the man who held his uncle's life in the balance.

'Very well,' said Shaw, turning to go. 'I shall take a room at the, the Benmurie Inn. Would you be so kind as to give me the particulars of my uncle's solicitor? I should like to gain permission to stay in the house as soon as possible.'

'Certainly,' said Keller, opening the front door. Shaw noticed Miss Graham looking at him from the top of the stairs, from which point, he assumed, she had been eavesdropping on the conversation in the drawing room.

'We were expecting him to visit this morning, but he appears to have been delayed,' said Keller, smiling as he led Shaw on to the front step. 'I shall send word to you the moment he arrives. His name is Lewin.'

Chapter Four

On his way to the Benmurie Hotel, Shaw stopped at the little post office and general store in the village high street. He purchased a sheet of paper and an envelope and, with the scratchy pen made available for the use of customers, wrote a brief letter to his wife outlining his uncle's situation. He handed the missive over to the elderly, bespectacled lady at the counter, and paid for a stamp.

As the post-mistress was about to place the envelope in a mailbag, her eyes lit upon the name and address written upon it.

'Pardon me sir,' she said, 'but I couldnae help noticing this name and address. Would that be the same place I sent that telegram to yesterday, about Colonel Shaw being taken ill suddenly?'

Shaw was well-versed in the ways of village life, and knew that evasion of such questions would often lead to more gossip and speculation than a direct answer.

'Yes, that is correct,' he said. 'I am Lucian Shaw, the colonel's nephew. It was his physician who sent me the telegram, and I came as quickly as I could.'

'Oh dear,' said the lady. 'I hope the Colonel's all right. He comes in here frae time to time for his wee messages.'

Shaw was confused for a moment until he remembered that 'messages' was the Scots expression for purchases.

'We will know more by tomorrow,' replied Shaw. 'He has undergone a surgical procedure and his recovery is not yet certain. But thank you for your concern.'

He turned to go but as he opened the door, with its jolly tinkling bell, the post-mistress called out to him from behind her counter.

'Did ye say his doctor sent the telegram?' she asked.

'Yes,' replied Shaw. 'Mr Keller, a surgeon from Inverness.'

'Och, that's strange. It was the minister who sent the telegram. Mr McKechnie. My memory's not whit it was these days, but I remember that much.'

'I expect Mr Keller had been to see the minister and passed the job on to him,' replied Shaw.

'Aye, that'll most likely be right,' concluded the lady. 'Well, guid day to you, sir, and I hope your uncle gets better. I'll be rememberin' him in my prayers the night.'

Shaw raised his hat and stepped out into the little high street. He walked towards the Benmurie Inn, a whitewashed, two-storey building with a grey slate roof and dormer windows. It appeared to be the only such establishment in the village. There were no public houses as such, and he remembered from previous visits to Scotland that the village pub was less of an institution here than in England.

He stepped up to the front door; it was locked, and the place appeared deserted; he rang an electric bell by the door but no sound came and he wondered if it was even in working order.

He looked around and saw that, tucked away in the trees opposite the road, was a little grey-stone church with large, clear Georgian windows on either side of its forbidding grey door. He approached the building and saw a faded sign in front of it which read 'Inverbrodie

Parish Church.' Underneath were the times of services and then the name of the incumbent: C. McKechnie MM. Shaw was intrigued by the idea of a clergyman winning the Military Medal, the British army's decoration for gallantry awarded to non-commissioned ranks. He also recalled the conversation in the post office and realised this must be the minister that had sent him the telegram. He decided it was time to meet this gentleman.

A few yards away from the church stood the manse, or minister's house; another grey stone building with a slate roof, looking much the same as the Benmurie Inn on a smaller scale. Although it was still fairly early in the morning, Shaw decided it would not be too early to call, and rang the old-fashioned ring-pull by the door.

He expected a servant to answer it, but instead, a man in shirt sleeves with a clerical collar appeared. He was heavily built and had a bristling red moustache. Shaw was surprised to see the man was holding a high-calibre hunting rifle and a cleaning rag; a pull-through dangled from the end of its barrel.

'What is it?' asked the clergyman.

Shaw noticed the man's eyebrows raise slightly as he noticed he too was wearing a clerical collar.

'Mr McKechnie?' asked Shaw.

'Aye, the same,' said the man taciturnly. 'You'll be Mr Shaw, I'm guessing.'

'Indeed,' said the other. 'I assume you are aware of the reason for my visit to your town.'

'Aye,' said McKechnie gruffly. 'Will you come in?'

A few moments later Shaw was sitting in the cosy study of the manse, looking out on to an expanse of woodland with towering mountains beyond. Mrs McKechnie had been despatched to make tea – the manse had no servants – and Shaw felt for some reason rather nervous.

He pulled out his pipe.

'Would you mind if I...?'

'Be my guest,' said McKechnie, who had propped his rifle against the chimney-piece and was now wiping gun oil off his hands with a rag. 'A pipe's all right, though I don't hold with the cigarette habit,' he added. 'After some of my experiences in the war, all I want in my lungs is clean Highland air.'

'Oh dear,' said Shaw, as he put his pipe back in his pocket. 'Gas?'

'Nothing as bad as that,' said McKechnie dismissively. 'Enjoy your tobacco, Mr Shaw, don't hold back on my account.'

Shaw puffed at his pipe and the astringent aroma of Dunhill's Standard Mixture filled the little room; he kept a small packet of this for smoking in the mornings as he found it more refreshing than his usual brand of Three Nuns.

'Talking of the war,' said Shaw, 'I noticed the MM after your name on the signboard.'

'Och, that!' laughed McKechnie, and the atmosphere suddenly became more relaxed. 'I was in the Fifty-First before I entered the church.'

'The Highland Division?'

'Aye, the Gordons. Don't worry, I didn't put the "MM" to cover myself in glory. That's a wee dig at the Covenanters in the chapel up the road, after one of them told me to my face that no man who had taken up arms against another should be a preacher of God's word. It's also a subtle reminder to the local gentry of my humble origins. Some of them worry I'm not top-drawer enough to be their minister.'

'They would expect you, I suppose, to have a DSO rather than an MM,' said Shaw. 'The former being the decoration for officers, and the Military Medal for Other Ranks.'

'I see you know a bit about the army,' said McKechnie. 'Were you in the services yourself, Mr Shaw?'

'Only as a chaplain. I was attached to the Third Army – under General Woolcombe – for most of 1917.'

'God help us all,' breathed McKechnie in a tone of saddened admiration. 'That means you were at Cambrai.'

'If you count giving Holy Communion to a handful of men in a trench just before the big push, then yes. Not quite the stuff of Military Medals.'

McKechnie slammed his fist on the table; the tin of gun oil jumped slightly. 'Don't you dare put your calling down,' he said angrily. 'The Lord's Supper is worth more than a piece o' tin and ribbon when a man's about to meet his maker.'

'You are of course right,' said Shaw, somewhat alarmed by the man's violent outburst. 'I hope I was able to offer some comfort. It was, however, a long time ago. Ah, here is Mrs McKechnie with our tea, I presume.'

Shaw stood up as the minister's wife entered the room and fussed about with the tea things. She asked several questions about England, his journey and so on as if he were an old family friend rather than someone she had only just met. Shaw realised this must be the famous Highland hospitality, and noted that it contrasted sharply with the reception he had received at his uncle's house.

After Mrs McKechnie had gone, Shaw decided to come to the point. 'Has Mr Keller informed you of the full picture?'

'Mr who?' said McKechnie, draining his cup of tea and smacking his lips.

'Mr Keller. My uncle's physician.'

'I'd no idea he had one. I assumed he was under the local doctor.'

'It seems not. He has appointed Keller, a surgeon from Inverness, who specialises in his ailment.'

'I've never heard of the man. Wait a moment. Is he a well-dressed fellow, with striped trousers and eyeglasses?'

'Yes, that sounds like him.'

'Aye, that'll be him I saw coming up to the house after I went over yesterday. He was taking a dog for a walk, though I didn't know the Colonel had one. The housekeeper didn't want to let me in. Maybe if I'd waited that man would have been more welcoming.'

'That must have been Keller,' said Shaw. 'He told me it was he who sent the telegram.'

'Well that's not right, it was me,' replied McKechnie. 'Somebody stuck a note through the door in the night asking me to send it.'

'Ah….then I assume *that* was what Keller was referring to when he claimed to have sent the telegram.'

'Then why didn't the man knock on the door and tell me, or send the thing himself?'

'I have no idea. I assume – again – that he did not wish to leave my uncle for too long, and perhaps did not wish to wake you, as it would have been pointless before the post office was open.'

'Hmm…I suppose so. He might have left a more informative note, all the same. It wasn't signed. How did he seem when you met him, your uncle?'

'I have not yet seen him. Keller says it is too much of a risk, and that I should return tomorrow morning. That is why I was on my way to book a room at the Benmurie Inn. If you will pardon me I ought to go there now, perhaps they will have opened.'

McKechnie glared alarmingly at Shaw.

'You'll do no such thing,' he said, with the same gruff tone he had used to chide Shaw for his lack of pride in his chaplaincy service. He got up and opened the study door and called out loudly into the passageway.

'Jeannie! Make up the wee room at the back. Mr Shaw's staying with us.'

Shaw felt at something of a loose end for most of the day. McKechnie allowed him use of his study and reference books to begin work on his sermon for Sunday, but something told him he might not be back in Lower Addenham in time to deliver it. He disliked being left in limbo, and by the time lunch at the manse had finished, he was tapping his fingers on the dining room table in frustration.

'What you need is a spot of fresh air,' said McKechnie. 'Come on, I'll show you around a wee bit. You'll likely not remember much of the place after 18 years. I've little on today and the weather's braw. We might even pot something. Care to take a gun?'

'Does the manse stretch to a game estate?' asked Shaw.

'Lord no,' laughed McKechnie. 'Should be a pheasant or two around on the common mosses though, and they're ours to take.'

'Common mosses?' asked Shaw.

'Aye, what you'd call a peat bog,' replied McKechnie. 'The landowners around these parts are awfully particular about who shoots and farms or does anything on their land. It's been that way since the Highland Clearances. But the common mosses round here are similar to the common lands in England.'

'You have a right to shoot game there?'

'Aye, if the brutes land there long enough.'

McKechnie shrugged on an ancient mackintosh and continued his explanation.

'The only reason the lairds allow it is the land's no good for proper shooting or farming or anything else. Few folk bother with peat gathering now either, what with coal being so easy to get.'

He opened the gun cabinet in the hall and took out a shotgun from next to his hunting rifle which he had placed there earlier. He cracked it open and squinted through the barrels before offering it to Shaw.

'Ah, no, thank you,' said Shaw. 'I shall be content to watch.' Although a moderately good shot, he had still not quite recovered from a rather too close proximity to such a weapon the previous year.*

The weather was indeed beautiful, thought Shaw, as the two men, plus Campbell, McKechnie's jet-black gun dog, reached the summit of the gentle hill at the edge of the town after a couple of hour's walking. The weather had cleared; watery sunlight shone down and a gentle breeze rippled through the remaining golden leaves on the trees; there was none of the chilling mist and driving rain he associated with Scotland in autumn, or indeed at any time of year.

'You can see pretty much everything from here,' said McKechnie, pointing downwards to the expanse of purple heather which led down to the little village. The high street was a small grey ribbon running through the valley; beyond it was more purple moorland running down to the gleam of the railway line. Still further on were the dark, brooding peaks of the Benmurie Braes. Shaw noticed a small building on the edge of the town and realised it was Auchentorrin Lodge, his uncle's house.

*See *The King is Dead*

Shaw gazed around himself at the impressive landscape.

'Is the land around Colonel Shaw's house part of the…"common mosses", Mr McKechnie?' he asked.

'Not down there. That's all his land, as far as I know, right down to the railway, more or less. But it might as well be common mosses with the amount of bog on it. More black and foul smelling than most of the bogs round here, to tell the truth. Nobody would want it.'

'I assume that is why he was able to buy such a large acreage on his army pension.'

'Aye, he's always seemed canny with his money, your uncle,' said McKechnie with an admiring smile. 'Folk around here admire that. The land's no good for anything much though. Too wet for shooting.'

'Uncle bought it, as far as I know, in order to watch birds. That has always been an interest of his.'

'He's certainly a rare one for talking of them when we've shared a dram. I don't know much about birds myself other than the difference between a game bird and a hunting bird. But the Colonel spends hours on his own out with his binoculars watching them.'

Shaw noticed a gleam of light to the eastward beyond the railway line. 'That surely is not the sea?' he asked.

'No,' replied McKechnie. 'That's Loch Nairn. She's a sea loch, mind. Links with the Moray Firth. Folk used to come round the coast from Edinburgh that way by boat before the railway was built.'

'Of course, that must have been the body of water I saw from the train,' mused Shaw. 'What is that house over there?'

He pointed to a large, bow-fronted Georgian mansion a mile or so across the valley from Auchentorrin Lodge. Its large, plate glass windows looked out like two blank eyes on the moorland in front of it.

'That's Balnacurin House,' said McKechnie. 'Owned by our laird and master, Sir John Debayle-Bradley. He wouldn't have been here the last time you came. His father was an absentee landlord, and so was he until recently.'

'I met him this morning. He was kind enough to offer me a lift in his motor car from the station.'

'Aye, he's around a lot these days. On the bench as a JP and standing for Parliament too. I didn't care much for him at first, but I'm warming to him.'

'He seems ambitious.'

'That's what put me off him. But I've heard him speak and he seems to be one of the few men around here willing to see that the men need work. They'll not live on crofting and eat tatties and herring the rest of their lives like their forefathers. And if they don't get something soon, we'll likely go the way of Russia. Not much fun for the likes of us ministers.'

Campbell yelped. McKechnie shouted 'Mine!' and suddenly there was an enormous explosion as he let off both barrels of his shotgun; then there was a whirring noise as a colourful pheasant disappeared rapidly into a clump of pine trees a few yards away.

'Ach, luck's not with us today, Mr Shaw,' said McKechnie. 'Come on, let's away home. It's nearly tea-time.'

After they had finished tea, Shaw caught sight of the Inverness evening newspaper that had recently been delivered. He frowned as he noticed a small article on the front page. It read:

Businessman found dead on night train

A man was found dead in a sleeping compartment on the London night train when it arrived in Inverness this morning. Harold Moffat, 39, of 25 Poolewe Gardens, Inverness, is thought to have died of heart failure following a business trip to London. Police are not treating his death as suspicious.

'In the midst of life, we are in death,' he said to himself, as he undressed in the little back room of the manse. He knew all too well that someone's death, someone with only the tenuous connection of having travelled on the same train as him, would not play on his mind for very long, but it reminded him of the fragility of life and he resolved that he would not miss the opportunity to be with his uncle as soon as possible.

The next morning Shaw awoke early and, after a splendid breakfast prepared by Mrs McKechnie, he strode to Auchentorrin Lodge and clanged the bell loudly.

This time it was Keller who opened the door. Dressed immaculately in a morning coat as before, he flashed a professional smile and ushered Shaw in to the hall.

'Good morning, Mr Shaw,' he said. 'We tried to relay a message to you, but the staff at the Benmurie Inn claimed never to have heard of you.'

Shaw cursed himself silently. He realised he ought to have left a message at the inn to intercept any communications coming from his uncle's house. No wonder he had not heard anything about the man's condition.

'How is he?' asked Shaw.

'Still touch-and-go, I am sorry to say.'

'May I see him now?'

'I would rather you did not – there is still a risk of infection.'

'I am afraid I must insist. I wish to pray with him.'

'Very well. Come this way, please.'

Keller led the way up a creaking, ornate staircase past stuffed animal heads and ancient, soot-darkened oil paintings of Highland landscapes, until they reached a landing with an expanse of threadbare red carpet. It was all just as he had remembered it from his last visit. He recalled that his uncle's bedroom was at the far end of the corridor. Keller's assistant, Miss Graham, stood guard outside.

'Mr Shaw has come to see his uncle,' said Keller.

Shaw noticed Miss Graham glare at him. 'He is sleeping,' she said curtly. 'I gave him the sedative as you asked.'

'Thank you, Miss Graham, you may go,' said Keller, and the woman tramped off down the stairs into the hallway.

Before he opened the door, Keller turned to Shaw. 'I must warn you, he is unlikely to recognise you or be aware of anything. I have had to sedate him as he will be in considerable pain as he recovers from the procedure. He has also had to be heavily bandaged due to bleeding. If it becomes more serious I shall have to take him to hospital.'

'He will recover?' asked Shaw.

Keller fixed Shaw with a steady gaze. 'I do not believe doctors should make such predictions, but I am sorry to say, Mr Shaw, that I do not think he will survive much beyond this night. Please be aware of this.'

'Thank you for your candour,' said Shaw, as they entered the room. The light was dim in the room, as the window was obscured by heavy curtains; dark wood panelling covered the walls which were sparsely decorated with regimental photographs. The furniture had a barrack-room simplicity about it, with a heavy wooden bedstead in the centre of the room. Next to it was a trolley with surgical paraphernalia on it, and a strong smell of antiseptic filled the air.

Shaw felt a certain sense of trepidation. Though he had been present at many death-beds, he realised he had not witnessed the passing of a close relative; his father had died while he was in France during the war, and his mother was still living. He took a deep breath and approached the bed. He looked at the thin form of the man lying on it, whose face was partly obscured by bandages wrapped around his throat and jaw. A shock of white hair stuck out from his head and his eyes, though closed, flickered slightly.

'Uncle? Uncle James?' said Shaw gently. 'It is your nephew, Lucian.'

'I am afraid he cannot hear you,' said Keller. 'I have tried various methods but none have worked in reviving him.'

'Surely he should be in hospital,' protested Shaw.

'As I said before, Mr Shaw, it would not do him any good. He is too ill and the journey would merely hasten his end.'

'Very well,' said Shaw. 'I had hoped to offer him Holy Communion.' He pointed to the small bag he had brought containing his miniature portable altar and communion vessels he had used on the Western Front.

'Impossible,' said Keller bluntly. 'He is unable to move his jaw due to the procedure.'

'Then let us pray,' said Shaw, kneeling at the bedside. Keller stepped back and busied himself with arranging some of the instruments on the trolley, while Shaw recited from his prayer book.

'"O Father of mercies, and God of all comfort, our only help in time of need: we fly unto thee for succour in behalf of this thy servant, here lying under thy hand in great weakness of body. Look graciously upon him, O Lord; and the more the outward man decayeth, strengthen him, we beseech thee, so much the more continually with thy grace and holy spirit in the inner man."'

Shaw opened his eyes and looked at his uncle's face.

There was no sign of recognition or even that he was hearing anything. He resumed the prayer.

'"Give him unfeigned repentance for all the errors of his life past, and steadfast faith in thy son Jesus; that his sins may be done away by thy mercy, and his pardon sealed in heaven, before he go hence, and be no more seen. We know, O Lord, that there is no word impossible with thee; and that, if thou wilt, thou canst even yet raise him up, and grant him a longer continuance amongst us…"'

Shaw thought he heard something like a laugh, and looked up to see Keller, standing by the window, put his hand to his mouth and clear his throat. Then he sighed and looked ahead blankly.

Shaw looked back at his uncle. Of course, it had been some time since he had last saw him, but there was something different about his appearance he could not put his finger on. He decided it must be age and ill health which had altered his features; the mind's eye could be deceptive. He took his uncle's hands in his own and concluded the prayer.

'"…Yet, forasmuch as in all appearance the time of his dissolution draweth near, so fit and prepare him, we beseech thee, against the hour of death, that after his departure hence in peace, and in thy favour, his soul may be received into thine everlasting kingdom, through the merits and mediation of Jesus Christ, thine only Son, our Lord and Saviour. Amen."'

'Amen,' echoed Keller peremptorily. 'If you will excuse me, Mr Shaw, I think your uncle should be left alone now.'

'I should like to stay longer,' said Shaw. 'If, as you say, the end is near…'

'There is still a chance he may recover,' said Keller, 'as you so eloquently pointed out in your prayers – and I do not wish him to be tired unnecessarily. In the event that he is able to hear you, he will have been overly stimulated, which could be harmful.'

Shaw bridled slightly at the man's attitude. He was beginning to take a strong dislike to Keller. 'I would hardly call prayer for a sick man to be "overstimulating".'

Keller smiled again and ushered Shaw to the door. 'Please, Mr Shaw; I would not presume to question your professional practices and I would ask you extend the same courtesy to me. Rest assured we will get word to you the moment your uncle's situation should change.'

'Very well, but I intend to stay in this house for as long as is necessary,' said Shaw as they stepped out on to the landing.

'That, I am afraid,' said Keller, 'is the province of yet another professional gentleman, namely your uncle's solicitor.'

'Ah yes,' said Shaw, 'this Mr Lewin.'

'Indeed. Come with me please, I shall introduce you to him and you can discuss the matter.'

Shaw was introduced in the drawing room to a tall, sleek man, who was well dressed, though not quite as punctiliously as Keller. He shook the man's proffered hand. For a fleeting moment he thought they may have met before, but he could not place him.

'I am sorry we meet at such a sad time, Mr Shaw.'

'There is yet hope, I believe.' Shaw said, as he noticed that Lewin did not invite him to sit down. He also noticed another man – dressed like some sort of gamekeeper, standing motionless in a corner of the room by the door.

'Oh, this is Tench, by the way,' said Lewin, pointing to the man. 'As Colonel Shaw's executor I have engaged him to help around the house. The Colonel rather let things go, I am afraid.'

Tench merely nodded at Shaw, and remained silent.

'You speak as if my uncle is already dead,' said Shaw.

Lewin sighed. 'We must face facts. Mr Keller informs me it is highly unlikely he will recover; even if he does his faculties are likely to be considerably impaired. It is, in my experience, advisable to arrange one's legal affairs as early as possible in such cases. Your uncle was prescient enough to grant power of attorney to me when he knew he would have to undergo a risky surgical procedure.'

Shaw felt an instinctive dislike for the man in the same way he had felt Keller. There was something unctuous and vaguely manipulative in his manner; and why, wondered Shaw, was Tench, who appeared to be some sort of servant, remaining in the room?

'I was given to understand,' said Shaw, 'that it was in your power to grant permission for me to stay here in case my uncle's condition should worsen. Is that the case?'

'In theory, yes,' said Lewin smoothly. 'But in this particular instance I regret I cannot allow you to. Rest assured we will get word to you immediately his condition changes.'

'May I ask why I am not permitted to stay?' asked Shaw.

Lewin smiled and sighed again. He shrugged his shoulders in a gesture which seemed to say 'it is out of my hands' but which also had in it something ancient and foreign, a hint of sun-bleached market places in walled Levantine towns.

'Unfortunately the rules of the trust are clear, that nobody is to stay in the house.'

'What is this "trust", exactly?' asked Shaw.

Lewin gave another enigmatic smile.

'Your uncle desires that, upon his death, or upon him losing capacity to manage his affairs, that the whole of his estate be handed over to a consortium set up to create employment for local people. The details are rather complex, I am afraid, and must remain confidential for the time being.'

Shaw wondered just what sort of employment a crumbling house and a few acres of bog could provide. 'So it seems,' he said. 'Why, however, should that preclude his next of kin from staying here?'

'In this particular instance,' Lewin explained, 'due to the large number of small items of personal property in the house, the trustees of the estate, whom I represent, have insisted that no outsiders are to be allowed to stay. They are all too familiar with cases of relations turning up and claiming that certain valuable items were promised them by the deceased, and so on. I am sure you understand.'

Shaw bridled. He did not normally get angry, but this oleaginous man was beginning to annoy him intensely.

'I do indeed understand, sir,' he said evenly, 'and I resent the implication,'

'There is no implication, Mr Shaw. Merely legal protocol. Why, even Tench here has to submit to the indignity of a personal search every time he goes home. Is that not so, Tench?'

Tench merely nodded, and looked out of the window.

Shaw breathed deeply and regained his temper. It would not do, he realised, to create scenes or stir up legal trouble whilst his uncle was lying gravely ill upstairs.

There was a moment of silence, and he could tell Lewin wanted him out of the house. He was determined not to give him the satisfaction of rushing him out, and so looked around the room admiringly. It felt strange, he reflected, to be in the house of a relative without that person being with him. Then something caught his eye. It was a framed photograph on the chimney-piece of himself and his uncle, and he realised it had been taken at the school reunion, the last time he had met his uncle.

Shaw strolled to the photograph to examine it. 'This brings back memories,' he said. He picked it up and looked at it. There was something about his uncle's appearance that did not seem right, but he could not put his finger on what it was.

Then his eye fell upon a small table near the fireplace, on which sat a large tome bearing the title *Limelight Illustrated Theatrical Directory.* Strange, thought Shaw. His uncle had never shown much interest in the theatre. He went to pick up the book but was interrupted by Lewin, who attempted to guide him away from the fireplace.

'If you will excuse us, Mr Shaw,' said Lewin firmly, 'we have rather a lot of work to get on with.'

'Very well,' replied Shaw, as he replaced the photograph and turned to face the lawyer. 'I will await word from you whilst I stay at the manse. You will not object, I trust, should I seek independent confirmation on the matter of your powers of attorney?'

Lewin shrugged in that ancient manner once more. 'Of course not, Mr Shaw. Be my guest. My offices in London, and the relevant paperwork are open for inspection by appointment at any time. Here, take my card.'

With a flourish he presented Shaw with a business card, giving an address in Mayfair. There was nothing more to be said, or so Lewin's manner suggested. With a perfunctory exchange of greetings, Shaw left the house and walked into the village.

Chapter Five

Sergeant Allan Nesbitt of the London and North Eastern Railway Police, the force charged with the protection of persons and property on the railways, sighed as he looked through the pile of reports on his desk in the police office in the bowels of Inverness station.

He ran a hand through his greying hair and turned over some of the pages; it was the usual litany of petty thefts, fare-dodgers and the growing problem of vagrants on railway premises. He smiled grimly at the memory of an article he had read in his Sunday newspaper about a similar problem in America, where 'hobos' hitched free rides on the trains; at least things were not as bad as that here, he reflected.

Before he could read any further, there was a tinkling sound from the telephone on his cluttered desk, and he picked up the earpiece and receiver.

'Nesbitt.'

'I've a call for you, sergeant. Dr McReady.' It was the young probationary constable at the switchboard, his voice unnecessarily bright and chirpy.

'Aye, put him through.'

McReady was the police doctor assigned to the division, young, enthusiastic and wanting to make a mark for himself. Silly fool, thought Nesbitt, remembering he had felt much the same way thirty years previously. He'll soon learn, he said to himself, as he waited for the call to be connected.

'Good morning Sergeant,' said the doctor in his well-spoken Edinburghian tones.

'Doctor. What can I do for you?'

'Remember the fellow that you found on the train yesterday?'

'Aye. What about him?' Nesbitt felt his heart sink. He had thought that was over and done with, but he suspected more work – a lot more work – was about to come his way.

'You did right to let me to have a proper look at him,' said the doctor.

Here it comes, thought Nesbitt. He just wished he had not told that reporter that there was nothing suspicious about the man's death. He had a feeling he was going to look stupid when he had to call in the Criminal Investigation Department.

'Meaning?' asked Nesbitt curtly.

'Meaning I think your chaps might need to have a further look. I've found a few things of interest.'

Nesbitt also now wished he had not given permission for a post-mortem examination of the man. It was only because the doctor was so insistent that he had conceded; Moffat had no next of kin to give permission and the only person who seemed to know him was his landlady, whose main concern was for when she could start to rent his room out to someone else.

'That mark on his neck that I mentioned,' continued McReady, 'which was what aroused my interest in the first place, is indeed fascinating. The bruising and puncture mark, although small, is consistent with someone administering an injection.'

'How on earth can you spot a wee pinprick like that?'

'As I said, the bruising gives it away, and I noticed that when I first examined him. One doesn't normally see that sort of mark with a hypodermic injection when administered properly, but this one appears to have been done by a rank amateur. Even a first year medical student would not have done it as crudely as that, and considerable force was used.'

Nesbitt sucked his teeth. 'Could he no' have just cut himself shaving?'

'It looks like he was injected with something.'

'Maybe he had to visit a doctor afore he travelled.'

'If he did, the man should be struck off for malpractice. And there's a couple of other things.'

'Go on.'

'Your theory was he had a weak heart and keeled over due to too much drink.'

'Aye, that's right. The steward said he had a bottle or so of wine and that he was so tight he had to be put to bed by a couple of other passengers, and he reeked like a distillery.'

'Indeed. I distinctly remember you mentioning a distillery. The strange thing is I found no traces of whisky or any other spirits in his stomach. Only a considerable amount of red wine. A claret, I'd say, though it's hard to tell after exposure to stomach acid.'

Nesbitt winced and felt his own stomach lurch slightly. He wished now he had not had those eggs and bacon at the station canteen, especially if he was going to have to look at a cadaver.

'The only place I did find traces of spirits,' continued MacReady, 'was in his oral cavity – his mouth – and down his neck. I noticed it straight away by the smell alone, and a swab test confirmed it was whisky. Now I can't tell much with the limited time and equipment available, but judging by the amount of additives in it, it was rather a nasty cheap blended whisky. Bells, or something like that.'

'Good God, what self-respecting Highlander would drink that? He wasnae a Glaswegian.'

'Well, quite. But it looks as if he *didn't* drink it.'

'What the hell did he do with it then? Brush his teeth in it?'

'Not really my area, Sergeant. There's one more thing that you ought to know about.'

Nesbitt sighed. 'I suppose you're going to tell me you've opened his lungs up and found out what brand o' cigarettes he smoked.'

'Player's Navy Cut.'

'Dear God man, I was only joking.'

'So was I. I saw the packet in his top pocket when I first examined him. But seriously, I found some traces – some quite considerable traces – of a certain drug in his blood. I won't bore you with the name, but it's a type of fast-acting sedative, usually used by alienists to subdue unruly mental patients. I know because I've administered it myself once or twice when I was at Craiglockhart.'

'The loony bin?'

'I wouldn't use that term myself, but yes. In normal use one wouldn't notice it in the blood, but he's got at least twice the safe amount. Enough to bring on a heart attack.'

'Do you think,' said Nesbitt, 'it could have been that drug which killed him?'

'I certainly think it's possible. He was forcibly injected with something all right. And I'll wager it was done on the train because if he'd had it beforehand for some inexplicable reason – say, at a doctor's in London – he'd not have been able to get off the surgery couch, let alone eat his dinner in a moving train. '

'Good God,' breathed Nesbitt.

'So that's where we are. I'll leave the rest to you, shall I sergeant? Do telephone me if you need me.'

Nesbitt sighed as he replaced the telephone on his desk. A moment later he picked it up again and spoke to the constable at the switchboard.

'Get me the Inverness CID.'

'You'll understand, Mr, ah, Shaw, that I cannot divulge personal information about your uncle's medical records?'

Dr Sneddie, Inverbrodie's ancient family doctor, looked at Shaw quizzically over his half-moon spectacles as he sat comfortably far back in his surgery chair. His old, greenish frock coat seemed too big for him, as did his wing collar, giving the impression of a tortoise poking its head out from its shell.

'Of course,' said Shaw. He had expected this when he had called in at the surgery, hoping to shed some light on his uncle's condition.

'Would ye care for a pinch of snuff?' asked the doctor, extending an open silver box containing a brown powder exuding the smell of camphor.

'Thank you but no,' said Shaw. 'I find it makes me sneeze.'

'That's all part of the joy of it,' said Dr Sneddie, taking a large pinch and then sneezing violently into a spotted handkerchief. 'Ah, that's better,' he exclaimed. 'Clears the nasal passages and has an antiseptic effect. I'm certain it was what kept me from catching the Spanish 'flu back in 1918. Cheaper than smoking, too.'

'I will not take up too much of your time, Doctor,' said Shaw, anxious to get to the matter in hand.

'I realise of course that you cannot divulge information from my uncle's records. I have outlined his situation, however, and wondered if you would be kind enough to furnish me with some general medical information regarding it. Nothing personal need be said.'

'I was sad to hear of the Colonel's condition when you told me about it just now,' said the doctor, shaking his head. 'And I can see you're not the sort to report me to the General Medical Council. I'll tell you as much as I can.'

'Thank you. I will of course pay your usual fee.'

'Nonsense,' said Dr Sneddie, waving his hand. 'Don't get the idea all Scots are always after money. This is no' Aberdeen, you know. I've an empty waiting room as you've seen, and it'll be a pleasure to talk to someone. The trouble is people around here are too well,' he chuckled. 'Now, what did ye want to know?'

'Firstly, whether you had heard of a surgeon called Keller, from Edinburgh. He is the man treating my uncle.'

'Keller…Keller…' said Dr Sneddie thoughtfully. 'Aye, I've heard the name I think. Wait a moment.'

He turned to a dark wooden bookcase behind his desk and took down a large medical directory. He thumbed through the pages.

'Keach…Keane…ah, here it is. Keller. George Emanuel. Qualifications as long as your arm, Bucharest 1890, Paris 1893 – he's been around a fair bit – ah, accepted FRCS Edinburgh 1895, Royal Edinburgh Infirmary and private practice, oesophagal and thoracic specialist; also psychiatric medicine. Hmm, member of the Royal and Ancient Golf Club too. Quite impressive.'

He closed the book and replaced it on the shelf. 'The Colonel's certainly in good hands then,' he said. 'It'll cost him a pretty penny though, with a nurse too like you said. It's strange though that he didn't mention anything to me about his condition. Ah, well, it would have been a bit much for me to deal with here, all the same.'

'Is it usual,' said Shaw, 'for a condition such as the one my uncle is suffering from, to be treated at home in this way?'

'Aye, it could be done,' mused Dr Sneddie. 'Without knowing the exact nature of the complaint it's hard to say. A small tumour could be removed at home, though nowadays most doctors like to refer patients to hospitals to be on the safe side. I certainly would. Time was when I'd do some operations on a crofter's kitchen table by oil lamp, but we didn't do the complicated things they do now.'

'And is this the sort of thing that could come on quickly?' asked Shaw. 'My concern is he never wrote to me about it.'

'From what I know of your uncle he's a retiring sort of fellow,' said Dr Sneddie. 'Apart from his visits here, we've spoken briefly after morning service at the Kirk a few times, that's all, but he seemed the sort of man who wouldn't make a fuss. I do find it a wee bit surprising he didn't come to me first, though.'

'Do you think there is hope?'

'There's always hope, Mr Shaw, as a minister you should know that more than me. If you're asking me if I think the Colonel can pull through, well, again it's hard to tell without seeing him – and I wouldn't dream of interfering with another doctor's patient by having a look at him, before you ask – I'd say he's a good chance. He was fit as a fiddle the last time I saw him.'

'He did mention being treated for an injury on his leg, the last time he wrote,' said Shaw.

'Aye, well if you know about that I suppose it's all right for me to mention it. Old wound from his time in the army. He got it at Khartoum or somewhere like that. Tiny bit of shrapnel – British I think – in his leg, giving him a bit of trouble from time to time. Too near the knee to get out without permanently damaging the ligaments, I told him, so he left it.'

'Was it serious?'

'Och no, or they would have invalided him out of the army. It looked worse than it was. I prescribed a sedative to help him sleep and that was that. Nasty lot of old scarring on the knee, though. It was a good job he was an Englishman as if he ever wore the kilt he would not have been a pretty sight for the lassies. Not that many men who wear the kilt ever are,' he added with a chuckle.

After parting cordially with the doctor, Shaw stopped at the telephone box by the village post office on the way back to the manse. After a considerable delay and with the expenditure of a large pile of pennies, he was able to make a telephone call to the Royal Edinburgh Infirmary.

'Mr Keller is not available at the moment,' said a secretary crisply. 'Would you like to leave a message, sir?'

'Oh, it's not important,' said Shaw. 'Could you tell me perhaps when he will return to his office?'

'Mr Keller is residing with a patient near Inverness at the moment. We are not sure when he will be back. Whom shall I say called?'

'That's quite all right, thank you,' said Shaw quickly. 'Good day to you.'

Shaw frowned as he stepped out of the relative shelter of the kiosk into the brisk Highland autumn air. It was good to have it confirmed that his uncle was receiving the best possible professional care, but there was something, something he could not put his finger on, that did not seem quite right about all this.

'You look a bit under the weather, Mr Shaw,' said McKechnie as they sat in the dining room of the manse, having just finished lunch. After Mrs McKechnie had cleared the plates away and the left the room, Shaw had fallen into deep thought, his source of polite conversation largely used up. He felt, however, that he could trust McKechnie, and outlined the situation with his uncle.

'Aye, it seems an annoyance,' said the minister, sitting back in his chair and folding his hands over his barrel-like stomach. 'This lawyer fellow in particular – Lewin – sounds like one or two staff officers I knew in the war – over fond of rules and their own place in enforcing them.'

'A type not unknown in the church also,' replied Shaw.

McKechnie chuckled. 'I came across some like that a year or so ago when the Kirk was having most of its legal powers transferred to the council. I had to put a lawyer in his place then, as well.'

'I do not wish to make a fuss,' said Shaw, 'but it does seem strange that Lewin is such a stickler for protocol. Do you know, he even implied I might steal the family silver if left alone in the house?'

'Did he?' said McKechnie with a snort. 'Some men just don't seem to have any fellow-feeling, do they?'

There was a moment of silence. Shaw was already feeling as if he had intruded on the McKechnie household too long. Perhaps McKechnie sensed this, as he placed a hand on Shaw's arm.

'Listen, Mr Shaw, if you're worried about staying on here, don't be. Jeannie loves looking after people and we Highlanders are known for our hospitality. Take as long as you like, and if you've a mind to take the silver, be my guest, it's all tin anyway.'

Shaw was uncertain for a moment whether McKechnie was joking or not, until the man burst out laughing and slapped him on the back. He joined in with the laughter briefly.

'That's better!' exclaimed McKechnie. 'Now, here's another thing. You say your uncle's in good hands with that surgeon, as far as you can tell. But if you're worried about this lawyer fellow, you could try having a word with Sir John Debayle-Bradley about it. You know, the man who drove you from the station.'

Shaw nodded as McKechnie continued. 'He's a Justice of the Peace and will know a thing or two about powers of attorney and suchlike. That'll give you a bit of a leg to stand on if this Lewin gets pushy again. I know Sir John's helped one or two people around the village with legal problems of one kind or another, those that couldn't dream of affording to pay a lawyer, I mean.'

'I will bear it in mind,' said Shaw thoughtfully. 'I am not sure I trust them to bring word should my uncle's condition change, quite frankly. They seemed to view me as an unwelcome intrusion.'

'They sound like uppity Edinburgh types to me,' said McKechnie. 'As the apocryphal surgeon once said, "the operation was a success but the patient died." Vainglory, Mr Shaw. I've seen men fall prey to that sin too many times in the army *and* the church.'

'Very well,' said Shaw. 'I am resolved that if I should not hear from Keller by this evening, I shall call again at the house. And if there is any more obstruction I may well take up the matter with Sir John.'

'And talking of sin,' said McKechnie, 'I've a sermon to write for Sunday, so you'll have to amuse yourself until supper time.'

In the small back bedroom of the manse, as McKechnie was working on his sermon downstairs, Shaw took pen and paper and sat at a little table in the corner of the room.

He wrote a brief letter to his wife, stating that there was no change in his uncle's condition but that he hoped he would not have to wait much longer. He was about to write 'for the funeral' but decided, after remembering Dr Sneddie's words about hope, to put 'for a recovery' instead.

Something was still nagging at him in a corner of his mind, some detail he had missed. Dark suspicions began to circulate in his thinking. He stopped and rubbed his eyes. Had his experiences of the recent past – his involvement with three murder cases in less than two years – led him, he wondered, to become unbalanced, to see plots and intrigue where there were none?

He pushed the thoughts back down into the recesses of his mind by reciting the twenty-third psalm to himself, and went to the pillar box to catch the last post.

Supper time came and went, and by eight pm Shaw had received no word of his uncle. He shrugged on his coat and hat and announced to McKechnie where he was going.

'Would you like me to drive you over there in the car?' asked the clergyman. 'It'll not take a moment to take her out of the garage.'

'That is quite all right,' said Shaw. 'I have put you to enough trouble already. Besides, it is a pleasant evening, and a walk will do me good.'

Shaw strode through the darkened main street of the village, noticing the only major source of light were the windows of the Benmurie Inn. He hurried on, and within twenty minutes or so had arrived at his uncle's house. There was a low moon, and the whole valley was softly lit by a silvery glow.

He suddenly remembered something his uncle had said; that the valley had a peculiar climate of its own; the bad weather that Scotland is famed for often tended to pass over it without stopping, making conditions ideal for his hobby of bird watching.

He could see now the attraction of the area; it would be a good place to spend one's last days, looking out upon that valley. He resolved to do his best to ensure his uncle was well cared for and not prey to the caprices of professional care-givers.

The house was dark; he pulled the ancient bell pull and after a few moments, the door was opened by Miss Graham, who gave him the same impassive stare as last time.

'What is it you want?' she asked.

'Good evening,' said Shaw firmly. 'I wish to see my uncle. May I come in?'

'I have orders not to allow anyone in the house.'

'I am sure you do,' said Shaw. 'Would you kindly therefore fetch the person who gave you those orders? I imagine it was Mr Keller or Mr Lewin.'

Miss Graham looked at him as if he were something nasty on the sole of her shoe, and disappeared within the house. A few moments later, Lewin appeared at the door, with Tench hovering a few feet behind. Lewin cracked a professional smile.

'Mr Shaw, please come in,' he said unctuously.

Shaw was ushered into the drawing room where, once again, Tench stood impassively near the door. Shaw could not help thinking he had the appearance of a jailer about him.

'Thank you, I will stand,' said Shaw, after Lewin had offered a chair to him. 'I have not heard any news of Colonel Shaw and would appreciate it if you would let me know his condition.'

'I regret to inform you,' said Lewin, his smile now gone, 'that your uncle died earlier this evening. I am assured it was very quick and he felt no pain.'

Although the news was not unexpected, Shaw nevertheless felt a deep sadness and depression come over him.

'Why was I not told earlier?'

'Forgive me but there was rather a lot to do for all of us. Tench was about to go out to give you the news, but since you are now here…'

'I should like to see him, please.'

'Unfortunately that is not possible.'

'Mr Lewin, I am beginning to think you are deliberately obstructive.'

'Mr Shaw, I understand you are upset. If it were up to me…' Lewin again gave that shrugging gesture, which for some reason was beginning to annoy Shaw intensely.

'I assume you will at least have the decency to allow me to organise his funeral?' he asked.

Lewin's smile was now fixed, and he spoke slowly as if to a person of limited mental capacity. 'The terms of trusteeship do not permit any involvement in the trustee's funeral arrangements. I am sorry. Now, unless there is anything else…'

Shaw turned to go. 'There is something else,' he said. 'You ought to know that I will be seeking legal advice on this matter. To be frank, I am concerned about the legality of this trust you mention. I am also concerned as to why you are required to spend so much time in this house on this particular matter.'

Lewin bridled, but then regained his composure. 'There is a large amount of paperwork to be done – inventories to be taken, deeds to be found, and so on, which regrettably takes up much of our time. And, if you are concerned about legality, as I said before, you are most welcome to examine any paperwork concerning the case.'

'It will not be I who will examine it,' said Shaw briskly. 'I intend to inform the local Justice of the Peace. No doubt you will hear from him in due course.'

There was a moment of silence, then Lewin smiled again and opened the door of the study to show him out.

'Very well, Mr Shaw. You must do what you think is best.'

The two men in tightly-belted raincoats and bowler hats who climbed the metal stairway of the Peabody Buildings flats in a back street of east London knew that they stood out a mile.

They had already noticed the twitching of grubby net curtains and a sour glance from one of the men idling in the courtyard, who had spat theatrically on the ground as they passed.

If not exactly regular visitors at the Buildings, plain-clothes police officers were there often enough for the residents to know what they looked like.

The larger of the two men knocked loudly on the door of a certain apartment; a portly, harassed-looking woman, visibly pregnant, opened it and two slightly grubby little boys peered from behind her apron.

'Evening, madam,' said the detective. 'Mrs Loake?'

'Yus,' said the woman warily. 'What do you want?'

'Is your husband in?'

'Why?'

'We'd like to ask him a few questions.'

'What's he done?'

'Nothing, as far as we know. Could we speak to him, please?'

'He's listening to the wireless.'

'What's that to do with the price of fish?' asked the other policeman, in a tone rather less polite than his superior.

'Is he selling fish, mum?' asked the older boy.

'All right, I'll get him,' sighed the woman. She turned and shouted into the gloomy corridor behind her. 'Loake! Come here!'

Mrs Loake opened the door a little wider. The older boy looked up at the detective and piped up.

'Are you a copper, mister?'

The officer of the law ignored the boy.

'Hurry up Loake, it's freezing out 'ere!' shouted Mrs Loake in stentorian tones.

''Ave you got a gun, mister?' said the smaller boy, his eyes wide with curiosity.

'Hush, Tommy,' chided Mrs Loake. 'Oh, here he is.'

She stepped back from the door and bustled the children through a doorway off the corridor. Loake swayed into view in his shirtsleeves, his waistcoat partially undone and with the remainder of the buttons strained to bursting point across his enormous stomach.

'Mr Loake?'

'Just Loake will do, thanks. What can I do for you, gents?'

'My name's Inspector Thorpe,' said the taller man, 'and this is Sergeant Hollis. May we come in?'

'How do,' said Loake affably. 'I won't invite you further than the hallway if you don't mind. The parlour is the only room for entertaining and I'd rather the family didn't hear the details of what I think you want to talk about.'

'Very well, Loake,' said Thorpe as the two men stepped into the tiny corridor, lit only by a forty watt bulb. Loake squeezed past them to shut the door, muffling the sounds of the piano rising up from the public house on the street below.

'You're the one who found the deceased party on the train in Inverness?' asked Thorpe.

'Yes, but I told all that to the Scotch police,' protested Loake. 'I'm on my day off now and I've got to get the morning train up there tomorrow. What are London coppers involved for?'

'There's been a development,' said Thorpe. 'The railway police asked us to look into it because half the people working on that train live in London.'

'Lumme, they could have waited until I was up in the frozen north again tomorrow. What's all the fuss for a poor chap dying of 'eart attack?'

'Because the Inverness police think it's murder,' said Hollis bluntly.

'Strewth,' said Loake. 'Who done it?'

'If we knew that we wouldn't be here,' said Thorpe. 'You were one of the last persons to see the man – Moffat – alive, according to the details the Inverness chaps gave us.'

'Was I?' asked Loake. 'Yus, I suppose I was,' he added thoughtfully. 'Here, you're not suggesting I...?'

'Just eliminating you from our enquiries,' said Hollis. 'We got most of your statement read out to us over the telephone.'

He looked down at a notebook. 'You say the last time you saw the deceased was when he was being put to bed by two men.'

'Yus, that's right,' said Loake. 'Business acquaintances, they said they was.'

'That's who we're interested in,' said Thorpe. 'Not you. Can you describe them?'

'Oh, now, that's a tall order,' said Loake, rubbing his jowls. 'I see a lot of gentlemen on that train and they all sort of blend into one, if you get my meaning.'

'Do try a bit harder, won't you?' sighed Hollis.

'All right, let me think,' said Loake. 'Tall order. That's something. One was a tall gentleman.'

'How tall?' asked Thorpe.

'Over six feet, I should say,' replied Loake. 'He was what you might call a well-dressed fellow. Expensive, like. You pick up a bit of knowledge about that sort of thing in my line of work, as I'm what you might call a "gentlemen's gentlemen" in a small way.'

'All right,' said Thorpe impatiently. 'Can you describe him?'

'Not really much to say,' said Loake. 'Clean shaven, average looking, wore a tweed overcoat and a white silk scarf.'

'And the other one?'

'Ah, now him I do recall a bit better as he looked to me not quite the type we usually have on the *Flying Caledonian*. Sort of rough looking, if you know what I mean. Could have done with a shave, and wore an 'at with a sort of feather in it.'

'Did they mention any names?'

'No, not them. And we don't keep a record either, afore you ask. We only 'as a list of names for them as booked sleeping compartments in advance. Those two weren't in the sleeping carriage anyway. I know because I checks all the tickets for the sleeping compartments, and they wasn't in any of them.'

Hollis looked at his notebook again. 'You said they put Moffat to bed and told you he shouldn't be disturbed.'

'That's right,' said Loake. 'I remember because…' he stopped talking and looked towards the door through which his wife had recently passed.

'Because what?' asked Thorpe.

'Because he give me a good tip,' Loake whispered.

Thorpe smiled. 'Don't worry, we won't tell the wife. All right, we've got most of this in your statement to the Inverness police. Did you see Moffat talk to anyone else on the train? Apart from the waiter in the dining car – we've already seen him.'

'No…no wait,' said Loake, smiling. 'Now that you ask, the poor fellow did speak to someone else. He was sat opposite a man in the dining car. A parson, he was.'

Thorpe and Hollis exchanged looks. 'The waiter mentioned him,' said Hollis. 'You didn't happen to catch his name, did you?'

'Oh, now…just a moment. No, it's gone. He did tell me, but I don't recall it.' Loake looked downcast. 'You'll have to check the manifest at the station.'

'Are you sure?' said Thorpe.

'That's it!' exclaimed Loake brightly. 'I *do* remember it. That's his name. Shaw.'

'What is?' asked Thorpe in a confused voice.

'Shaw's his name,' said Loake. 'S-H-A-W. Reverend Shaw. Seemed a nice gent as well. Tipped me two bob he did, which is more than I can recall getting from a churchman before. Some of them's as tight-fisted as …here, you don't think he had anything to do with…?'

'Well thank you, you've been very helpful,' interjected

Thorpe crisply. 'You might be getting another visit from the Inverness police tomorrow when you're up there so don't go off on your holidays just yet, will you?'

A sound of boys yelling followed by a scolding from Mrs Loake drifted out into the passageway. Thorpe winced and the two men turned to go.

'Holidays, me?' laughed Loake. 'With that lot in there to look after? Cor, work's the only rest I get. You can tell them Scotch police I'll be 'appy to see them. And if they can give me a night in a quiet cell I'll tell them anything they want to know.'

Chapter Six

Shaw strode through the darkened village in something of an angry mood; not a condition he was used to. He enjoyed, he realised, something of an elevated social position in his own village of Lower Addenham, and was generally not hindered in the duties of his day-to-day life; most of the people he dealt with in an official capacity had known him for years.

It was a long time since he had come up against obstructive bureaucracy; in fact, he had probably not experienced it since the war. He took a deep breath and slowed his pace slightly. It would not do to appear out of breath and red-faced at the house of a Justice of the Peace. There was no solicitor in the village and he did not think it a matter for the police; he noticed, anyway, that the lights of the little village police house were all extinguished.

He decided he was letting his emotions get the better of him. His uncle had just died; he had seen enough of death to know that people often got the wrong end of the stick in the heightened passions of a bereavement. Although he had not been close to his uncle, it was still something of a shock. Should he simply acquiesce to the wishes of Lewin?

No, he decided. The man was, for some reason, being deliberately obstructive. He would not himself dream of behaving in such a manner to the next of kin of a deceased person, and he decided Lewin needed to be put in his place. As he passed the Balmurie Inn, he heard laughter and a booming voice. The saloon bar was bathed in light and the large plate-glass window afforded a full view of the interior.

It was unusual, Shaw thought, in Scotland to see such a window without curtains; drinking normally went on in semi-secret in small towns such as this. He glanced through the window as he passed, and saw something so fantastical that he blinked, thinking it must be an illusion of some sort. No, he was not seeing things!

He looked again through the window of the Benmurie Inn. He breathed deeply and gathered his thoughts. Was he dreaming? He was often able to will himself to wake up from bad dreams, because some part of his subconscious was sufficiently aware that what he was experiencing was not real. This time, he did not wake up despite willing himself to, and so he resolved that there must be a logical explanation for what he was seeing.

Inside the public house, standing at the bar as large as life, was his uncle James!

Shaw rushed inside and was greeted by a wave of warm air laced with tobacco smoke. The room was empty except for the barman behind the bar and the elderly man, who was talking loudly and appeared rather the worse for drink. It looked like his uncle, but how could it be him? The man was dead. Surely it was some strange coincidence? Then the man began speaking tipsily in a booming Scots accent while he waved his arms expressively, a glass of whisky held in one hand.

'Then there was the time I played the Dane. *Hamlet*, you know. "Oh, that this too, too solid flesh would melt…," etcetera, et…cete…ra,' he declaimed. 'I had the honour of performing that particular part in the presence of Her Majesty the…' The man suddenly stopped talking as he caught sight of Shaw standing close by him. His arms stopped waving and some whisky splashed out from his glass on to the wooden floor.

Shaw stared at him open-mouthed. The man looked like his uncle – and yet it was clearly not him. His voice and manner were that of someone else.

The old man swallowed hard and drained his glass. 'If you will excuse me, my good man,' he slurred, 'I must away. *Exeunt, omnes!*'

He slammed the whisky glass on to the bar and strode past Shaw, staggering slightly as he went out of the door. Shaw raced after him.

'Wait!' he shouted. He looked down the street, which was now wreathed in a light mist, making the dimly-lit main street appear even dimmer. The man was nowhere to be seen.

Shaw returned to the bar; the barman looked at him with benign curiosity as he polished a glass.

'Who was that man?' asked Shaw loudly.

'Are ye all right sir?' asked the man. 'Ye look as if ye've had a bit of a shock.'

Shaw swallowed hard. 'Quite all right thank you.' He breathed in deeply, and spoke more politely this time.

'I wonder if you happen to know the name of that gentleman who just left. I should like to speak to him. Is he a guest here?'

'Him?' replied the man nonchalantly. 'I've no idea who he is. He doesnae stay here. Just passing through, he said. Kept me entertained for a while though. A wee bit too much in his cups for a week night, mind. Ah well. What can I get you, minister?'

'Nothing, thank you,' said Shaw distractedly. He walked briskly out of the bar and out on to the main street. There was no sign of the man anywhere; nor had he heard the sound of a motor car. The man seemed to have vanished into thin air – like a ghost.

Sir John Debayle-Bradley was in his sitting room at Balnacurin House, enjoying a large after-dinner brandy while reading the newspapers. His wife was still at their Edinburgh flat and the children were away at boarding school, so apart from his servants and dog, he had the place to himself.

A fire crackled in the grate, the orange light casting flickering shadows over the high, ornate Georgian ceiling. There was no sound except for the fire, and the loud, rhythmic ticking of a long-case clock in the corner of the room.

He turned to the financial pages of the newspaper and scanned the information on share prices, frowning. He then tossed the broadsheet away and picked up the Inverness evening paper. He frowned even more when he saw one of the articles on the front page.

Night train death: police to open murder enquiry

The police have announced a murder enquiry following the discovery of the body of Mr Harold Moffat, 39, on the London to Inverness night train on Tuesday morning. The death was previously thought to have been from natural causes but new evidence has come to light suggesting foul play. Detectives wish to speak to anybody who travelled on the train, particularly two men who claimed to have been acquaintances of the deceased, and a clergyman whose name is believed to be Reverend Shaw, who was seen speaking with Mr Moffat.

There followed details of the detective investigating the case; Sir John sipped his brandy and looked into the middle distance, thinking about what this could all mean. Enquiries would have to be made, he decided. Shaw – that was the man he had picked up on the road from the station.

It was fortunate, he thought, that through his political connections he knew certain senior members of the Inverness police. Now that Moffat was dead – murdered – this cast a new light on things. He cursed himself for not reading the evening paper yesterday. That was sloppy; when he became an MP he was going to have to keep watch on local events far more closely. He decided he would have one more drink, and then get to work.

Shaw felt uneasy about calling at Sir John's house at a relatively late hour, but remembered the man's cordial invitation to call on him should he need anything. He did not strike Shaw as the sort of man who would turn down a request for help.

Sir John's butler showed him into a large, shadowy sitting room and the man himself stood up to greet him.

'Mr Shaw, good evening,' said Sir John amiably. The two men shook hands and Sir John showed Shaw to a leather armchair facing his own across the fireplace. 'I would say "talk of the devil" but that would seem inappropriate in your case. Brandy? I shan't bother McKie again so allow me to pour you one myself.' He walked over to an ornate drinks cabinet in the corner.

'A small glass, please,' said Shaw. He did not quite know what to make of Sir John's remark about the devil.

'I'll pour you a large one,' said Sir John. 'I expect you'll need it.'

'Why?' asked Shaw, as Sir John handed him a heavy crystal glass. He took a sip of the warming liquid and felt instantly better.

'You've come about the murder, I assume?' said Sir John.

'Murder…?'

'You have seen the evening newspaper?'

'Today? No.'

'Ah. Well then. Take a look.'

Sir John handed Shaw the newspaper and he read the article on Moffat's death.

'Moffat must have been the little man in the raincoat,' mused the cleric. 'He did not tell me his name, but I did not speak to anyone else on the train apart from the steward. Murder…how terrible. I read the previous article about the death when it was assumed to be from natural causes, but since I did not know his name, I did not make the connection.'

'I must have missed that article but I'll keep a closer look in future,' said Sir John. 'A magistrate needs to be aware of this sort of thing. Sloppy of me.'

'But…why do detectives wish to speak to me?' asked Shaw. 'I barely said anything to him, the poor man.'

'They'll want to eliminate you from their enquiries, as the saying goes,' said Sir John.

'I must telephone to them immediately,' said Shaw, looking around the room. 'May I…'

'Just sit back for a bit, Mr Shaw,' said Sir John in a calming voice. 'You've had something of a shock. There's plenty of time to telephone later. If I know the Inverness police they'll be at home by the fire by now and won't be answering any telephones.'

'Yes, perhaps you are right,' said Shaw. He took another sip of brandy.

Sir John looked quizzically at Shaw. 'If you were not aware of the news of the murder, why *did* you come to see me?' he asked.

Shaw took a deep breath. He had not wanted to burden the man with too much detail, but after the incident at the Benmurie Inn, he decided he had to tell somebody or he feared he would take leave of his senses.

The long-case clock struck nine and Sir John looked into the fire. 'It's a peculiar thing,' he said. 'This man you saw – you are certain it was not your uncle?'

'In appearance he was, as far as I could tell, identical,' replied Shaw, 'but his voice was completely different.'

'Very well,' said Sir John. He took a couple of puffs on his cigar, and then replaced it in the ashtray on the small table beside his chair.

'So to summarise: you are summoned to Scotland by a telegram sent by Mr McKechnie which he claims he was instructed to send by a note which was delivered anonymously through his door in the night.'

'That is correct.'

'Have you seen this note?'

After a pause, Shaw replied in the negative.

'Let us go on,' said Sir John. 'You arrive at Colonel Shaw's house, and are told you may not see your uncle because he is recovering from an operation. You return, and meet his physician, who allows you to sit with your uncle for a while and pray with him.'

'Correct.'

'You are then introduced to a solicitor or lawyer of some sort claiming to be your uncle's attorney, by the name of Lewin, who claims your uncle has passed his property on to him for the purposes of some sort of trust.'

'That is right.'

'And did you see any *bona fides* or legal paperwork relating to this matter?'

'No, but Mr Lewin said that it would be provided if asked for. I have also established that the doctor, Keller, is who he claims to be.'

'How so?'

'By telephoning to his office at Edinburgh.'

'Very good. That is at least one thing out of the way. Then, you are informed that your uncle has died but it is not possible to view his body.'

'Yes.'

'Now we come to the strange part. On the way here, to discuss the matter of overcoming this obstruction, you see a man who appears to be, without wishing to sound too fantastical, the shade of your uncle.'

'It sounds fantastical, but yes.'

'Fantastical indeed, and we shall come to that later, but there is now another strand to the web, remember?'

Shaw thought for a moment and puffed on his pipe reflectively. 'The death of Moffat?'

'Very good. I can see you have the makings of a legal brain.'

'But how does that connect with...?'

'There's something you may not be aware of, Mr Shaw, and under the circumstances, I'll come clean with you. Let us just say I have had cause to have dealings with this Moffat fellow. He is – or was – a private investigator in the field of fraud. I believe he may have found out a few things of interest.'

'Of interest to whom?'

'Myself. I will be frank with you Mr Shaw. I have had my eye on this man Lewin for some time now. Your uncle chanced to mention him one night at the Benmurie Inn, and it piqued my interest. Unlike our cousins in the United States of America, judges here do not formally investigate crimes. But we do keep our ears to the ground and try to help the police where possible. I have not been able to prove anything, but he seems to be mixed up with some very shady characters in the financial world.'

'And you believe he is somehow involved in something…shady…with Colonel Shaw's estate?'

'I don't know. I do think it is possible that Moffat found out something about Lewin. Did he by any chance mention anything of interest while you had dinner with him on the train?'

'No. We merely exchanged a few pleasantries about the journey, and so on.'

'A pity,' said Sir John. 'I'm beginning to wonder if somebody had Moffat…well…let us say…*dealt* with.'

Shaw breathed in sharply. 'Are you suggesting Lewin had the man…murdered?'

'Again, I don't know Mr Shaw. And I would be wary of such utterances in public. I'm just looking at all the possibilities before we open Pandora's Box.'

'But where does the man in the Benmurie Inn fit in with all this?'

Sir John sighed. 'Mr Shaw, are you certain you saw this man?'

'Quite certain.'

'Any witnesses?'

'Are you suggesting I am making this up?'

'Not at all Mr Shaw. I am merely trying to establish if what you are saying will hold up under cross-examination in a court of law, should it come to that. Now, did anyone else see this man?'

'Yes, the barman at the Benmurie Inn.'

'A young man, with fair hair and a moustache?'

'Yes.'

'That would be Thomas McAllister. I have spoken to him a few times. He's a reliable witness, I should say. All right; now here's the important part. Could you swear in a court of law that the man you saw in bed *was* your uncle?'

Shaw's mind whirled. Had it been him? What was the man implying? He began to speak, then hesitated. 'I… but why should it *not* be my uncle?'

'Never mind that for the moment, Mr Shaw,' said Sir John, his eyes fixed on Shaw's. 'Do you, or do you not, have some doubt that the man you saw was your uncle?'

'I did not, until…'

'Until you saw the man in the Benmurie Inn?'

'Yes. Up until then it never occurred to me to doubt it was my uncle on his deathbed. Why should it not be? But seeing his…his double…made me wonder…but why in the Lord's name…?'

Sir John puffed on his cigar several times and blew a long stream of smoke up towards the darkened ceiling. He looked thoughtfully into his brandy glass, which glinted with orange light reflected from the fireplace.

'Mr Shaw, I am an analytical man. A financier, a magistrate and, hopefully, soon a Member of Parliament. I must deal in concrete realities. I do not pretend to have your spiritual insights and there may be some explanation for all this which is beyond our understanding. But until such explanations are vouchsafed to us, I think we must face the two most likely explanations.'

'Occam's Razor,' murmured Shaw.

'What?' asked Sir John.

'Nothing,' said Shaw. 'Please continue.'

Sir John put his glass down and pointed to his palm. 'The two most likely explanations are as follows: One: that a person or persons unknown, for some nefarious reason, employed someone who looked like your uncle to act in his place.'

'But why…?'

'Wait, please, Mr Shaw,' said Sir John, raising his hand and then placing two fingers in his palm.

'Two: that your uncle is not dead, and perhaps not even ill, but for some reason is going about alive and well and did not, or would not recognise you when he saw you in the Benmurie Inn.'

Shaw thought for a moment. The implications were horrific. 'But,' he protested, 'would not the landlord have recognised my uncle? I believe he attended the Benmurie Inn quite regularly.'

'McAllister is new, I believe,' said Sir John, 'and one of several barmen there. Perhaps he has not met the Colonel before.'

'Perhaps…' mused Shaw. 'But the man I saw looked like my uncle, but certainly did not sound like him.'

'So it was only his voice that jarred with you?'

'Yes. In appearance, he was identical. That is why it was such a shock to see him.'

Shaw was about to add a remark about understanding now how the disciples must have felt when seeing the risen Lord for the first time, but something stopped him. He had a strong sense that there was nothing mystical about any of this.

'Very well then,' replied Sir John, draining his brandy glass. 'I think we can rule out the second possibility, that the man you saw was actually your uncle. Which leaves us with the first possibility; that he is some sort of "double".

'Posing as my uncle? But why…?'

'I do not know, Mr Shaw. My guess is, he was used in some way to sign legal papers or withdraw money from a bank, because the Colonel refused to comply.'

'Then why on earth was the man drinking whisky in a local pub?' asked Shaw in an exasperated voice.

'Again, I do not know. It seems however there is a way to settle this. If Lewin can be persuaded to let you view your uncle's body, it will put your mind at rest that he is not somehow still alive and wandering around the public houses of Inverness-shire.'

'It would be a start, at least,' mused Shaw. 'I should like to see him for the last time, despite all this.'

'Quite right,' said Sir John. 'Lewin is on pretty shaky legal ground denying you that right anyway, if you ask me. Leave it to me, Mr Shaw. I'll see to it that you are allowed to say a proper farewell, and then we can speak to the police about these other goings on. We will get to the bottom of this, rest assured.'

'Speaking of the police,' said Shaw, 'I really ought to make a telephone call to them. It says quite clearly in the newspaper that they wish to speak to me about Moffat's death.'

Sir John smiled and raised his hand. 'As I said before Mr Shaw, we can leave that until tomorrow. "Sufficient unto the day is the evil thereof", as the good book says. In my experience of these matters there is no point in bothering the police at this late hour. One is liable to be held on the telephone for a very long time.

'No, leave this to me; I shall call on this Mr Lewin tomorrow morning and explain in no uncertain terms that he is not to forbid you access to view your uncle's body. I shall then call on you at the manse at noon and we shall go down there together. Once that is done, you and I shall begin a little investigation into these other matters. We need to get our case in order before we go blundering in to police stations with stories of conspiracies.'

Shaw got up to go. 'You have been very helpful, Sir John.'

The baronet waved the compliment away. 'Not at all. I shall get McKie to drive you in the Bentley.'

'No need,' said Shaw. 'It is not far to walk, and I should like to have some time to think.'

'Very well,' said Sir John. 'Oh...and a word to the wise...how well do you know the minister, McKechnie?'

'Not well,' replied Shaw. 'He and his wife have been most hospitable.'

'Of course, of course,' said Sir John with a smile. 'It's just that...one hears rumours in small towns like this, and, well, suffice to say I wouldn't go telling him about our conversation this evening.'

'Rumours, Sir John?'

'I've said too much, I fear. I am sure our minister is an upstanding man. Best not to mention any of this to him or anyone else for that matter. *Sub judice,* and all that.'

They walked to the hallway and McKie impassively opened the large front door with its fan window above. 'I understand, Sir John,' said Shaw. 'Goodnight,' he added, and stepped out into the misty Highland evening.

Keller was in his room at Auchentorrin Lodge, packing instruments into a medical bag which he had placed on the bed. The woman known as Miss Graham stood beside him, a carpet bag on the floor next to her.

'We are leaving?' she asked.

'If you mean together, then no,' said Keller. 'I have already explained that.'

'You said this would be the last time of working together, and that after this we would be married.'

'I know…but things are…complicated. We need to wait.'

'I have been waiting too long.'

'This is a complicated business matter. It cannot be hurried.'

'I do not talk of business,' said Miss Graham, her eyes flashing fire. 'I mean our marriage.'

'Cosmina, my dear…'

'You said we should not use our names in this house.'

'I know, but your Christian name does not matter, and besides, who will now hear it?'

'Very well. But I have waited long enough to become your wife.'

'And so you shall be, my dear,' said Keller, reaching out to stroke her cheek. She pulled away.

'Yes, your *wife*.' she said angrily. 'Not your…what is the word…concubine.'

'Please, Cosmina,' replied Keller testily. 'Spare me your middle-class morality. There is my wife to consider.'

'And that is not middle class morality also?'

'I am speaking in practical terms. Divorce is difficult.'

'I thought here it was not forbidden. Which is why we had to leave the other country.'

'It is allowed but difficult. It requires lawyers, court cases, a staging of adultery in front of paid witnesses in sordid hotel rooms.'

Miss Graham's eyes widened. 'You mean others are required to watch while we…?'

'No, no,' said Keller with a bitter laugh. 'It is entirely a pretence, a fabrication in order to satisfy a judge. It also is likely to mean disgrace for a man in my position, even in today's supposedly more tolerant society, which is why we need to have the money first.'

'I suppose so…' said Miss Graham, her voice softening. 'But I do not like this business.'

'Nor I, my dear, but think of the money.'

'Very well. I shall see you again in Edinburgh?'

'Most certainly. As soon as I can get away.'

Miss Graham appeared placated, and lifted up her carpet bag. Suddenly, there was a sound from downstairs, as if someone was thumping on the French doors at the rear of the house. Keller led the way cautiously down the stairs, with Miss Graham following behind.

'Fetch the others,' he whispered. 'They are in their rooms.'

Miss Graham turned and walked back up the stairs, while Keller reached the hall. There was another sound from the drawing room, as if somebody were rattling the French doors.

Keller hesitated at the door of the drawing room and flicked on the hall lights; Tench and Lewin appeared behind him with Miss Graham at the rear. He was relieved to hear the crisp sound of Tench loading a shotgun.

Keller turned the handle of the drawing door and flung it open. Ahead, lit by the light of a dim bulb on the garden terrace, they could see the figure of a man pressed against the patio doors.

Miss Graham screamed, and then the doors both gave way inwards. The man collapsed face down on to the dusty, ancient Persian carpet.

There was at the same time a crash and tinkle of broken glass as the man dropped a bottle from his hand, which landed on the hard parquet floor next to the carpet.

Lewin stepped forward and looked down. His lip curled in disgust as he pushed the man over on to his front with his booted foot. 'You damned fool,' he hissed. 'What the hell are you doing back here?'

'You're back just in time,' said McKechnie, as Shaw entered the darkened manse. 'I was about to lock up for the night, and getting worried about you. How is the Colonel?'

'My uncle is dead,' said Shaw simply.

'"Rest eternal grant him O Lord and let light perpetual shine upon him",' said McKechnie solemnly. 'Come and sit down, man,' he added, patting Shaw's shoulder and leading him into his study.

'A Catholic prayer for the dead,' said Shaw with a smile. 'Not very Calvinistic.'

'We Calvinists are a wee bit too dry when it comes to death if you ask me,' said McKechnie. 'Your uncle wouldn't have minded.'

The two men sat down in the armchairs in McKechnie's study. The Scotsman took a bottle of whisky and two glasses from a cupboard.

'Will you have a dram?'

'Thank you but no,' said Shaw. 'I had a drink at Sir John's.'

'You've been to see him then? Is that lawyer still causing problems?'

'Yes. He refused to allow me to see my uncle's body.'

McKechnie's face curled in disgust as he took a sip of whisky. 'Disgraceful. You were right to see Sir John about it. What did he say?'

Shaw hesitated. He remembered Sir John's warning about divulging too much information.

'He is going to use his influence to persuade Lewin to allow me access. I hope, also, that he will be able to allow us to begin funeral arrangements.'

'You'll want to officiate?'

'I think not, Mr McKechnie. It is your parish and the duty should go to you.'

'Aye, very well. It will be an honour.'

McKechnie's dog padded into the room and sat down beside him; he stroked his head and then took another sip of whisky.

'There is one thing…' began Shaw. 'You said you received a note asking you to summon me here.'

'That's right.'

'I don't suppose you recognised the handwriting?'

'I can't say I did. It was a sort of scrawl, as if it were done in a hurry.'

'Do you still have the note?'

There was a pause; McKechnie scratched his chin.

'Now let me think. I know I took it to the post office, but…it must be around here somewhere. But I'm not the tidiest of men, as you can see.'

He pointed to his desk which was piled with various papers and letters.

'Do you need to see it this instant?'

'No, thank you. If it turns up I shall be interested to see it.'

'Why?'

'No particular reason,' said Shaw.

In the little police office at Inverness railway station, Sergeant Nesbitt buttoned up his tunic and decided to call it a night. He should have ended his shift hours ago, but had been asked – ordered, if truth be told – to help on the Moffat murder case. He had begrudged it at first but now he was beginning to feel something approaching enthusiasm for his job, something he had not felt for a long time.

The railway police were more used to dealing with crimes of petty theft and trespass than murder and rarely ventured off railway property. The regular police detective appointed to the matter – Inspector Walter McLeish – had, however, seconded Nesbitt due to much of the investigation taking place on the railway. There was a risk, McLeish said, that if they did not clear this matter up quickly, detectives from Edinburgh or even Scotland Yard would be sent to take over, and they would be reduced to the status of lackeys. If they managed to crack the case quickly, however, it could mean promotion for both of them.

Nesbitt looked across the desk of his little office at McLeish, who was still brooding over various reports that he had brought in with him when he had taken over Nesbitt's office.

He had a perfect detective's face; neither thin nor fat, his hair neither fair, dark nor grey. It was a face which could fit in anywhere and be forgotten immediately, making him an ideal 'undercover' man. He looked back at Nesbitt and spoke to him.

'How did you get on with that clerical directory?'

'*Crockford's*? Aye sir,' replied Nesbitt. 'I managed to get hold of a copy from the public library. They didn't want to let it out of the building at first so I had to be a bit stern with them.'

'Good man. Found anyone called Shaw?'

'There are four of them in the whole country, sir.'

'Try to eliminate all of them. Shaw could be a valuable witness and apart from those two men who helped Moffat to his bed, he's the only person we know to have spoken to the deceased that we haven't spoken to yet.'

'I will do, sir. I'm starting with the ones closest to London. One's in central London, another's in a place called Pinner, which I think is close. Then the next one's in…' He looked down at his notes and looked up again. 'In a wee village somewhere in Suffolk. The last one I found is in Cornwall.'

'Right, the London boys we spoke to before can deal with the first two. Get on the telephone first thing tomorrow to them. Then telephone to the Suffolk and Cornwall police.'

'I'll need a priority clearance for the telephone exchange,' said Nesbitt. 'That's a lot o' trunk calls needing to be put through.'

'Don't worry,' replied his superior, 'I'll give you a chit. The calls can be routed through Inverness central police station. They'll not keep you waiting.'

'Thank you sir. Can I be away home now? Only the wife…'

'Yes, yes,' said McLeish distractedly, then he looked up. 'Wait a minute, let me see that directory.'

Nesbitt passed the heavy book over to McLeish and he looked at the cover. 'This says Anglican clergy. How do we know he was Anglican?'

'I've thought about that, sir,' said Nesbitt proudly. 'Chances are he is Anglican. We know he's English, so that rules out the Scots churches, most probably. We know he's no' a Roman Catholic.'

'How so? Aren't they called Reverend?'

'I think they call themselves Father, and Loake never mentioned that. Said the fellow called himself Reverend.

Anyway, the Catholics wear awful strange clothes. Black robes and wide-brimmed hats and the like. This fellow was in tweeds, according to Loake.'

'Hmm, what if he was a, what do you call them, Methodist, or Baptist or something? You'll need to get another directory for them.'

'I don't think so sir. Many of them never wear a clerical collar. And, he was seen drinking wine in the dining car and I'm pretty sure those types dinnae approve of that.'

'You may be right,' said McLeish in a tone of grudging admiration. 'That's a clever theory but don't get carried away with yourself. I'd say a lot of these chaps take a drink when they think nobody they know's watching. All right, let's start with these Anglican ones and if we don't find him we'll move on to the other ranks.'

'All right, sir. But do we stop there? There's a Reverend Shaw in the Irish Free State as well.'

'Are there any Protestants left there?' replied McLeish jocularly. 'Must be a lonely beggar. Och, don't worry about him for now – if it was him he would most likely have come on the ferry from Stranraer, not the train from London. Away you go home.'

Chapter Seven

October, thought Mrs Shaw as she walked back from the churchyard of All Saints', Lower Addenham, was really one of the nicest months in the calendar. The evenings were still relatively light, and in Suffolk on the dry side of England it was sometimes even mild enough to sit in the garden. The long roll-call of Sundays after Trinity seemed to go on and on, into the 'teens and then the twenties, until… now how did Keats put it, she thought to herself, then remembered the line of poetry. 'Until they think warm days will never cease.'

The sun shone and the countryside was bathed in gold, the churchyard strewn with bright yellow leaves; from a field somewhere beyond the village came a whiff of bonfire smoke. That lowered her spirits slightly, as it made her think of Bonfire Night, which always seemed a rather forced festival of jollity, a rearguard action against the encroaching dark of November, a month made more solemn in recent years by the commemoration of Armistice Day.

Stop brooding and make the best of it, she said to herself. She realised she was missing her husband and hoped that he would soon return. She longed for news – the most recent letter from Shaw had been uncharacteristically terse. She tried to recall the last time they had been separated for more than a night, and could not.

She had just returned to the vicarage and was taking off her coat in the hall, thinking to herself what instructions to give Hettie regarding luncheon. Then the door bell rang.

'It's all right, Hettie, I'll go,' she called out to the kitchen, thinking it would be somewhat pretentious to affect that she had not heard it, and then wait for the servant to arrive.

When she opened it, she was surprised to see Fred Arbon, one of the church bell-ringers who worked also as a Special Constable, towering in front of her. He still had on his bicycle clips, she noticed, and perspired slightly as he fumbled to remove his helmet.

'Sorry to disturb you ma'am,' he said, in broad Suffolk tones, tucking the helmet under his arm and smoothing back his thinning hair. 'I wondered if the vicar was at home.'

'Oh…' replied Mrs Shaw. 'I'm sorry, Fred, but he's away at the moment.'

'It's "PC Arbon" while I'm on dooty if you don't mind, Mrs Shaw,' said the policeman awkwardly.

'Of course, PC Arbon,' replied Mrs Shaw politely. 'I wouldn't want to get you into trouble.'

'Ah, that's all right,' said Arbon, still looking slightly worried. 'May I ask, ma'am, where the vicar's gorn? Only, that's rather important, like.'

'He's visiting a sick relative in Scotland.'

'That's awkward,' said Arbon. 'Didn't happen to leave an address, did he?'

'Yes, I can fetch it for you if you like. What's all this about, constable?' Mrs Shaw was beginning to feel rather concerned.

'May I come in for a moment, ma'am?' said Arbon.

'Of course. Would you like to bring your bicycle into the garden?'

Mrs Shaw pointed to the machine, black and official looking, propped up against the vicarage wall.

'That's all right there ma'am,' said Arbon as he stepped into the hall. 'Nobody's likely to nick that old thing.'

Mrs Shaw closed the door. 'Now, may I offer you a cup of tea?' she asked.

'Er no, thank you Mrs Shaw, I'll come straight to the point.' Arbon took his notebook out of his top pocket.

'Fact is,' he continued with some hesitation, 'your husband's wanted to help the police with their enquiries.'

'Oh dear…in what regard?'

'I'm not in possession of all the facts myself, but I got a telephone call this morning from the Midchester station who in turn got a call from the police in Scotland. They want to talk to your husband in connection with…well there's no other way of putting it ma'am, seeing as you are 'is wife and all – that's in connection with a murder.'

'Oh dear,' repeated Mrs Shaw, this time more forcefully. 'Not *again*.'

At noon, Shaw took a light luncheon provided early by Mrs McKechnie, which was followed by a glass of whisky from her husband. 'You'll not view a corpse without a drink inside you,' he had said, despite Shaw's protestations at the earliness of the hour.

Sir John arrived in his Bentley right on time, and he and Shaw drove the short distance to Auchentorrin Lodge.

'I trust you won't find these people as obstructive now,' said Sir John as he awkwardly double-declutched while changing down gear on a tight bend.

'How did you manage it?' asked Shaw.

Sir John chuckled. 'By putting that chap Lewin in his place. He's a jumped-up barrister's clerk, if you ask me. To tell you the truth, I'm not exactly sure of his rights in this matter – it's not my area – but one thing I do know is when someone's trying to pull the wool over my eyes. I quoted a few legal precedents at him and he backed down without a murmur.'

'Then we have right on our side,' said Shaw.

'Don't be sure of that,' replied Sir John. 'The legal precedents I quoted were made up off the top of my head. That's how I knew he was shamming. I'm sceptical as to whether he's had much legal training of any kind. Seems to be more of a jack-of-all-trades as far as I can make out. Anyway, that investigation is for another day.

'The important thing is you can say your farewells. And, I've told him there's to be no funny business about his trust or whatever it is arranging a funeral either. The Colonel will be buried in the local churchyard by Mr McKechnie according to the rites and ceremonies of the Church of Scotland as by law established.'

As if to drive home his point he pressed down the accelerator of the car which surged forward up a short incline before turning into the driveway of Auchentorrin Lodge, where it stopped amid a spray of gravel.

Before they alighted from the car, Shaw remembered something.

'Did you manage to speak to the police?' he asked.

'Police?'

'Yes. About them wishing to speak to me regarding Moffat's death.'

'Oh, that. Yes, I telephoned to the Chief Constable this morning. You'll probably have a visit from them today, or tomorrow, I should imagine. They probably have dozens of people they wish to speak to.'

'Thank you,' said Shaw. 'That puts my mind at rest. Did you mention to him your suspicions about Lewin?'

'Not just yet,' replied Sir John. 'I want to get some watertight evidence before I start anything. That's partly why I'm coming along with you today. Gives me a chance to keep an eye on these people. But don't mention any of this to them, will you, Mr Shaw? We don't want them getting wind of us and clearing off.'

'Certainly not,' said Shaw. 'Let us attend to the matter in hand.'

'Good show. Let's get cracking then.'

The two men approached the door and Sir John rang the doorbell; quicker than usual, the door was opened by Miss Graham who looked at them suspiciously. She looked tired and her eyes were red rimmed, noticed Shaw, as if she had not had enough sleep or had been crying.

'Hello again, ma'am,' said Sir John jovially, but Shaw noted the authority in his voice. 'Back again as promised.'

'Come this way please,' said Miss Graham in a clipped and professional manner, as she showed them into the hallway. Keller and Lewin stood before them, but Tench, Shaw noted, was nowhere to be seen.

'You still here, Keller?' asked Sir John. 'Thought you'd be off by now. No sense hanging around a dead patient, surely? Rather bad for business, I'd think.'

Keller scowled. Sir John is enjoying this, thought Shaw, and if truth be told, so was he. It was always satisfying to see the tables turned on deliberately difficult people.

'Colonel Shaw may be dead,' said Keller calmly, 'but he is still my patient and I intend to see his body is removed in a decent manner. I shall be remaining here until the undertakers arrive later today.'

'Don't look so upset, Lewin,' said Sir John affably. 'Haven't you some papers to tie up in pink ribbon?'

Lewin's face remained impassive, but Shaw noticed a flicker of distaste as the lawyer stepped aside into the study. Keller followed him, and Sir John led Shaw up the stairs to the Colonel's bedroom.

'I expect you'd like to be left alone,' said Sir John in low tones, sounding more respectful than he had downstairs. 'I'll wait for you out here.'

Shaw thanked the man and stepped into the room. His uncle's body lay under a sheet on the bed, and with some trepidation he turned it down to reveal the familiar shock of white hair and lean features, now drawn taut and waxen in death, a clean bandage still in place over his throat marking where Keller had performed his unsuccessful operation. He was filled with an intense sense of sadness.

He knew the subject of praying for the dead was a contentious one in his church, and his own views on it were mixed; petitions for the repose of souls were rather too Roman Catholic, he decided, and so instead he knelt and said the Lord's Prayer.

He stood up and was about to replace the sheet over his uncle's face when something stopped him. The words of a passage from St John's gospel suddenly occurred to him, almost as if they had been spoken out loud by someone in the room.

'Then saith he to Thomas, reach hither thy finger, and behold my hands; and reach hither thy hand, and thrust it into my side: and be not faithless, but believing.'

It was the moment when Doubting Thomas had encountered the risen Lord and had refused to believe who he was until he could touch the spear-mark upon Jesus' body. Why had this passage occurred to him? Then his nose began to itch and he fought back a sneeze, which in turn reminded him of the snuff-loving Dr Sneddie.

It was then that he remembered. Dr Sneddie had mentioned heavy scarring on one of his uncle's knees. Without pausing to think of the propriety of the act or even why he was doing it, Shaw gently lifted the sheet from the lower part of the body. He looked closely for a few moments until he was sure. The knee of each white leg was smooth, hairless, and utterly devoid of scarring.

After Sir John had dropped him off at the manse, Shaw was left to his own devices as McKechnie had to make a parish visit and his wife was busy with her church ladies' group.

After posting a short letter to Mrs Shaw informing her of the death of his uncle (but leaving out any hint of his suspicions) he was left alone in the house, and spent the morning dipping into McKechnie's extensive library on military history.

Shaw took out the letter from his uncle and read it again. It seemed strange, he thought, to read the words of someone who was now lying cold and dead, but at the same time oddly comforting; a sense of the continuity of life stretching from the past, through the present and then beyond, into God's mercy and the world to come.

He sighed and put the letter back into his rucksack. He then noticed, tucked into the inner pocket of the bag, a piece of paper. He took it out and found an envelope, with 'the occupant' on the front. How on earth had it got there? he wondered. He opened it and found a note and underneath it another envelope. With increasing alarm he read the note.

Dear Sir,
Apologies for the scrawl and for pushing this under your door. I have reason to believe my life may be in danger. I intend to claim the enclosed letter back from you before you alight the train at Inverbrodie.

If I do not, please assume the worst. The letter must be delivered to the addressee as soon as possible. You will of course also need to inform the police.

Please accept my apologies for this intrusion – I do not even know your name but from our conversation I assumed you were a trustworthy man and you may be the only hope I have.

Yours faithfully
H.R. Moffat.

Shaw felt fear rising in the pit of his stomach. He now realised where the letter had come from – the steward on the train had seen it on the floor of the compartment, and put it in his rucksack, and Shaw had assumed the man was referring to his uncle's letter instead.

It was horrific – like something, he suddenly thought, from the novels of Thomas Hardy – one man's fate hinging on a tiny accident or misunderstanding. He breathed deeply; no, he thought; the universe did not operate like that. There was a divine order and it was not for him to question it, only to trust and obey. Now, he decided, he must deliver this letter.

Perhaps, he thought, Sir John would be able to drive them in his motor car to whoever the letter was intended for. He turned over the enclosed envelope to look at the address. He felt the fear rise again in his stomach. It was addressed to his uncle, Colonel Shaw.

Later in the afternoon, Shaw sat in an armchair in McKechnie's study, the room in which he had been given free access to the minister's library, and puffed on his pipe reflectively. McKechnie sat opposite him, his parish visiting finished for the day.

'You're looking glum again, Mr Shaw,' he said. 'Remember your uncle's in a better place, in the arms of the Lord until the last day. '

'Yes…' replied Shaw hesitatingly.

'Is it the funeral arrangements you're concerned about? You need not be, I'll be happy to organise everything if you are needed back in England. You can always come up again on the train for the ceremony.'

'No, it is not that, I am sure you are most capable and it is kind of you to undertake the task.'

'What then?' asked McKechnie in his characteristically blunt manner. 'I can tell when something's troubling a man.'

Ought he to divulge his suspicions?, wondered Shaw. Sir John had warned him about mentioning too much lest it could prejudice an investigation, and yet…he decided to risk it. Experience had taught him that if he kept his theories to himself, they were liable to expand in all sorts of directions that perhaps might not lead to the truth.

'I am concerned that my uncle's body has been substituted.'

'What on earth…?' said McKechnie with alarm.

'I am convinced the man I saw in the bed just now is not my uncle.'

'How can you be sure? You've not seen him for a year.'

'Yes, I know,' replied Shaw, 'and the man did closely resemble the photograph of my uncle which I saw in Auchentorrin Lodge. But there is one vital difference.'

Shaw explained about the scarring on the Colonel's knees and the absence of the same on the body's legs. McKechnie looked concerned.

'But why, Mr Shaw? What would be the point?'

'It is my belief that some form of fraudulent activity is in progress. A conspiracy, if you will. Sir John is in agreement with me.'

'You told him all this?'

'Yes. He was most considerate, but has asked that I refrain from further investigation until the police have had a chance to talk to me. They may call at some time today or tomorrow.'

'What do the police know?'

'They wish to talk to me in connection with the death of a man named Moffat on the train on which I arrived here.'

Shaw went on to explain the suspicions of Sir John regarding what Moffat may have discovered about Lewin. After some hesitation, he also mentioned the letter addressed to his uncle.

'And you've not opened it?' asked McKechnie.

'It ought to go to his executors, I feel.'

'For the Lord's sake man, after what you've told me about this Lewin? I'd open it myself this minute, and devil take the executors.'

'Perhaps later.'

'Aye, I hope so. So you think your uncle's been murdered?'

'I do not know what to think. It seems the most obvious explanation – that the conspirators killed him and substituted a man of very similar appearance in his place.'

'But why?'

'Presumably to carry out some form of financial transactions posing as my uncle.'

'But then…why's the double dead as well?'

'I dread to think. I believe it's possible the gang killed him also.'

'To stop him talking, once he was no use to them?'

'Something of that sort. I also think they may have found out I saw him in the Benmurie Inn.'

'What? You mean the man was wandering around a public house?'

'Yes. I am certain it was him now. My guess is that after I saw him, he returned to Auchentorrin Lodge, admitted to the conspirators that he had seen me, and then…'

'I see…it sounds devilish, Mr Shaw – devilish. They couldn't risk him being seen alive. And that's why they suddenly became co-operative when Sir John told them you'd a right to see your uncle's body. It didn't matter to them by then, because they really did have a dead body for you to look at.'

Shaw nodded, and McKechnie slammed his fist into the arm of the leather chair.

'I've a mind to take my gun and go down there right now and get the truth from them,' he growled.

Shaw raised his hand. 'No, Mr McKechnie, if you please. "Put up again thy sword into his place: for all they that take the sword shall perish with the sword."'

'Yes, yes, St Matthew's gospel,' sighed McKechnie. 'You're right of course. But do you not feel righteous anger, Mr Shaw?'

'It has its place, perhaps, but let us not rush into anything. I have some experience in these matters and believe me it does not do to run anywhere with guns blazing. We are not on the Western Front any more.'

'Perhaps you're right,' said McKechnie.

He sank back into his armchair. 'I've been a soldier for a while longer than I've been a minister. Sometimes I forget which I am.'

'As Sir John said, it is best to leave the matter to the police. They will soon call, I have no doubt.'

McKechnie moved in his seat. Shaw could tell the man was filled with nervous energy like a coiled spring.

'But we've no idea when they'll speak to you,' he said. 'As far as they're concerned, you'll just be one of a long line of potential witnesses. They might not even bother speaking to you. Why don't you telephone them now?'

'Thank you but no,' said Shaw firmly. 'I think that would constitute a similar, albeit less dramatic blunder, to attempt to force a confession from Lewin by force of arms. There are still some things I am unsure of.'

'Such as what?'

'Such as, why would Keller, as he claimed he did, deliver a note to you asking you to send me a telegram stating that my uncle was gravely ill? It makes no sense.'

'Aye, there is that. I thought it mighty strange at the time. Why not just send a telegram from the post office himself?'

'If there was a plot to conceal my uncle's murder, why summon me at all? The whole thing could have been done in my absence and I would have been none the wiser. By the way...have you found the note?'

'Oh, yes, I did that,' said McKechnie, fumbling in his jacket pocket. He handed Shaw a crumpled piece of paper.

Shaw looked at the note and read the scrawled pencilled inscription: "Send urgent telegram Rev Shaw Lr Addenham Suffolk: Uncle James gravely ill come at once."'

'Do you recognise the handwriting, Mr Shaw?'

'No. May I retain this? It may be required at some later date as evidence.'

'Be my guest.' McKechnie leaned back in his chair.

'It's lucky you reminded me of it,' he continued, 'as it might have gone on the fire otherwise. Jeannie's always tidying my desk and throwing wee bits of paper out. Och, I wish I could be of more help, but I've got a baptism later and after that a parish meeting. Not that many will come mind, as they're all going over to the Old Covenanters' kirk, for some popular hell-fire preacher from Carlisle they all want to hear...a dour windbag from what I've heard...but here's me havering on. Should you not be down to the police house right away?'

'I think not, just yet,' replied Shaw. 'In order to build a case, we must play the conspirators at their own game and use legal means to thwart them. Then, if all this has been some terrible mistake, nobody's reputation need suffer.'

'All right then. How do we do that?'

'If I may, I will use your telephone, but rather than call the police directly, I intend to call upon the services of Sir John again.'

Shaw put through a telephone call to Sir John, asking to speak with him on a matter of some urgency. The magistrate invited Shaw to call at his house at his earliest convenience, rather than discuss it over the telephone, and Shaw agreed.

McKechnie had to motor out to some remote corner of the parish to baptise the aforementioned baby which was too sickly to attend church. Shaw's offer to assist Mrs McKechnie with any chores she might have was dismissed out of hand. 'I'll not have any guest in my house lift a finger to work,' she said, 'especially not someone who's grieving.'

Shaw was once again left to his own devices. In the little back bedroom he placed the mysterious note asking for a telegram to be sent, alongside the last letter he had received from his uncle. There was no resemblance in the handwriting. It had been something of a long shot to think his uncle might have written the note – if he had the means to do so, why not explain the situation more fully?

It had to be someone else, but who? There was no reason for Keller's gang to attract attention by summoning a relative who might endanger their plot – if indeed, there *was* a plot.

Shaw sighed, and replaced the note and letter in his jacket. Then his eye lighted on the letter from Moffat. The one which was to be delivered to his uncle post-haste. He knew that, strictly speaking, it ought to be given to Lewin as the Colonel's executor, but under the circumstances, he decided it would be best to open it.

He slipped his little finger under the corner of the flap and opened the envelope. His eyes widened as he read the contents, and he nodded to himself with a grim and unwelcome sense of satisfaction.

'Mrs McKechnie!' he called, as he bounded down the stairs. The minister's wife emerged from the kitchen, wiping her hands on a towel.

'Aye Mr Shaw, what is it?'

'Would you kindly tell your husband when he returns,' he said breathlessly as he put on his coat, 'that I have decided to call on Sir John immediately. New evidence has come to light.'

'New evidence…?' asked Mrs McKechnie in a confused voice.

'I cannot explain now,' said Shaw as he stepped out into the bracing Highland afternoon. 'He will understand. Tell him that the matter in hand can now be resolved.'

Twenty-five minutes later he was ringing the heavy wrought iron bell-pull of Sir John Debayle-Bradley's front door.

McKechnie emerged from his little car in the driveway of the manse and paused for a moment before entering the house. His mind was pre-occupied; he had performed the baptism of the sick child perfunctorily, his thoughts straying to the conversation he had had with Shaw earlier that afternoon. Could it really be true that a monstrous conspiracy was taking place under their very noses? It was a terrible thought. He decided he would question Shaw a bit further about just exactly what he knew – or thought he knew.

He looked into his study, and finding that the man was not there, he called his name up the stairs.

'He's gone out, dear,' said his wife from the kitchen doorway. 'Are you all right?'

'Out? Was it with the…' He was about to say 'police', but checked himself. He did not want his wife to know about any of this, until she had to.

'With the what?'

'Nothing.'

'Oh, he did say something about telling you "the matter in hand can now be resolved."'

McKechnie frowned. 'Did he say where he was going?'

'Aye, to Sir John's house.'

McKechnie breathed a sigh of relief. He was concerned that Shaw might have decided to single-handedly expose the supposed conspiracy at Auchentorrin Lodge with some rash act of amateur detection.

'That's all right then,' he said, unbuttoning the Geneva bands from his neck as he began to change out of his clerical clothing.

'What's he wanting with Sir John?' asked Mrs McKechnie.

'Nothing to worry about, dear,' replied her husband. 'Just…legal matters to do with the Colonel's death. I'll away into the kitchen with you in a minute for some tea.'

As he changed in his study, he thought he caught sight of a face peering at him from the hedge outside, but when he blinked and looked again, it was gone. He shook his head. Imagining things, he thought to himself. Shaw and all his plots. All this talk of murder was probably, he decided – or rather, hoped – a huge misunderstanding.

Shaw was shown into Sir John's study by McKie, the impassive butler, and the two men were left alone in the large, high ceilinged room. Sir John sat in his armchair by the cold fireplace and rose to greet Shaw.

A panting sound came from beside the chair and Shaw noticed a large, black Doberman Pinscher seated between the chair and the fireplace.

'I trust you like dogs, Mr Shaw?' said Sir John as he rose to greet the clergyman. 'Don't worry about Blucher here, his bark is far worse than his bite.'

The dog looked disinterestedly at Shaw and then settled back down and closed his eyes.

'I have a terrier myself,' said Shaw.

'A wise decision. Far easier to look after and much more economical to run. Have a seat, won't you?' Sir John gestured towards the armchair opposite him.

Shaw sat down and looked intently at Sir John. 'I apologise for the call,' he said, 'but something rather important has come up.'

'Not at all, dear chap, not at all,' said Sir John. 'Have the police got hold of you yet?'

'Not yet, and I fear we must wait at their convenience no longer.'

'What has happened?'

Shaw explained about the lack of scarring on his uncle's knees, and then about the letter and how it had come into his possession.

'May I see it?' asked Sir John. His voice was calm as usual, but Shaw detected a hint of "the game is afoot" excitement in his tone. He handed the letter over, and Sir John read it aloud.

> Dear Colonel Shaw…this is to let you know that the enclosed letter may be of the utmost importance in the case. Without going into too much detail, suffice to say it was found in the offices of Mr Lewin in London.
>
> I believe the names at the bottom may refer to two members of a known criminal organisation wanted for fraud in more than one European country. Whilst any further investigation will be a matter for the police, let this be warning to you to have no further dealings with Mr Lewin and his organisation.
>
> I believe therefore my duty to you is discharged and will provide you with my account in due course.
>
> Yours etc, H. Moffat.
>
> PS, for reasons I will not go into I have entrusted this letter to be delivered by a third party. Once received please do not reveal the contents to anyone but contact me directly at my offices. Should anything happen to me, please notify the police.'

Sir John frowned and looked at the attached typed letter. He then read out the contents.

> To all concerned parties:
> Reference: sale and development of trust property.
> All is in place and ready to proceed. Kindly inform all relevant staff to carry out agreed plans.
>
> CC: Mr Keller, Mr McVitie, Miss Petrescu.

Sir John was quiet for a moment. 'Has anyone else seen this?' he asked. 'Mr McKechnie, for example?'

'Nobody,' said Shaw. 'If truth be told I was doubtful as to the legality of my opening it, but that seems rather a moot point now.'

'Quite so. Strictly speaking of course it should have been delivered unopened to Colonel Shaw's executors – namely, Mr Lewin – but I agree that would be a point of legal pedantry now.'

'Do you think this, along with the medical evidence regarding the scarring, constitutes sufficient evidence to have the people at Auchentorrin Lodge arrested?' asked Shaw.

'Hmm,' replied Sir John, tapping the letters against his palm. 'It's not my area of law really, but yes, I think so. As I said to you before, I've had my eye on this Lewin chap for a while. I knew there was something not quite right about him, but had nothing to prove it. Now however it looks as if this poor chap Moffat found out something conclusive, which is to link Lewin, and possibly Keller, with some known criminals. You're certain nobody else could have seen this?'

'Quite sure. The letter has not been opened nor, indeed, out of my possession since it was delivered to my compartment on the train.'

'Did you see, for example, this Moffat talk to anybody else on the train other than yourself?'

'Not that I am aware of.'

'Very well. Now listen carefully Mr Shaw. What we will do is this. I will telephone to the Chief Constable, and get him to send the detectives working on this case to Inverbrodie immediately. I will then telephone to the local police house and ask the constable to meet us at Auchentorrin Lodge. We must not delay.'

'And then…surely we cannot accuse them of murder?'

'No need at this stage. If as you say you can affirm the body in the house is not that of your uncle, my intention is in the first place to levy a charge of interference with a legal burial, namely, the substitution of a body. I believe it comes under the Burial Act but would need to consult a solicitor to be sure. However, it will give us sufficient grounds, I believe, to have the lot of them arrested, and then the police can get working on them and find out what's really going on.'

'Very well. Ought we to fetch Dr Sneddie, in order to confirm the presence of scarring on Colonel Shaw's leg?'

Sir John chuckled. 'Old Sneddie will be on the golf course by now if I know him – and besides, we don't have time. We can fetch him later. Please keep your seat, Mr Shaw – I will telephone to the police and then we will go to Auchentorrin Lodge immediately. I trust you will not object if I hold on to the letters for the time being?'

'Not at all.'

'Very well.' Sir John carefully placed the letters in his jacket pocket and strode to the door.

'I shall return as quickly as possible. It may take some time to get hold of the Chief Constable, but in my experience it is best to speak to the head man rather than his minions. Orders travel faster with the aid of gravity.'

Shaw was left alone, with only the dog, Blucher, for company; but the animal lay sound asleep in his place in the corner. He could hear the indistinct sounds of Sir John speaking on the telephone in the hallway, and then there was silence, while he was presumably kept waiting on the line.

Shaw felt relief that, at last, action would be taken on the suspicions he had been harbouring for the last two days. Within an hour or so it might all be over…and yet, he felt he had missed something. Something that he could not quite put his finger on, which irritated from a corner of the mind like an alarm clock ringing in a distant room.

He felt his stomach rumble and realised that despite having had luncheon, he was again feeling hungry. It must be the Highland air, he thought, giving him an appetite. But was that also what he had been trying to remember? It was something Sir John had said about food…but what on earth, he thought, had the man said on that subject of any relevance?

In his musings he lost track of time and was brought back to the present moment by the sound of Sir John hurriedly re-entering the room.

'Time to go, Mr Shaw,' said Sir John energetically. 'The Chief Constable's people are sending a motor car from Inverness, so that means...' – here he consulted his wrist watch – 'they should be at Auchentorrin within thirty minutes. I have told Constable Murdoch from the police house to leave straight away. He only has a bicycle but is rather nearer, so ought to arrive the same time as we do in the car. Come along. No, not you Blucher. Sit.'

Shaw and Sir John arrived at Auchentorrin Lodge in the Bentley, which was left on the drive outside the front door. Shaw swallowed hard; if his suspicions were correct, they might be putting themselves in considerable danger. He resolved not to let on about their true intentions until it was absolutely necessary.

Sir John rang the bell and looked around the carriage turn while he waited.

'I don't see Murdoch's bicycle here,' he said in a concerned voice. 'We'll have to keep them talking until he and the others arrive. Leave it to me.'

'Very well,' said Shaw.

Once more the door was opened by Miss Graham, who gave the two men her usual look of suspicion and disdain. Sir John touched the brim of his hat.

'We've come to see your masters,' he said.

'What is this about?' asked the woman suspiciously.

'Never mind that. Just tell them the local magistrate is here on a legal matter. A question of *habeus corpus*.'

'Of *what*?'

'Never mind. Just tell them I want to see them.'

A few moments later Shaw and Sir John stood in the drawing room by the chimney-piece with Lewin and Keller facing them by the door; Tench and Miss Graham stood by the French windows. Shaw realised any escape for the two of them was blocked off, and he wondered if this was deliberate.

Once again he felt a pang of hunger in his stomach, mixed partly with a sense of foreboding. Then he suddenly realised what it was he had been trying to remember in Sir John's study earlier. It was about his evening meal with Moffat on the train. He felt an ice-cold sensation creep down his spine as he realised if he was right, he was in terrible danger.

Shaw was momentarily distracted from the feeling as the silence was broken by Keller.

'What on earth is this intrusion for?' he demanded angrily. 'We have had quite enough of your meddling, sirs!'

'It's all right, Keller,' said Sir John airily. The jovial, well-fed face had become hardened with a new expression of restrained malice. 'You can drop the pretence now. Shaw here knows everything, or at least, far more than we can let him get away with. Tench – oh hang it, we can drop that as well – I mean, McVitie, take him upstairs while we discuss what to do with him. There's a good chap.'

Before Shaw could move, he felt his arms pinioned behind his back in a vice-like grip by the servant.

'The police have been called…' said Shaw, but he already knew it was hopeless.

'Your naivete is touching,' said Sir John. 'A little bit of play-acting on a disconnected line was enough to convince you I had telephoned for the police. There's no help coming, so you may as well stop struggling'.

'You…' said Shaw with a growing sense of realisation and alarm as he felt Tench – or rather, McVitie – grip him more tightly around his arms. 'You are one of them!'

Chapter Eight

'Can you hear me? I'm looking for a Reverend Shaw. Shaw. S..H...yes, that's right.'

Sergeant Nesbitt held the earpiece of his candlestick telephone close to his ear; the long-distance line to the vicarage in Pinner was terrible. He had been waiting for the operator to connect him for what seemed like hours, and now hoped he might have got somewhere, but the man's wife did not seem to understand what he was trying to say. Bursts of static kept drowning out the indistinct feminine voice on the other end of the line.

'Hello...?' he called loudly into the telephone. 'Are ye still there? I'm looking for a Reverend Shaw.'

The woman said something incomprehensible.

'I do have the right place, I hope?' said Nesbitt, more loudly. 'Hello? The vicarage at Pinner, Middlesex? I'm looking for Middlesex!'

There was an outraged squawk from the receiver and Nesbitt held it away from his ear. He wondered whether it would have been easier simply to write a letter.

'I said *Middle*-sex madam. I was'nae saying I was looking for...Madam I am a police sergeant, no' a...yes I am aware that some men make calls of that nature...none taken, now could you kindly put your husband...oh I see. In the hospital. Unable to walk? Since when? Och, I'm sorry...no, that's all I need to know. Thank...yes, thank you madam. From Inverness, yes….yes I do know a Mrs McDonald…but we've a lot of them in this part o' the world and I doubt she's the same one to whom you're…hello…?'

The line went dead and Nesbitt replaced the telephone with a sigh. He crossed the Reverend Augustus Shaw of Pinner, Middlesex, off his list and looked at his notebook again; the one in central London had said he had been at a prayer meeting the night Moffat was killed, so that left the one in Suffolk, the one in Cornwall and the one in the Irish Free State. He hoped he would get to the right man before that final one, because he was not even sure if there was a telephone line across the Irish Sea.

He had been unable to get a trunk call connected to the vicarage in…now where was it, he thought…ah yes, that was it, somewhere called Lower Addenham in Suffolk, but he had managed to get through to the nearest branch of the CID, in Midchester, who had said they would look into it for him.

He tapped his pencil thoughtfully on his chin and wondered whether to call again and hurry them up. There was already talk of Scotland Yard taking over the Moffat case, but if he could crack this one, he might make Inspector and the prospect of that spurred him on with an energy and enthusiasm he had not felt in years.

The telephone tinkled again, and he picked it up. 'I have a long distance caller from Midchester on the line,' announced an operator brightly, and he accepted a call from a constable with an impenetrable English accent of a kind he had not heard before. As far as he could make out from the man, the Reverend Shaw he had been trying to find was staying in the manse at Inverbrodie.

Nesbitt thanked the man and hung up the telephone. Inverbrodie! That was only a few miles away, the last stop on the railway line before Inverness. He looked at his watch; the next local train would be leaving soon and he could take that. He rubbed his lower back, wincing slightly; he was getting too old for this kind of running about and wished he had use of a motor car.

As if in answer to his prayers, the door opened and Inspector McLeish, his bland features obscured by a brown trilby hat pulled down low over his forehead, walked in.

'Any news on that minister?' he asked tersely.

'Aye, I've just been on the telephone to the station in Suffolk,' answered Nesbitt. 'The man came up on the night train and is staying at the manse at Inverbrodie.'

'That must be the one we want, then,' said McLeish, pushing his hat back and then placing his hands in his trouser pockets. 'Good work, Nesbitt. You'll be wanting to go along there the day, I imagine?'

'Yes sir, well, if I can catch the next train…'

'Och, don't bother with the train. I've the car outside. I'll drive us there.'

'That's awfy guid of you, sir. But is it no' a bit of a way for you?'

'Normally I'd say yes,' said McLeish with a conspiratorial grin, 'but not today. I'll be wanting to drive over there myself right away. I just dropped by to let you know.'

'Let me know what, sir?'

'Fetch your cap and raincoat, I'll tell you a bit more in the car,' said McLeish as he turned to the door. 'I've been over at Moffat's wee office in town,' he continued, with barely disguised enthusiasm. 'It's hard to make out some of his notes, but from what I can gather, he'd found out something big going on in Inverbrodie. Something *really* big.'

In the drawing room at Auchentorrin Lodge, Keller was looking at Shaw quizzically, as if he were examining a patient on his morning rounds. McVitie still held his arms behind his back, albeit now with lessened force.

'What do you propose we do with him?' asked the surgeon to Sir John.

'We'll come to that in a minute,' said the baronet, who leaned nonchalantly against the sofa. He took out a gold case, extracted a hand-made cigarette and lit it. Breathing out a long plume of blue smoke, he looked Shaw up and down.

'I've got a nasty feeling I let something slip with you that I didn't notice at the time,' he said. 'But it can't have been particularly serious or you wouldn't have come over here with me. Care to enlighten me?'

Shaw's initial fear had ebbed, and he felt oddly calm. He had been in tighter spots before, and as he was not in imminent danger, he felt reasonably confident that he could somehow extract himself from the situation. He decided the first thing to do was to encourage conversation.

'It was something you mentioned about me taking dinner with Mr Moffat on the train.'

'Yes? What about it?' asked Sir John.

'I never mentioned that I had dinner with him. Merely that I spoke to him. It was not mentioned in the newspapers either.'

Sir John clicked his fingers. 'Of course. It was Lewin who mentioned it to me. Careless of me. But up until then, I think you trusted me entirely, no?'

Despite Sir John's cut-glass English accent, there was something foreign and strange in the placing of the negative at the end of the question like that. Shaw had the impression the man wanted to flatter himself at his ability to deceive.

'I must admit you seemed to me to be a perfect British gentleman,' said Shaw casually. 'I wonder however, since your gang has international connections, whether you are in the pay of some foreign power?'

Sir John laughed bitterly. 'My dear Shaw. How quaint you are. Do you really think this is all in aid of some rotten tin-pot government, that I…we…are employees of some drab espionage department?'

'I do not know. Are you?'

'Suffice it to say I am as British as you are.'

'Perhaps,' replied Shaw, 'and Mr McVitie is a genuine Scotsman, I concede. One could hardly expect a foreigner to imitate his accent with such accuracy. I do not believe Miss Graham, however, is British. Or should I call her Miss Petrescu? A Roumanian name, I think?'

Shaw heard a gasp from Miss Graham, or rather, Miss Petrescu, who stood in the corner of the room watching them. 'How does he know this?' she asked.

Shaw looked at her steadily and continued. 'And Mr Keller here trained in medicine in Bucharest. I imagine he may be a fellow countryman of yours, Miss Petrescu. And who knows where Mr Lewin may hail from?'

'How the hell does he know all this?' asked McVitie gruffly.

'All in good time, all in good time,' said Sir John, with a tinge of amusement in his voice. 'Quite the detective, aren't you, Shaw?' he said, blowing smoke at the clergyman's face. Shaw flinched and felt anger rising in his chest but fought it; now was not the time to lose his temper.

He prayed, briefly and silently, and then spoke again, playing for time.

'I wonder if I might explain my theory of what all…this…is about.'

'There's no need,' said Sir John. 'I think you've already told me everything.'

'Damn it, Deb,' said Lewin, using Sir John's nickname. 'He may have told you but he hasn't told us. This plan was supposed to be foolproof, so what went wrong?'

Sir John turned to face Lewin and his eyes flashed fire. 'What went wrong? You tell me. It was your bungling that started the whole sorry mess.'

'*My* bungling?'

'Yes. With Moffat on the train. You were only supposed to knock him out – if absolutely necessary – and get back that memorandum. Instead you let him slip the letter to Shaw here and then to add insult to injury you killed the damned man!'

'That wasn't my fault,' said Lewin. 'Tench…McVitie I mean… gave him the wrong dosage.'

Shaw felt hot breath on his neck as McVitie exhaled loudly. 'The doc gave us the wrong dose in the phial,' he said. 'Must have been that. I'm no' stupid.'

'How dare you impune me,' said Keller, stepping forward. He adjusted his *pince-nez* and looked McVitie and Lewin up and down. 'I gave precise instructions to you of how to administer the sedative if you should be required to use it in self-defence. One of you at least must have got it wrong. It was not intended to be used as a murder weapon.'

'Gentlemen, gentlemen, let's not argue amongst ourselves,' said Sir John smoothly. 'Suffice to say, Moffat was able to give the letter to Shaw. The letter containing evidence which has led him here to us.'

'And how the devil did Moffat do that?' asked Lewin. 'McVitie and I were watching him the whole time. We never took our eyes off him.'

'He slipped it under Shaw's compartment door,' said Sir John. 'The one next to his. You can't have been watching that closely.'

'Damn it,' breathed Lewin. 'It was just before we got to him. When he fell. That must have been deliberate.'

'How does this priest know my name?' asked Miss Petrescu. 'It is supposed to be secret.'

'That, my dear Cosmina,' said Sir John, 'is another fault of Mr Lewin.'

Lewin bridled. 'I had no idea that private detective was going to wheedle his way into my office, and certainly no idea that he would be able to steal a letter from my secretary's desk.'

Sir John replied more harshly this time. 'Forgive me but I must disagree. You told me that Moffat had been asking questions about your organisation and had even been to your offices previously. You should not have permitted your secretary to leave confidential letters lying around. And you certainly should not have dictated a letter using anybody's real names, you *damned fool.*'

'But it was a confidential memorandum,' countered Lewin weakly.

'Nothing is ever truly confidential,' replied Sir John firmly. 'I'm just glad you didn't mention my name.'

'What about *my* name?' asked Keller with concern.

'Yours is also on the letter,' replied Sir John blandly.

'Good God,' breathed Keller, who then turned to Lewin. 'You imbecile…' he hissed.

'Now, now,' said Sir John. 'Do let us try to keep civil. Don't worry, Keller, your precious reputation as a surgeon is unlikely to be besmirched. There isn't anything definite in the letter to link you or I with…them. Even if the police had got hold of it, which they have not.'

'That is at least something of merit in this whole fiasco,' said Keller, with relief in his voice. 'But these three,' – he indicated Lewin, McVitie and Petrescu – 'are known to have been involved with criminal activity.'

Sir John raised his hand. 'Suspected, Keller, not known,' he said. 'But of considerable interest to the police in more than one country. The names Petrescu, McVitie and Lewin would not arouse suspicion on their own, but when linked together were sufficient to be noticed by someone – Moffat – who was *au fait* with recent cases of financial irregularity. If the letter had been brought to the attention of the authorities, or, God forbid, the newspapers, it would have resulted in unwanted interference – something we do not want at this crucial stage.'

'So you would just blame everything on us, if the police got involved?' demanded Lewin, who looked about to explode with anger. Then Shaw noticed the man checked himself; Sir John was clearly the leader of the outfit and Lewin his inferior. Lewin breathed deeply and spoke in a calmer tone to Sir John.

'With respect, Deb, we are not the only ones to blame. It was not I who came up with the idea of using an actor to impersonate Colonel Shaw, for example. It was your suggestion that we procure a theatrical directory to find him.'

Shaw suddenly now realised the significance of the book full of actors' photographs which he had seen earlier in the drawing room.

'Very well,' said Sir John. 'I concede that point. I agree that expecting a veteran of the stage with a fondness for drink to be able to carry off a part such as that was rather a tall order. But he was only supposed to be employed *once,* for the signing of those papers with Colonel Shaw's solicitor. I did not expect him to be dragged here at short notice and made to play the part of a corpse!'

'We had no choice,' hissed Lewin. 'He was supposed to go straight home to Glasgow but instead the damned fool rolled in here drunk and told us he'd been spotted by Reverend Shaw. Instead of leaving, he demanded more money to keep quiet. If we hadn't stopped him he could have given the whole game away.'

Shaw gazed in horror at Lewin. 'And so you had the poor man killed…'

'Be quiet, you,' said Keller. 'Yes, we disposed of him. He had advanced cirrhosis anyway and would have been dead in a few months. I merely helped him painlessly on his way.'

'But surely the police will suspect…' countered Shaw.

'They will suspect nothing,' snapped Lewin. 'He has no relations, and we have paid his landlord and informed him the man has moved to London.'

'And so in death, as well as in life, he will play the part of my uncle,' said Shaw.

'Correct,' said Sir John. 'I trust his body has been taken to the undertakers, ready for burial?' He looked at Lewin and stubbed his cigarette out under his foot on the carpet. 'Or have you managed to get that wrong as well?'

'It is all in order,' said Lewin testily.

'And…the body of Colonel Shaw…?' asked Shaw with growing horror.

'At the bottom of a peat bog,' said Keller bluntly, 'from which it is unlikely ever to surface. I would like to say he did not suffer, but I would imagine a high-calibre bullet from a hunting rifle must have caused at least some discomfort.'

'You…you fiends…' breathed Shaw.

'Oh that reminds me,' mused Sir John, as blandly as if he were passing the time of day with a neighbour. 'Thank you, Keller, for giving Blucher a wash after we were hunting for the Colonel the other morning, and then taking the brute back home to me.'

Miss Petrescu spoke up. 'It was I who washed it. I do not think it part of my duties but I did it anyway.'

'Thanks awfully,' said Sir John. 'Now, I think we've had enough polite conversation,' he added, standing up. 'Take Shaw upstairs and lock him in the small bedroom. Keller, get your medical bag and draw up the same concoction these two used on Moffat. And make sure it's another "wrong" dose this time, won't you?'

The enormity of his situation hit Shaw like a hammer blow to the stomach. There was going to be no reprieve. He tried a final attempt at forestalling them.

'You mean, you are going to kill me?' he asked.

'I'm afraid we've got no choice,' replied Sir John casually. 'You know far too much.'

'I won't tell anyone,' Shaw was about to say, but he chased the thought away as cowardly. He was not going to lie, and anyway, he did not think they would believe him.

'Thank you for not debasing yourself by pretending you won't tell anyone about all this,' said Sir John with a vulpine smile. 'And as a man of God, you'll doubtless be treated well when you arrive at the pearly gates, and so on.'

'I beg of you not to have this on your conscience,' said Shaw earnestly. 'Think of your immortal souls.'

'Oh please,' said Sir John, waving his hand dismissively. 'Spare me the sermon. Get it over with, Keller. I'll wait down here.'

'At least tell me *why,*' said Shaw. 'What is it all for?'

Sir John chuckled and shook his head.

'I'm not a villain from some yellow-backed novel from Boots' Library,' he said. 'I'm not about to tell you all our plans, even if we are going to kill you. I think it infinitely more amusing if you go to your grave not knowing why.'

Shaw swallowed hard as he felt McVitie begin to steer him to the door. He had one last hope; if he could keep them talking, perhaps some chance would make itself known; some caller or tradesman might arrive or he would see some means of escape. He tried a final appeal to Sir John's vanity.

'There is something wrong with your plan, however,' he said as calmly as he could.

'Oh yes?' asked Sir John. 'Do tell, but make it quick, won't you? I'm all ears.'

Shaw felt McVitie's grip relax slightly, and he turned his head to face Sir John. 'One of you is a traitor.'

'Be quiet you damned idiot,' said McVitie, and once again pushed Shaw towards the door.

'Wait,' called Sir John authoritatively, and McVitie stood still. 'What do you mean?' he asked.

'Somebody summoned me here by telegram,' said Shaw. 'I cannot believe that was part of the plan, so there must be one of you who wishes it to fail. Why go to the trouble of presenting me with a double of my uncle, at the risk of me seeing through the trick? Why not simply kill my uncle, get Mr Keller to sign a death certificate, and have a coffin loaded with bricks buried?'

There was a pause and Shaw could tell Sir John was slightly worried. 'I told Keller here to send the telegram, didn't I, Keller?'

There was a pause, and then the physician bowed slightly and replied. 'That is correct, Sir John,'

'But why? Why?' asked Shaw.

'I am a gambling man,' said Sir John. 'Are you?'

'No.'

'I thought not. I am often at the tables in Monte, Deauville, and so on. I tend to do quite well. After a while one becomes rather bored with winning, and so one tends to take greater and greater risks. It was the same with this plan. Things were going rather well and I wanted a little *frisson* of excitement. So I had Keller invite you to add a hint of danger and to see how well the plan would hold up under scrutiny. If one of us was a traitor, he – or she – would surely have summoned the police instead of a whimsical vicar.'

'I don't believe you,' said Shaw.

'Believe what you like,' said Sir John. 'Your own religion worships a God who was so bored with omnipotence that he had to create something he could not control – human beings with free will – so the idea is not without precedent.'

'Then the risk was not worth it,' said Shaw. 'You have been found out.'

'Yes,' replied Sir John, 'but in a short while that won't matter, because you will be out of the way. And don't think I'm worried about what you might have told McKechnie or his wife, as we'll be dealing with them as well, if necessary. Take him upstairs.'

Shaw struggled but McVitie's grip was relentless and he was propelled forwards to the door. There was to be no help, he realised. It was time to make his peace with God.

Just then, from outside the room there was the sound of an engine, and the crunch of tyres on gravel. From the corner of his eye Shaw saw a black saloon car pass by the window on the front drive. Keller hurried over and looked out from the corner of the bay.

'My God,' he exclaimed. 'It is the police!'

'Tell me again what this Colonel Shaw fellow's got to do with anything,' said Nesbitt to McLeish as the powerful Austin Twelve police car slowed to a halt outside Auchentorrin Lodge. 'I just want to be sure we're singing from the same hymn-sheet, as they say.'

'Look, as I said before,' said McLeish as he let go of the steering wheel and applied the hand-brake, 'I couldn't make out much from Harry Moffat's records. I've put a man there to have a proper comb through them, but from what I can tell, Moffat found out something about a criminal gang wanted in London – and abroad – operating in the area. Involved in land appropriation.'

'In what?' asked Nesbitt.

'Stealing land.'

'God's sake,' breathed Nesbitt, shaking his head. 'Did the lairds not do enough of that in the Clearances? Do you think this place is the gang's headquarters, sir?'

He looked doubtfully at the decaying country house and noticed the large Bentley parked outside. 'Well somebody's got some money here anyway. A car like that costs a bomb.'

'Aye,' said McLeish, glancing over at the motor car. Then he turned back to face Nesbitt.

'I don't know if this Colonel Shaw's anything to do with it. He may well be an entirely innocent party. But there's some correspondence at Moffat's office between the two of them. The Colonel asked him to look into the people behind a potential land deal. Moffat warned the Colonel that they were a bit suspicious, and that he was trying to find some hard evidence against them in London.'

'On the trip he never came back from,' replied Nesbitt.

'Right,' said McLeish.

'But the fellow *I'm* looking for is called Shaw as well,' said Nesbitt thoughtfully. 'There's a connection, do you think? The Suffolk police said he was here visiting a relative.'

'I'd say so,' replied McLeish. 'Too much of a coincidence for two men with the same English name in a wee place like this.'

'All right then. So we have a wee word with this Colonel,' said Nesbitt, placing his cap firmly on his head. He felt a sense of excitement; this was rather different to his usual work of poking around railway sidings or escorting rowdy association football fanatics on excursion trains.

'Softly-softly,' warned McLeish as he opened the car door. 'Don't let on anything the now, just that we're making routine enquiries. You know the sort of thing. But keep your eyes peeled. I've got the Chief Constable wanting Scotland Yard to take over and I'd like to get this cleared up quickly. By rights you shouldnae even be working with the CID – your gaffer's only lending you as we need everyone we can get on this – so don't mess anything up.'

Nesbitt felt a slight sense of wounded pride as he was put in his place. He was about to speak, but looked up to see that the Inspector had already walked across the gravel drive and was pulling hard on the bell by the front door.

'Don't open it,' whispered Keller to Sir John, in response to the urgent-sounding ring at the entrance of the house. 'For

God's sake, if I'm found here with you people I could be ruined.'

Shaw felt nausea rise in his throat as McVitie's ape-like, moist palm was clapped hard across his mouth.

'Make a sound and I'll snap your neck like a twig,' he hissed in Shaw's ear. The captive clergyman then looked in alarm as Lewin pulled out a slim automatic pistol from his trouser pocket and pointed it towards the window.

'Don't be a damned fool!' whispered Sir John. 'Put that thing away. And Keller, stop acting like an old woman. Everybody stay still, or they might see you through the window. Leave this to me.'

The doorbell rang again.

'They must not find me here,' urged Keller, almost plaintively this time. 'Let us just wait for them to go away.'

'My car's parked right outside,' said Sir John. 'They'll know something's amiss if nobody answers. Just keep quiet and try to at least remain continent.'

Keller reddened with anger but Sir John ignored him. He crossed the drawing room floor, crouching down so as to be unseen by anyone outside the window. He then disappeared into the back of the house.

The doorbell rang a third time, and this time somebody banged on the knocker as well. A voice called out 'anybody home?' from outside; the rickety front door enabled the policeman to be clearly heard from the drawing room. Shaw felt McVitie's grip tighten on his mouth and Lewin drew his pistol again. Keller and Miss Petrescu stood stock-still, listening intently.

Shaw could not see anything through the window, but could clearly hear the footsteps of Sir John crunching on the gravel as he emerged from the back of the house.

'Hullo,' he called out jovially. 'I don't think you'll have much luck with that bell. There doesn't seem to be anyone at home. I've just had a try of the servant's entrance but no joy there either.'

'May I know who you are, sir?' said one of the men.

'My name's Debayle-Bradley.'

'Sir John Debayle-Bradley, the magistrate?' asked the second man. Shaw noticed with a certain irony that the man sounded slightly in awe.

'That's right,' replied Sir John. 'I've seen you somewhere, haven't I, sergeant? Now where was it. Ah yes. At the police burgh court in Inverness. Something to do with…a stolen purse on a train. I remember you because I don't see the railway police chaps before me very often.'

'Indeed you have, sir,' said the second man proudly. 'You passed a very fair sentence in that particular hearing, if I may say. My name's Sergeant Nesbitt, and this is Inspector McLeish of the Inverness CID. '

'How do you do, Inspector. Cigarette?'

'Not just now, thank you,' answered McLeish. 'That'll be your motor car over there, I take it?'

Shaw heard the snap of a case and the clicking of a lighter. 'That's right,' said Sir John. 'Doesn't seem to be anyone else around.'

'May I ask,' continued McLeish, 'what you are doing here, sir?'

'Well it's all rather strange,' said Sir John. His voice became inaudible for a moment, as if he had turned away from the door, but then Shaw could make out what he was saying again.

'…called here on a formality to do with Colonel Shaw's death. Witnessing a signature of some kind. Tedious sort of thing we Justices get asked to do from time to time. But the man doesn't seem to be here.'

'Wait a minute,' said McLeish. 'You're saying Colonel Shaw is dead?'

'Oh yes,' replied Sir John. 'I'm sorry, was that the man you were hoping to find? If he's done anything he shouldn't have, you're too late, I'm afraid. He died yesterday evening. His body's already been removed.'

'What did he die of?' asked McLeish. Shaw noticed a hint of suspicion in the man's voice, and saw Keller looking distinctly nervous.

'Some sort of throat complaint, I think,' said Sir John. 'I gather he was elderly and had been ill for some time. His doctor could tell you better than I.'

'His doctor?' asked Nesbitt. 'And who would he be?'

Shaw noticed Keller's eyes bulge and the man hold his breath.

'No idea,' said Sir John with a slight chuckle. Shaw got the distinct impression that the man had said it more loudly so that Keller could hear. He seemed to be treating the whole thing as a joke. Keller breathed an almost audible sigh of relief.

'You said the man doesn't appear to be here,' said McLeish. 'Which man would that be?'

'Oh, that's Reverend Shaw,' said Sir John airily.

'Wait a minute,' said Nesbitt. 'You mean Reverend Lucian Shaw, of…' – here Shaw heard the sound of a notebook's pages being turned – 'All Saint's church, Lower Addenham, in the county of Suffolk?'

'That sounds like him, yes,' replied Sir John. 'Colonel Shaw's nephew. Next of kin, I think. As I say, he came over to my house looking for a JP's signature on some burial form or other and so I said I'd oblige later as I was going this way anyway.'

'And you've no idea where he might be the now?' McLeish again.

'Not a clue,' said Sir John. 'Oh, he did mention something about going out for a spot of shooting on the common mosses later. I remember because he didn't look the sort of chap who would know one end of a gun from the other. Perhaps he got tired of waiting and went off. I hope he hasn't lost his way back. I got here rather later than expected, you see. Damned sheep all over the road!'

'Aye, well, that's the Highlands for you,' said Nesbitt with a chuckle. 'Sorry to have troubled you. A wee bit strange though.'

'What is?' asked Sir John cautiously.

'Well sir,' said Nesbitt, 'we were given an address for where Reverend Shaw's staying, but it wasnae this house.'

'Oh? May I ask what the address was?'

'He's over at the manse, it seems.'

'Ah yes, come to mention it he did say something about that.'

'Did he say why he was no' staying here?' asked McLeish. Shaw had the impression from his voice that he was not quite as in awe of Sir John as was Nesbitt.

'I would imagine he took one look at the place and decided to find somewhere warmer and dryer, which didn't have a corpse laid out in it,' said Sir John in a wry tone. 'And he did mention something about Mr McKechnie – that's the local minister – taking the funeral, so he may well have been invited to stay there instead.'

'Aye, mebbe,' said McLeish thoughtfully. 'Well thank you Sir John, we'll not trouble you further.'

'I'll wait here a little longer in the hope of finding the elusive Mr Shaw,' said Sir John. 'Perhaps you would care to give me a message about this matter, so that I might pass it on to him if I see him?'

'I don't think so sir, thanks all the same,' said McLeish.

'One does like to keep abreast of criminal proceedings in one's judicial purlieu,' said Sir John.

'One's what?' asked Nesbitt.

'One's area of responsibility as a Justice of the Peace,' replied Sir John, 'and one's potential parliamentary constituency.'

The man is fishing by trying to pull rank, thought Shaw.

'Nothing to worry yourself about sir,' replied McLeish firmly. 'Just wanted some help with an ongoing enquiry. Doubtless you'll hear if it comes to court. We'll get a hold of the Reverend ourselves at some point. Good day to you.'

'And the best of luck wi' the election,' said Nesbitt.

'Thank you! Good day, gentlemen...' replied Sir John, with the faintest hint of irritation in his voice.

Shaw heard the crunch of police boots on gravel, doors slamming, and then the sound of a car moving away. His heart sank as McVitie relaxed his grip on his arm and removed his hand from his mouth. It seemed as if rescue was not to come after all.

Chapter Nine

'What do we do now, sir?' asked Nesbitt as McLeish steered the police car out on to the road and accelerated away from Auchentorrin Lodge. McLeish changed gear and turned briefly to look at Nesbitt, then directed his eyes back to the road.

'We'll look for this Reverend Shaw,' he said.

'So we'll away to the manse, then?' replied Nesbitt.

'Did you not hear? That man said he was no' there but had gone shooting.'

'Aye, right enough. Would it not be easier to wait for him at the manse?'

'We could be there a long time. I'd rather find him first. He'll be easy enough to spot if we drive around for a wee bit. Have you any idea where the common mosses are around these parts?'

'Not really,' said Nesbitt. 'We'll maybe stop at a croft and ask.'

'Good idea,' said McLeish. 'There's a but-and-ben over the valley – you can ask there.'

McLeish steered the car up a narrow, rutted track towards a small cottage about half a mile distant.

'What do you think to that magistrate?' asked McLeish.

'Sir John? A proper gent, as far as I know. Always gets a good write up in the papers.'

'I'm no' so sure,' mused McLeish. 'There's something

about him I don't like. Acting like the Lord President of the Court of Session, when he's just a lay magistrate probably spending most of his time fining drunks and poachers.'

'He cannae be all bad – he's a Labour man after all,' said Nesbitt proudly, folding his arms. 'He'd get my vote if I was living here.'

'Och, how old are you?' said McLeish. 'He knows he stands more chance of getting elected under Labour, that's all.'

'I don't believe it,' said Nesbitt. 'A man cannae just change his principles like that.'

'Come on, it's a flag o' convenience for gentry like him,' replied McLeish. 'Look at that other one, what's his name. Mosley. Used to be Tory, then he was Labour, now he's away starting some party of his own taking bits o' doctrine from both sides, like Mussolini's mob in Italy.'

'I'll take your word for it, sir,' said Nesbitt. 'Seems you know a bit more about politics than me.'

'Dinnae worry about it,' muttered McLeish, slowing the car down as they approached the cottage. A man in a flat cap, slowly digging in a far corner of the garden, looked up and watched them.

'All I'm saying,' continued McLeish, 'is just keep an open mind about our Sir John.'

'You don't think…he could be mixed up in this, this land grab thing?' asked Nesbitt slowly.

'Unlikely, but it wouldn't be the first time an English laird has done something like that, now would it? Anyway, what's more important the now is finding this man Shaw. I've a few things I'd like to ask him.'

'Such as?' enquired Nesbitt, as the car stopped outside the cottage gate.

'Such as, did he no' think it a bit odd that a man he met on the train ends up murdered, and now the uncle he's gone to visit, who by the way the murdered man was working for, is dead too?'

'You think this Reverend Shaw might be involved himself in some way?' asked Nesbitt, his eyes widening. McLeish had cast suspicion on a magistrate and now he was doing it to a man of the cloth. It was a level of cynicism that was somewhat new to the sergeant, who realised that up until now he had led something of a sheltered life.

'All I think,' said McLeish slowly, 'is there's something strange going on and this minister mebbe knows a wee bit more than is good for him about it.'

Shaw felt McVitie's iron grip relax slightly further as the sound of the police car's engine gradually ebbed away.

'They have gone, thank God,' said Keller with a sigh. 'Do you think they suspect anything?' he asked Sir John.

'I doubt it,' said the baronet airily as he re-entered the drawing room. 'The Inspector didn't seem to take to me but the other one, the sergeant, ought not to be any trouble. Let's not let it worry us.'

'I do not like this,' said Miss Petrescu, stepping forward from the corner of the room in which she had been staying out of sight. 'We have had too much trouble with police before and nearly got captured. I say we go.'

'This isn't a democracy, my dear,' said Lewin sharply. 'Just like your home country in that regard, so get used to it. We'll give the orders, you follow them.'

Miss Petrescu gave a sharp glance at Lewin but said nothing.

'We've come too far to give up now,' said Sir John.

He paced up and down the drawing room carpet, then stopped and surveyed the group. 'There's no need to back out,' he said decisively. 'We can still go on. We just need to get rid of this…problem.'

He pointed at Shaw, who took a deep breath and tried to sound as calm as he could. 'Do I take it you intend to kill me, as you killed Moffat, my uncle, and the poor unfortunate paid to be his substitute?'

'You have a choice,' said Sir John. 'We can end it now – quickly and painlessly, I might add – or we can let you go.'

'On the condition that I say nothing, I assume?' replied Shaw.

'Of course,' replied Sir John. 'You can hardly expect that I would let you go without some cast-iron assurance that you would not cause trouble with the police.'

'This is madness!' said Miss Petrescu sharply.

'Quiet you,' urged McVitie. 'Your temper's got us into enough trouble in the past. Hold your tongue woman and let Sir John speak.'

'Thank you McVitie,' said Sir John. 'We all need a cool head at the present. Well, Shaw, *can* you assure me that you will not cause trouble with the police if we let you go?'

Shaw's head reeled. The man was asking him to bear false witness; to break the Ninth Commandment to save his own skin, to promise to say nothing, knowing that he would break that promise. Could he do it? *Should* he do it? In the few moments before he replied, he prayed more earnestly and fervently than he had ever done before.

After a moment of silence Sir John continued speaking. 'If you are thinking of lying to me about keeping quiet should I let you go – or let us assume for the sake of argument, that you somehow escaped – and you went to the authorities, we would simply follow the plan we had prepared for your uncle should he have got away alive.'

'And that is…?' asked Shaw.

'Keller here,' said Sir John, 'along with myself, would convince the police that you are insane and have you committed to an asylum for the rest of your natural life, or at least until you were no longer an obstruction to us.'

'You would not get away with it,' said Shaw.

'We already have, in the recent case that Moffat stumbled upon. There is an institution which tends to turn a blind eye to the reasons for its inmates' admissions should they be paid sufficiently well for their trouble. You may not be aware that a person can be committed to an asylum on the evidence of just a doctor and magistrate, and our little band has both in its ranks.'

'It would be quite clear that I am not insane,' urged Shaw.

'Not once Keller had administered certain substances to you,' said Sir John. 'He could turn you into a raving lunatic with one simple injection.'

'Very well,' replied Shaw, a strange sense of relief and calm spreading through his body. Was this how the first martyrs had felt, he wondered, when they refused to pay homage to the pagan gods by sprinkling a pinch of incense on an altar? Such a small act, but such a great betrayal of their faith had they done it.

'I shall not give you any such assurance that I shall remain silent should I be allowed to leave,' said Shaw slowly. 'I am not afraid to die. Either let me go unconditionally…or kill me.'

'Well, well,' said Sir John. 'A man of principle. So rare these days. But I notice you only made your decision once I had made it clear what would happen if you tried to talk to the police. Would you have made such a noble sacrifice before knowing that, I wonder?'

Shaw ignored the question. That, he felt, was a matter

between him and his maker.

'Who then is to be my executioner?' he asked instead. He looked intently at each member of the group in turn, apart from McVitie who still stood behind him holding his arms. He noticed that Keller, Lewin and Miss Petrescu looked slightly shame-faced; the woman more so than the men. Perhaps there was still hope, he wondered. Perhaps there was some weakness in the group he could exploit…he tried to focus, but nothing came.

'Take him upstairs and lock him up,' said Sir John, looking at the group in disgust. 'Perhaps you will find the topic of discussion less squeamish if the subject is not within hearing. As I can see none of you has the courage for the task in hand we'll draw lots for it.'

As the watery afternoon sun slanted across the wall of Inverbrodie manse, McKechnie finished his tea and sat back in his chair. His wife had gone out for some shopping in the village stores, and he was left alone in the house with only Campbell the dog and a pile of church paperwork for company. He wondered what had happened to Shaw; he seemed to be taking an awfully long time over at Sir John's house. Ah well, he thought, hopefully they will be getting to the bottom of the peculiar goings-on at Auchentorrin Lodge.

He heard a rustling sound from the corner of the room. At first he thought it was Campbell moving in his basket, but the dog was sitting at his feet under the desk. He looked towards the window, and this time there was no doubt about it. Somebody *was* looking at him through the window! He caught a glimpse of a pallid, moon-like face suddenly appear and then disappear, back into the foliage by the side of the house.

He grabbed his shotgun from the rack, stuffing a handful of cartridges in his pocket, and strode to the front door. A week ago he would have thought it an over-reaction to arm himself, but with all the strange activity lately, he felt it prudent to do so.

He pulled open the front door and saw another flash of movement to his left; an indistinct figure moved rapidly into the shrubbery and was gone, leaving a few branches springing back in its wake. Campbell appeared at McKechnie's heels and began barking.

'Seek him boy, seek him!' ordered McKechnie, and the dog raced ahead as quickly as if he were a greyhound at a racing track. Campbell crashed into the undergrowth and began to thrash around. He whined and yelped and McKechnie ran forward; the animal had become stuck on some brambles. After releasing him, the pair pushed through the undergrowth which marked the boundary between the Manse garden and the wooded area beyond.

Suddenly the light became dimmer as the canopy of pines overhead obscured the sunlight. McKechnie caught sight of the figure again, moving erratically behind some trees about fifty yards ahead; then he was out of sight.

'Stop or I'll shoot!' ordered McKechnie. He knew that a gun loaded with birdshot discharged at this distance would do little damage, even if he could see the target, but he hoped the warning would be sufficient to stop the man. He jogged along, hurriedly loading the weapon, and then stopped. Campbell seemed confused and looked at his master, wagging his tail.

'Where is he, boy?' whispered McKechnie. The man could not have gone far; about sixty yards away was open moorland and anyone trying to run out of the woods would be clearly visible. There was a soft soughing of wind in the pine trees; other than that, utter silence. The minister began to feel uneasy, and that he was being watched in some way.

He remembered the man he had seen on the moors near Auchentorrin Lodge; the well-dressed gentleman with a dog, and a hunting rifle with telescopic sights. Was he being watched through those same sights at this very moment? He felt a sudden stab of fear, and remembered his army training: Dash, Down, Crawl, Observe, Sights, Fire.

He raced forward and threw himself to the ground, thanking the Lord for the soft carpet of pine needles underneath him, then he cursed as he felt the tiny pin-like objects working their way into his elbows and knees as he crawled forward. He looked up and scanned the woodland ahead. There he was! A man was trying to conceal himself behind a tree on the edge of the wood; probably waiting, thought McKechnie, to make a dash for it.

He sighted the figure along the barrel of the shotgun; at this range he would not do much harm with his first shot, but could probably wing the target with the second, if he emerged. But was the man armed? He had no idea. After a deep breath, he decided to give the man a chance; after all, this was Scotland, not the Western Front; one could not just blast away at someone just because he had looked through a window.

'Come out, or I'll fire,' shouted McKechnie.

An indistinct voice called from behind the tree, shouting something which might have been 'don't shoot', accompanied by the fluttering of a white handkerchief.

McKechnie grunted as he tried to get off the ground, and as he did so, Campbell barked once and darted forward, wagging his tail.

'Campbell, come back!' shouted McKechnie. 'Heel!'

The dog ignored the command and sprinted to the tree, then leapt on the man as he emerged. He was thrown to the ground by the force of the animal and lay sprawled out on his back on the soft carpet of needles.

'Lord help us,' muttered McKechnie. He had held back from shooting the man, but then had allowed his dog to savage him; he just hoped the fellow was not too badly injured.

He jogged over to the prone man, who had his hands around Campbell's neck. He raised the shotgun, about to issue another warning, but then stopped, looking down at the dog. Campbell was licking the man's face.

'Campbell, off!' shouted McKechnie, and the dog stepped back, looking back and forth excitedly between his master and the figure on the ground.

McKechnie looked down and his eyes widened in disbelief. 'You…!' was all he could think to say.

'This door'll be locked and so is the window,' said McVitie, as he pushed Shaw into the small bedroom at the top of the stairs overlooking the front drive of the house. 'And don't bother trying to break it either to shout for help, as we'll hear you from downstairs. Any nonsense and the doctor'll tell anyone asking questions you're a dangerous lunatic, ken? Turn out your pockets.'

Shaw put the few objects in his jacket and trouser pockets onto the bed and McVitie scrutinised them; he picked up Shaw's little pipe-cleaning knife.

'I'll take this,' said McVitie. 'I don't trust you with it.'

'I am hardly likely to use it as a weapon,' said Shaw.

'True,' replied McVitie, 'but you might try and cut your throat with it and I'll be the one that has to clean up the mess. You can take the rest of your things.'

Shaw scooped the little pile of coins and keys from the bed and replaced them in his pockets. McVitie pulled the curtains across the window and the room was plunged into gloom. Shaw nodded silently and sat down on one of the twin beds. Could he, he wondered, somehow get the man on his side?

'A man like Sir John will not be loyal to you, you know, Mr McVitie,' he said slowly. 'You will most likely be sacrificed as a pawn in a much greater game, whatever it may be.'

'You know nothing about this,' said McVitie, 'so hold your tongue. I can look after myself.'

'Sir John will surely not want any surviving witnesses to the crimes he has ordered…'

'Quiet man. I'm not interested in what you've got to say. So don't think you can scare me into helping you.'

'One of you is a traitor. It must be so, as why else would I have been summoned here? How do you know he – or she – will not betray *you* also?'

'Haud your wheesht, minister,' barked McVitie. 'And stop talking rubbish about traitors. Sir John's already explained why he had you brought here.'

'Very well,' said Shaw sadly. 'If you would kindly leave me, I should like to pray.'

McVitie looked him up and down in disgust. 'Aye, that's all your lot ever do, and most of it's a load of nonsense dreamed up to justify the power o' the Kirk. I had to put up with your sort twice every Sunday as a laddie, and I can't say I'll be sorry to see one less o' you. Keep those curtains closed.'

McVitie left the room and Shaw heard him lock the door.

He looked around at the small bedroom and he suddenly remembered it was the room his children had slept in when he had last visited in 1913. The room, he now recalled, had not changed a bit, although the wallpaper seemed more faded and grimy than he remembered. He felt a certain strange comfort in knowing he was going to die in the same room in which his children had once slept so peacefully.

Or was he? Perhaps, he thought suddenly, I am being too fatalistic and there is still a chance. He looked around quickly; there was nowhere to hide or to run to, not even to delay the inevitable by a few seconds. Drawing aside the curtains a few inches, he checked the sash window; it was indeed locked with a heavy brass fitting on each side, and there was no key to be seen, nor was there any implement in the room with which he could force it; there was no poker next to the little fireplace, which contained nothing more than some very ancient and dusty dried flowers.

He tried to raise the sash; it was stuck fast. He looked down. A few feet below was the flat roof of the downstairs bay window, and next to that the canvas roof of Sir John's Bentley. Beyond that was the overgrown hedge at the end of the drive through which he could see a small patch of the road; in the unlikely event anyone walked past it was doubtful whether he could attract their attention, and even if he did, McVitie had made it clear what would happen to him.

He sighed and tried the sash a final time. On this attempt, he felt movement at the side of the window. It was of the Georgian style, with nine pieces of glass separated by glazing bars painted a chocolate brown colour. He pushed at one of the bars and felt his finger sink into a soft, spongy indentation coated with black mould.

He felt each of the glazing bars in turn – all of them were rotten, but the damage was concealed by the paint acting like the skin on a rice pudding.

Thinking fast, he took his latch-key from his pocket and used it as a makeshift saw on each of the bars; the damp and rotten wood crumbled like well-cooked meat. He left alone one bar on each side, and pressed gently at the centre of the window; it bulged slightly and little flecks of paint fell to the floor. A pane of glass cracked in its corner, but did not break.

Suddenly he heard footsteps on the stairs; he quickly used the key to lever the curtain rail away from the wall as far as he could without removing it completely, and then closed the curtains, leaving them just as McVitie had left them.

He was just in time. There was a sound of footsteps on the stairs, and he hurriedly knelt down by the bed in a position of prayer. A key turned in the lock, and the door opened. He looked up to see McVitie, Keller, Lewin and Miss Petrescu enter the room.

After helping the man in the woods to his feet, McKechnie broke open his shotgun and held it in the crook of his arm, listening to the intruder speak as they walked back to the Manse. McKechnie's expression gradually changed from disbelief to anger.

He offered the man food and drink but he waved it away; even the suggestion of a glass of whisky was rejected. A few moments later the man sat in McKechnie's study while the minister took out his hunting rifle from his gun cabinet and stuffed a box of cartridges into his pocket.

He slung the rifle over his shoulder and kept hold of the shotgun over his arm. He was just thankful that his wife was still out or else she might try to persuade him not to go; he scribbled a note to her telling her he had been called away urgently on parish business and would not be able to attend the meeting of the kirk session later that day.

'Come on,' he said to the man firmly. 'We'll take my car. If what you say is true – then Reverend Shaw *has got to be stopped.*'

'The common mosses, ye say?' asked the elderly, gnarled man with a ruddy nose and cheeks who opened the gate of the cottage garden. He had taken what seemed like an age to walk to it from his vegetable patch, and Nesbitt sounded a trifle impatient while he spoke to the man.

'Aye that's right. We're looking for them or anywhere with public shooting rights,' said the sergeant.

'If it's shooting you're wanting,' said the man, 'you're best speaking to the laird Sir John awa' up at Balnacurin. He's the best for the shooting around here. Owns most o' the land. Save the common mosses, o' course. But the shootings no' so good the day on them. The birds just dinnae seem to want to land. Something wrang wi' the peat, if ye ask me. It's mair drookit and glittie the day than it used tae be in the auld days, when it wis fair dry enough to toss on the fire richt away.

'Now, many a year ago, I had a wee gun mysel', a point two-two, and I had my fill o' my pot wi' the pheasants. But lately the birds are awa'. Aye, mebbe 'tis no' just the wet land. Mebbe this slump is the cause o' it. The young men have all gone tae England or America, and sae the birds could have gone the same way…'

The old man suddenly stopped talking and looked at Nesbitt, as if he were seeing the man's police uniform for the first time.

'What was it you were wantin' again, son?' he asked. 'Ah, the shooting. Well as I wis sayin', Sir John's the man to speak to…'

'It's no' shooting we're wanting, it's a minister,' cut in McLeish loudly, as if the man were deaf. 'Have you seen a minister round these parts, with a shotgun?'

'A minister?' exclaimed the man. 'Why, whit's happened? Is somebody deid?'

'Yes,' said McLeish. 'Colonel Shaw, over the way. Do you know him?'

'Colonel Shaw?' enquired the man. 'Aye, I know of him. That's a rare pity. He was a good man. You'll be wanting to find a minister for his funeral then?'

'No, no, we're just looking for a minister to help us wi' our enquiries,' said Nesbitt. 'We were told he might be out shooting round these parts and we wondered where the common land was.'

'Och, why didn't ye say?' said the man. 'That'll be Mr McKechnie you're looking for. He's aboot here sometimes for a wee spot o' shooting.'

'You've been very helpful,' interrupted McLeish. 'Where would we find Mr McKechnie if he were out shooting round here?'

Nesbitt sighed and turned to the Inspector. 'It's not Mr McKechnie we're looking for sir, it's a Reverend Shaw. Colonel Shaw's nephew.'

'I'll handle this, sergeant, thank you,' said McLeish firmly. Then he turned to Nesbitt and whispered. 'Just let the man speak, or we'll be here all day.'

'He'd be on the common mosses, most like,' said the old man with a smile, pointing with his stick up the hill. 'Up that way aboot half a mile on the other side o' the burn. That marks the end of Sir John's land.'

'You've been very helpful, sir,' said the McLeish. 'We'll bid ye good day.'

The two policemen turned to go but the elderly man took hold of McLeish's arm.

'Are you all right, son?' he asked. 'Only why are ye going aboot wi' a policeman? Have ye done something wrang?'

'As I explained before sir, when you came to the gate,' replied McLeish with a sigh, 'I'm a detective inspector. That's why I'm no' in uniform. The sergeant here is helping me on a case. Now if you don't mind….'

Before the old man could say anything else, Nesbitt had started the police car and McLeish jumped in, slamming the door firmly.

Shaw got to his feet slowly and faced the line of people in front of him in the small bedroom. Lewin stood impassively by the door and McVitie by the window; Keller stepped forward and placed a medical bag on the bed.

'I understood Sir John wished you to draw lots. It seems all of you except him drew the short straw,' said Shaw, with a grim attempt at humour. The group ignored him.

'Make up the formula,' Keller said to Miss Petrescu, who stood by him. 'As before. 25 centilitres of the serum and top up the remainder of the syringe with the tincture of cobalt pentaflouride.'

Miss Petrescu hesitated.

'Quickly now,' said Keller. 'We have other things to be getting on with and Sir John wishes to discuss them with us.'

Shaw swallowed hard. So this, he thought, was to be his end. No death or glory charge on the battlefield, no burning martyr's pyre…just an injection of an obscure chemical in a shabby back room, administered by a bored man who had 'other things to be getting on with.'

'There is perhaps one thing you ought to realise,' said Shaw. 'That you are perhaps not aware of.' It was a last, desperate gamble.

'Oh yes?' said Keller, disinterestedly, as he watched Miss Petrescu take out various phials and bottles from the bag and lay them on the bed.

'And what might…not the sodium, I said the cobalt,' he snapped, snatching a bottle from the woman's hand and replacing it in the bag. 'You were saying?' he continued blandly.

'Your substitution of my uncle's body had one flaw,' said Shaw. 'The scarring on his leg. There are others beside myself who know about it. The absence of it on the substituted corpse could raise questions.'

Keller sighed. 'Really Mr Shaw, do you think we have not thought of such things already? Why would these others ask questions about it? You will not be around to sound the alarm. Even if somehow they exhumed the body, they would not find any marks.'

'How…how so?' asked Shaw, his heart sinking.

'Anyone carrying out an exhumation,' said Keller with a hint of pride, 'would find that the corpse was in more advanced state of decay than normal, particularly around the area of the legs. You forget, Mr Shaw, that I am a surgeon and have some understanding of the processes of bodily decay, and how to accelerate it in particular areas. A first year medical student could do it, and remain undetected. Now, remove your jacket and roll up your sleeve.'

'But...what of dental records...it has been known to identify a corpse by them,' said Shaw.

'Dental records are irrelevant,' said Keller, this time with triumph in his voice. 'They would be no use. Both Colonel Shaw and Mr...his double...wore full dentures. His double's were removed. Believe me, there is nothing that can stop us now. Nothing. In a few hours you will be found dead from shotgun wounds on the moors.'

'The police have called,' said Shaw. 'They may already suspect something.'

'Sir John already primed them,' said Keller with a smile. 'He thinks of everything. By telling them you were an inexperienced shot who had gone out on his own. You walked carelessly with a loaded gun, you tripped, and you died. McVitie, his sleeve.'

Shaw felt his arms pinned to his sides as his jacket was pulled down by McVitie, so that the sleeves hung inside out around his wrists; he felt his right shirt cuff rip as McVitie pushed the sleeve roughly upwards. Miss Petrescu filled a syringe from a vial; she then peered at the numbers on the side of the vial. She replaced the syringe on the bed and went to draw back the curtain.

Shaw breathed in sharply; would they see what he had done to the window? Did it even matter now?

'Leave it,' snapped Lewin from the door. 'We don't want anyone seeing anything from the road.'

'But I cannot see what I am doing,' protested Miss Petrescu.

Shaw saw Lewin flick the light switch by the door, but no light came.

'The bulb has gone,' said Keller, looking up. 'You will just have to administer it as best you can. Quickly, now.'

'But I cannot see clearly,' protested Miss Petrescu as she stepped forward and held the syringe above Shaw's bicep. 'How am I supposed to…'

McVitie opened his mouth and roared. 'Just get on with it you stupid…'

Before he could finish his sentence, his jaw clamped shut, his teeth making a snapping noise as they collided, and he was silent. Miss Petrescu had stabbed the needle of the syringe about a quarter of an inch into McVitie's throat. A small trickle of blood dripped down the device and onto her thumb, which quivered above the plunger.

'That is the last time you tell me what to do,' she hissed. 'Any of you! I push this needle and he dies in a few seconds.'

'Put the syringe down Cosmina, there's a good girl,' said Lewin cautiously. Shaw, standing stock still, looked to the door and saw that Lewin was pointing his pistol at Miss Petrescu.

'No,' said the woman. 'I will not kill innocent people for you any longer.'

'You are just as much a party to it as we are,' said Keller angrily. 'If we make money, you make money. If we hang, so do you. Now, stop this nonsense and withdraw the needle before you do any more harm.'

'For God's sake get her off me,' whispered McVitie menacingly, his jaw still firmly clamped together. 'Shoot her if you have to.'

'I can shoot if you want me to, McVitie,' said Lewin blandly. 'I can hit Cosmina easily but that would probably mean the end of you as well if the bullet passes through her. So I'm afraid it's up to you old chap. It's entirely at your own risk.'

'You shoot and I press this syringe,' said Miss Petrescu.

'Come now, Cosmina, my dear,' said Keller unctuously. 'Let us talk about this in a civilised manner. What has upset you?'

'I will tell you,' said the woman. 'When we were in the other country we killed a man. I agreed because you said we needed the money for our new life together. Then we came here and you said we must kill again. I agreed but then I felt sorry for the Colonel and he asked me to help him.'

'Then it was you!' said McVitie. 'You were the one who got the minister to send that blasted telegram calling for his nephew. You're the cause of all this.'

'Well well,' said Lewin. 'And there was me believing Sir John's story about him sending for Shaw just for some sort of thrill. While all along it seems there was a traitor – Cosmina. I do wish you'd keep your woman under control, Keller.'

'I am not "his woman",' shouted Miss Petrescu. McVitie flinched visibly; a red stain was beginning to spread across the top of his shirt collar. Shaw wondered just how much longer this stand-off could last.

'I have had enough of you people,' she continued. 'You kill for money, you kill innocent people just because they stop your plans. There was no need to kill Colonel Shaw, we could have got his land by using the man who looked like him.'

'We had to kill Colonel Shaw because you let him escape,' said Keller slowly. 'Yes, I see it now. I told you to give him a strong sedative but he was still able to climb out of the window and run away while our backs were turned. You must have deliberately failed to give him that sedative. As well as leaving the window unlocked.'

'And what if I did?' said Miss Petrescu defiantly.

'Because that means it is your fault he is lying at the bottom of a peat bog with a bullet in his back,' replied Keller.

'That is *not* my fault,' said Miss Petrescu. 'You would have killed him anyway. Just like you killed that poor old man that you paid to pretend to be Colonel Shaw. A harmless old drunkard who would not hurt anybody. And also that detective, the one on the train. I saw, in the newspaper.'

'That was Lewin and McVitie's doing, not mine,' said Keller. 'And as for doing it to make money for our future, I can tell you now there is no "our future".'

'What…what do you mean?' asked Miss Petrescu. Her hand trembled slightly on the syringe.

'I mean I'm tired of you,' replied the surgeon in a bored voice. 'I cannot trust you any more. I was a fool to let myself get involved with some cast-off of Lewin's.'

'You…how could you…treat me like this…' said Miss Petrescu, her mouth gaping.

'Be quiet and pull that needle out,' barked Keller. 'I'll treat you how I wish. You're nothing more than a common…'

'Enough of this,' interrupted Lewin firmly. 'You can't possibly hope to escape, my dear. Either step back now or I'll shoot you where you stand.'

Miss Petrescu let out a bloodcurdling scream and she forced the plunger of the syringe to its fullest extent. McVitie's eyes bulged in horror, and then an enormous explosion filled the room. Shaw was momentarily blinded by a flash, and his ears sang with a high-pitched whine. He realised that Lewin had fired his pistol.

Miss Petrescu slumped forward and fell to the floor, her eyes already glazed over. McVitie clawed at his throat, pulling out the syringe, then he too, staggered forward.

The syringe dropped to the floor and was crunched into fragments under McVitie's boot as he tried to maintain his balance.

'Give me something...there must be something for it...' he gasped, looking imploringly at Keller.

'I'm sorry,' said Keller, shaking his head. 'Try not to struggle, it will be less painful.'

McVitie staggered towards the window, clutching his throat. 'Need...air. Let me...out,' he whispered.

'Stop him, before somebody sees,' barked Keller.

Lewin stepped forward and raised his pistol to fire. McVitie tried to pull open the curtain, but as he did so, the entire rod ripped away from the wall where Shaw had loosened it.

The heavy brass finial hit Lewin a glancing blow on the forehead, stunning him. McVitie took the chance to lunge for the man's wrist and forced the pistol down, causing Lewin to fire into his own midriff.

McVitie fell backwards on to the floor with a heavy thud as Lewin howled in pain, trying to extricate himself from the folds of the dusty curtain that enveloped him and which was now spattered with dark bloodstains. Then he was still.

Keller seemed frozen in horror in a corner of the room, but then sprang forward and began searching for Lewin's pistol under the curtain. It is now or never, thought Shaw.

Shrugging off his jacket, he ran to the window holding the garment aloft in front of his face for protection, and hurled his body against the glass as if he were meeting an enormous rugby full-back.

Expecting at least some resistance, he was shocked when the rotten, loosened frame gave way like paper and he found himself stumbling like a drunken tap-dancer on the roof of the downstairs bay window.

Slates, which had partly broken his fall, shattered and fell away under his feet as he staggered, momentarily surprised by the height of the roof. He quickly regained his balance then dropped the few feet down on to the roof of Sir John's car, his weight making two large rips in the canvas.

He rolled over and slid down the rear mudguard on to the running board, and after what seemed an age, his feet touched the gravel of the driveway.

Then he was running on to the road in his shirt-sleeves, still holding his jacket, as if he were being pursued in a dream; a dream punctuated by the sound of a pistol being fired repeatedly at him out of the shattered window.

Chapter Ten

'Do you know when your husband might be back?' asked McLeish of Mrs McKechnie as he stood with Nesbitt on the doorstep of the Manse.

'I've no idea,' the woman replied in a somewhat worried voice. 'I was out fetching a message, and came back to find a wee note saying he'd gone out on urgent parish business.'

'Did he say where?' asked Nesbitt, turning his cap in his hands.

'No,' replied Mrs McKechnie, 'but I'm guessing it's maybe to do with the kirk sessions meeting this evening at six. I'm not sure why he'd take the car, though, and the dog as well. Is anything wrong?'

'No, no, Mrs, er, McKechnie, nothing's wrong,' said McLeish. 'Actually we're more interested in the whereabouts of someone else. Am I right in saying a Reverend Shaw is putting up here?'

'That's right,' said Mrs McKechnie. 'He's here for a few days to deal with some family matters. His uncle died, you see.'

'Aye, we're aware of that, madam,' said Nesbitt. 'That's what we'd like to talk to him about. Is he in the now?'

'No,' replied Mrs McKechnie. 'I've no idea where he is. Is he in some sort of trouble?'

'Well…' began Nesbitt. Then McLeish interrupted.

'We'll not trouble you further, Mrs McKechnie,' said the Inspector, raising his hat. 'If Reverend Shaw should chance to turn up, will you kindly tell him to telephone this number. Good afternoon to you.'

Mrs McKechnie looked down at the card handed to her, with a puzzled frown.

'Oh there's one more thing, Inspector,' she said.

'Yes?'

'I noticed the gun cupboard in the study's empty. Calum – that's my husband – must have taken them with him.'

'How many guns does he have?' asked McLeish.

'Two I think, a rifle and a shotgun. He's often out looking for something for the pot, but he doesn't usually take the both of them.'

'All right, thank you madam. You've been most helpful,' said McLeish. The two policemen hastily returned to their car and drove off.

'This is turning out to be a wasted afternoon,' sighed Nesbitt. 'I suppose we'll away back to Inverness the now?'

'Not a bit of it,' said McLeish as he steered the car on to the main road through the village. 'Something I don't like about all this. Why would he go off shooting when he's got a meeting in an hour? And why take two guns, anyway?'

'Aye, well maybe he joined up somewhere with Reverend Shaw to try their luck.'

'But his wife said the note referred to urgent parish business, ' replied McLeish. 'What sort of urgent parish business is a minister going to be called out on at short notice like that? '

'Maybe it's a shotgun wedding,' said Nesbitt, and laughed. 'Do you get it, sir? A shotgun…'

'Aye, I get it,' said McLeish curtly. 'Now let me think. I cannae help thinking somebody's giving us the run around here.'

'Shall we call in at the police house in the village?' suggested Nesbitt. 'We could wait there for a wee while and have another look round. It's getting a bit cold the now.'

'Och, tell your mammy to give you a vest next time you come out,' chided McLeish as he turned at the junction, taking the road which led away from the road back to Auchentorrin Lodge. He slowed down briefly to pass through a small herd of sheep plodding along the highway, and then accelerated.

'I'll tell you what we'll do,' he said, as the sound of baa-ing faded away behind them. 'We'll have another wee look round the common mosses on the other side of the village – to see if we can find either o' these shooting clerics, and then another look over at Colonel Shaw's house in case Reverend Shaw's gone back there. By then it'll be six o'clock and McKechnie'll have to be back for his kirk meeting. Then if at least one of them hasnae come back by then, we'll send out a search party.'

Shaw thanked the Lord that he kept himself fit with regular walking, cycling and swimming, and that he smoked a pipe rather than clogging his lungs with cigarettes. He estimated he had run at least half a mile without stopping, at full pelt across the rugged moorland which rose upwards from Auchentorrin Lodge. He had heard the last of the pistol shots from the window several minutes ago; had he managed to get away?

He reduced his speed slightly to a fast trot and risked a look behind; he could not see anybody and even the house was now barely visible beyond the rising, tussocky ground.

He decided to rest for a moment, and threw himself down behind a rocky outcrop.

Shrugging on his jacket to protect himself from the damp ground, he cautiously peered through a gap in the rocks down into the valley. There was no movement of any kind, apart from the gentle waving of grasses in the breeze. The sun was now low in the west, and he checked his watch; five pm. At this latitude he realised it would not be completely dark, especially on a clear night such as this, until around eight pm or so.

He breathed deeply and tried to think. In his mind's eye he saw again the horror of the small bedroom and he forced the image out of his mind. 'I must remain calm', he said to himself. He thought of the men in his regiment. 'None of them flinched,' he muttered under his breath, 'not even in the face of certain death, and neither must I.'

He felt slightly calmer. McVitie was presumably, by now, dead with the injection meant for him; Miss Petrescu appeared to have been killed also, and Lewin must, at least, be seriously injured. That left just two possible pursuers, Keller and Sir John, assuming there were no other conspirators involved. Perhaps they had given up searching, realising they could not find him.

He looked again through the gap in the rocks, and this time he felt a cold trickle of fear run down his neck. A few hundred yards away, he saw Sir John's Bentley bumping and swaying along the rutted track that led away from the main road. They were coming towards him.

He had to warn McKechnie that dangerous men were after him and perhaps his wife also – they knew that he had told him of his suspicions, and he was therefore a target. Who knew what kind of dastardly lengths they would go to to silence him? He had to tell the police, but how?

It was imperative, he realised, to inform the authorities before Keller and Sir John got anywhere near him – if what they said was true, that they could turn him into a raving lunatic with one stab of a needle, it was hopeless – nobody would believe him and he would be shut away in some private asylum, perhaps for the rest of his miserable life.

Once more he looked down the valley. The Bentley had stopped, and a man alighted from it. His back was turned, and Shaw could not be sure who it was. He turned, and he saw it was Keller; he recognised the homburg hat and the well-cut overcoat which did not quite disguise the man's sedentary, slightly stooped physique. He slung a rifle awkwardly on his shoulder and began to walk off the track upwards towards Shaw; the Bentley then turned around and drove away towards the village.

Presumably, thought Shaw, they were separating in order to find him. He dare not risk going into the village in case he should be seen. Sir John might even convince the local constable of his story of a madman on the loose. In his mind's eye he saw lines of policemen with dogs combing the moorland, all convinced that the man they were looking for was a dangerous lunatic. Keller would be called for to 'sedate' him, and well, that would be that.

He had to somehow get to a telephone without being seen. But he could not risk staying here until dark; Keller would be likely to see him if he continued walking towards him. He had to make a run for it, but to where?

He turned and looked up the valley towards the line of pine trees, and could just make out a small whitewashed cottage, a twist of smoke curling from its chimney. A tumbledown dry-stone wall and rough hedging ran in a line between where he was hiding and the cottage. He realised it was the track from the main road; if he ran along it there was a chance that Keller would not see him.

Perhaps there would be a telephone at the cottage...it was a slim chance, but he had no alternative. Before Keller came any closer, he was off, running stooped behind the dry-stone wall, his body tensed for the impact of a bullet at any moment.

'Damned fool!' exclaimed McLeish, swerving slightly to the left as a large, expensive-looking motor car rushed past. Nesbitt clutched at the side of his seat to steady himself then looked round. He saw that the vehicle had stopped suddenly as a herd of sheep trotted nonchalantly across the road. There was then the sound of a klaxon being blown repeatedly, and a muffled shout from inside the car.

'Wait a minute...' said McLeish, looking into his rear view mirror. That's that Bentley from the house. Sir John whats-his-name. Where's he going in such a hurry?'

McLeish rapidly executed a three-point-turn and a few seconds later drew the police car up behind Sir John's Bentley.

'Off you go out and clear the road,' said McLeish, as the sheep crossed the road unhurriedly two-by-two, as if queuing for a Noah's Ark reserved exclusively for their species.

'What?' asked Nesbitt. 'They'll be across in a minute. Why've we turned round?'

'Dinnae ask questions,' snapped McLeish. 'Help those sheep over then check he's all right. Take your time till I get there.'

'Och...' protested Nesbitt as he opened the car door and walked forward to hurry the sheep across the road. McLeish smiled as he saw the man slip slightly on some droppings on the road, but quickly regain his balance. He began whistling and making the sort of noises that he had heard drovers use, which sounded something like 'Come by, come by!'

McLeish stepped out of the car and walked forward, as Nesbitt cleared the last of the animals out of the way. McLeish frowned as he noticed two large tears on the canvas roof of the car. The sergeant gave a little salute to Sir John, who leaned out of the car window.

'Thank you so much, sergeant,' said Sir John. 'I'm afraid I must dash.'

The Bentley's large engine revved. Before his head disappeared back inside, McLeish put his hand on the roof and leaned down.

'Just a moment, sir, if you don't mind,' he said.

Sir John flashed a smile. 'We meet again, Inspector.'

'Aye. Do you know what speed you were doing on that bend just now?'

'Really Inspector I…' Sir John's eyes briefly flashed annoyance, but then the professional assurance was back. 'Speed limits were abolished under the Road Traffic Act 1930. You ought to know that.'

'Aye, so I do,' said McLeish. 'But there's still a crime of "wanton and furious driving", under the Offences Against the Person Act of 1861. You could have caused an accident going that fast.'

McLeish could see Nesbitt's face burning red with embarrassment. He smiled inwardly but looked blandly at Sir John, waiting for a response.

'Look here, you're not going to give me a summons or anything tiresome like that, are you?' said the baronet. 'I can hardly appear before myself on the bench, now can I?'

McLeish continued to stare impassively at Sir John, who then clicked his fingers and smiled.

'I knew I recognised you the last time we met,' he said. 'You're a member of the Inverness Lodge.'

'Dinnae bother with any o' that, sir,' said McLeish with a sigh. 'I've never been in a Masonic Lodge in my life. I'll let you off with a warning, but be mair careful next time.'

'Very decent of you, Inspector. Won't go unremembered. Now I really must cut along.'

'Just one more thing, sir,' said McLeish. 'Did you happen to see that minister we were talking about earlier on your travels?'

There was a pause, and Sir John appeared momentarily confused. He then took a deep breath and smiled. 'Actually yes.'

'Where was this?' said McLeish.

'Oh dear,' replied Sir John. 'I suppose I ought to tell you. I really hoped I wouldn't have to.'

'Tell us what?' asked Nesbitt.

'It's a sad case, I'm afraid, very sad,' said Sir John, 'but it does, I hope, excuse my rather rapid driving. I'm sorry to say that Reverend Shaw has become…unhinged.'

'Unhinged?' asked McLeish.

'My…acquaintance, Mr Keller, could tell you more as it is one of his fields of speciality, but it seems the poor man is suffering from acute psychosis.'

'Acute what?' asked Nesbitt.

'You mean, like shell-shock?' offered McLeish.

'Something of that sort, at any rate,' replied Sir John. 'Keller can't give a full diagnosis at this stage, but the man appears to have gone stark staring mad, talking all sorts of nonsense about his uncle's death, and has run off across the moors. We're both looking for him now.'

'How did it happen?' asked Nesbitt, open-mouthed.

'Keller was on his way to Auchentorrin Lodge, on foot,' said Sir John. 'He'd come up from Inverness on the train –

and I was on my way back to the house to see if I could find Shaw. I offered the chap a lift and then found out who he was. Going to sign some papers for poor old Colonel Shaw, apparently, which was why I was supposed to be there too, if you recall.

'We got as far as the drive and then out dashes a clergyman in a state of dishabille, ranting and raving. Keller tried to calm the chap down, but he wasn't having any of it. Kept babbling on about all sorts of horrors, and didn't seem to make any sense.

'Keller seemed to think it might have been brought on by the strain of his uncle's passing. Then the next thing we know he's run off across the moors. Keller's up there looking for him, and I was on my way to the minister McKechnie, to…get his assistance. He knows him apparently, and we thought a friendly face might help.'

'Maybe that was why he was called away?' asked Nesbitt. 'We've been trying to find him but his wife said he'd gone out on urgent business. But who told him?'

'Damn,' said Sir John, ignoring the question. 'Then it's just me and Keller. I'm off to fetch my dog, he might be able to pick up the scent.'

'We'll help you,' said McLeish decisively. 'We cannae have a madman on the loose. We'll call in at the police house and telephone for reinforcements from Inverness. While we wait for them we'll get a local search party together, with dogs and horses if we can.'

'I…wouldn't do that if I were you, Inspector,' said Sir John firmly. 'Keller is of the opinion the man is in a highly fragile state. A large search party of policemen might just tip him over the edge, and cause him to do something desperate. I'm afraid he's armed.'

'Good God, I was forgetting that,' said McLeish. 'Now I remember you told me he'd gone out with a gun.'

'Keller thinks it may be shell-shock, as you say,' replied Sir John. 'The last thing we want is him thinking he's back in France and a line of bobbies are Huns about to mount a bayonet charge.'

'Aye, you may have a point,' said McLeish, rubbing his chin. 'I've had to pacify one or two men like that myself. What do you suggest?'

'I suggest,' replied Sir John, 'if you would be so kind, that you go one way and we will go another. If you search the area downhill towards the station, we will try upwards, towards the hills. If you see him, do not approach him, but send for us immediately. We're armed and Keller has sedatives. Rendezvous here, on the hour, every hour, until we find him. When he is found, Keller will need to sedate him, so he must be the first one to approach him.'

'But what if he attacks someone?' asked Nesbitt nervously. 'Wait a minute. This man Shaw was on the same train as Moffat…what if he…'

'Anything's possible with shell-shock,' said Sir John with a shrug. 'But it seems unlikely he'll attack anyone here – there's nobody around for miles. If he approaches the village, try to contain him until Keller can be found.'

'All right sir,' said McLeish. 'We'll try your way for a couple of hours, but no more – I'm not risking innocent lives for a madman.'

'Very well, Inspector,' said Sir John as he gunned his engine. 'But be careful. He was drifting in and out of lucidity when we spoke to him. Keller seems to think he might be able to appear sane if he has to, if you see what I mean. But it might be a trick.'

'Aye, I think I understand,' said McLeish, uncertainly.

'So don't trust him,' replied Sir John. 'See you back here in one hour.'

'Just one more thing,' said McLeish quickly.

'You seem to say that rather a lot, Inspector,' replied Sir John. 'What is it?'

'How did those tears get on the roof of your car?'

'Tears?' There was a pause and then Sir John smiled again. 'Oh that. That was Shaw's doing. Tore at the roof with his bare hands like a blasted ape when we tried to get him into the car. Poor devil.'

Nesbitt looked at the rips in the heavy fabric and swallowed hard, as Sir John drove off in a cloud of dust and exhaust fumes.

Shaw's knees ached as he ran awkwardly up the hill, his back bent forward to prevent Keller seeing him from beyond the dry-stone wall. After what seemed an eternity he reached the cottage. He checked nobody was in the garden, and then leaped over the low back wall and secreted himself behind the back door.

He looked cautiously round the rough whitewashed wall of the cottage, out over the valley. He spotted Keller straight away; the man had not moved but was still scanning the area in front of him with his binoculars. He must, thought Shaw, assume that I am pinned down here somewhere and he is waiting for me to make my move.

He looked behind the cottage up the hill to the dark line of pine trees at the summit; the track did not lead straight upwards, but passed by the back of the cottage at an oblique angle; the dry stone wall disappeared and there was no cover.

It would not be possible, he realised, to make a run for it to the cover of the woods without being spotted by Keller. He had no idea how good a shot the man was, but he did not wish to take a chance in open country against a high-powered rifle with a telescopic sight. There was only one thing for it. He took a deep breath and knocked softly at the back door of the cottage.

Almost instantly, the door opened and he heard a voice from within. 'Come in, Mr Shaw.'

'I don't like this one bit,' said McLeish as he steered the police car along the rough track down the hill away from Auchentorrin Lodge. 'An armed madman on the loose. And we two wi' nothing to protect us except your wee truncheon.'

'Ah,' said Nesbitt, looking sheepishly at his superior. 'There's a funny thing. I didnae bring it wi' me the day. It's an awfy weight in the pocket and well, I didnae think I'd need it…'

'God save us,' breathed McLeish. 'You're supposed to have your truncheon, whistle, notebook, indelible pencil and warrant card on you at all times. It's a wonder you ever made sergeant.'

'Sorry sir…' mumbled Nesbitt.

'Ach, never mind,' replied the Inspector. 'It wouldnae be much use against a shotgun anyway.'

'What'll we do if we find him?' asked Nesbitt.

'Like the man said. One of us'll have to keep an eye on him and the other'll have to drive back to the meeting place.'

'I'm guessing it'll be me you're wanting to stay with the man,' said Nesbitt, unhappily.

'Correct. Just keep your distance. Try not to let him see you.'

'But what if we find him in the next five minutes? I'll have to follow him for nearly an hour.'

'Ach, I'm not having that,' said McLeish. 'I'll drive as fast as I can in the other direction and find those two and bring them back.'

'I just hope they find him first,' said Nesbitt. 'It'll be getting dark in a couple o' hours. I'll not want to be chasing around the moors in the dark on my own.'

'You won't be,' said McLeish decisively, as he increased the speed of the police car along a relatively straight stretch of road. He looked from side to side across the desolate, empty moorland, with nothing in view except the enormous purple backdrop of the Benmurie Braes. Unless the man was lying down, he thought, there was no way he could remain unseen.

'We'll give it one hour,' said McLeish, looking at his watch, 'and then I'm calling in the cavalry from Inverness. Now keep your eyes peeled.'

'How on earth do you know my name?' asked Shaw incredulously, as he stepped into the cottage. A small, gnarled man with a ruddy face reached round him and drew the back door shut, bolting it top and bottom.

'I'll no' draw the curtains, as that'll attract attention,' he said. 'We'd best stay in the back room. One of them's oot the front. I noticed him just now and thought you might be coming in for a visit. You'll be safe enough in here for a while.'

Shaw looked around him in puzzlement. He was in a tiny back kitchen, which looked as if it had not changed for a century; it was dominated by a black cooking range and a well-scrubbed wooden table; two upright chairs, a stone sink in the corner with a pump handle and some pots and pans formed the rest of the contents.

'I know who you are all right,' said the man cheerfully, but in a rather quiet voice. 'The police were asking for you a wee while ago. I sent them on their way, dinnae worry. My name's Clelland by the way. Archie Clelland.'

'How do you do,' said Shaw. 'Look here,' he continued. 'This all must look fantastical, as if I'm some sort of wanted criminal. But let me explain…'

The old man held up a wizened hand, twisted with the marks of arthritis. 'Dinnae tell me,' he said firmly, 'because I dinnae want to know. If you're kin to the Colonel that's good enough to make me want to help you.'

'You knew my uncle?' asked Shaw.

'Aye, and my condolences,' said the old man, shaking his head. 'I only just heard the news. He was a guid man, and treated me respectful. Even stood me a dram from time to time at the inn.'

'But why did you invite me in?' asked Shaw. 'I could be a dangerous criminal, for all you know. Surely you trust the police?'

'I've been on this earth nearly ninety years, minister,' said the man, 'and I'd like to think I've got a wee bit judge o' character in me. You're no more a dangerous criminal than I am. Now him awa' down the hill,' he said, pointing his thumb over his back, 'I dinnae like the look o'him one bit. Dressed like he's having tea wi' Queen Mary but carrying a hunting rifle. Up tae no good. And I dinnae trust the police either, nor the gentry. They've made it clear over the years they dinnae want small crofters like mysel' getting in the way o' the shooting. I'm guessing they're wanting ye for something like that – poaching or the like. Sae let's jist leave it at that.'

'Something…along those lines,' said Shaw, 'and it is best I do not tell you exactly what is happening. Suffice to say, Mr Clelland, I need to send a message urgently. May I use your telephone?'

Clelland laughed, a hollow, rasping sound. 'Telephone? Och, no. We dinnae have one. Nor electricity, and the pump o' water there wis only put in when my late wife, God rest her, got too puirly to walk tae the well.'

'Very well,' sighed Shaw. He had hardly expected there to be such an instrument in a house like this, its walls darkened with the soot of centuries from the fireplace; the Crusie lamps flickering on either side. 'Where is the nearest telephone?' he asked.

'In the town, by the post office.'

'I cannot risk being seen there. Is there another one anywhere nearby?'

'Weel,' said the old man doubtfully, 'you could always ask at Balnacurin House, mebbe they'd let you use theirs.'

'Most certainly not,' said Shaw. 'That is Sir John Debayle-Bradley's house.'

'Och, I was right then about the poaching,' said Clelland. 'You've upset the laird himself. But whit's happened tae your gun? The police said you'd been out shooting roond this way.'

Shaw refused to be drawn. 'Suffice to say Mr Clelland, I must find a telephone immediately.'

'Aye, ask no questions, tell no lies I suppose,' said Clelland. 'The nearest other telephone is the public box over the other side of the woods. By the auld Covenantor's kirk. The minister there wanted a telephone in the vestry, but the elders wouldnae have one in the place. They dinnae like anything invented after they were founded in 1847, or some such palaver. They're no' a whistle-kirk for that reason.'

'A...whistle-kirk?' asked Shaw.

'Aye, they dinnae have an organ. Too modern for them. They sing the hymns on their own.'

'But the organ was invented centuries ago,' countered Shaw.

'Dinnae ask me aboot their reasoning, minister,' replied the old man, shrugging his shoulders. 'All ye need to know is they don't have a telephone in the kirk itself. But the minister dropped a few wee hints to the Post Office Telephones that he'd like one nearby and they put one in the lane.'

'Is it far?' asked Shaw.

'A mile or so,' said Clelland. 'Once you're in the woods they'll find it hard to follow you and you'll be away clear.'

'I don't suppose that you own a motor car?' asked Shaw.

Clelland laughed again. 'I can barely afford tae get ma boots repaired these days. Mind, there is something you could use. Can ye ride a bicycle?'

'Certainly.'

'Aye, well, there's an auld one out the back. I cannae use her any more on account of the arthritis in ma legs, but you're welcome to her.'

'You have been most kind,' said Shaw, turning to go. 'I shall return the machine as soon as I am able. Now, I must get to that telephone.'

'Had on, let me have a look out the front,' said Clelland. He walked into the front parlour and then called to Shaw.

'Come and have a look. And keep away frae the window.'

Shaw crossed the tiny parlour, which was a sort of bed-sitting room with a sleeping area in one corner and an armchair by the fire in the other; it was darker and more soot stained even than the kitchen. He looked carefully out of the window and saw to his horror, that a car was approaching slowly up the rough track that he had run up. It was Sir John's Bentley.

'Is that the fellow you'd like to stay away from?'

'Yes,' replied Shaw. 'I must go immediately.'

'Away you go then. Looks like they're coming up here. I'll try to keep them talking for a while. If they're in front of the house they'll not see you going up the brae to the woods.'

'You have been most kind, Mr Clelland,' said Shaw. He took out his wallet and extracted a five pound note which he rapidly unfolded.

'Please take this as a deposit for the bicycle, in case I should not be able to return it.'

'Keep your money, minister,' urged Clelland. 'I've no need for it.'

'I insist,' said Shaw, holding out the note to the old man.

'And I insist ye *go*,' said Clelland. 'The laird's nearly here. God be with you.'

Shaw heard the Bentley come to a halt outside the cottage and the noise of the doors slamming. He needed no further encouragement; he stepped out of the back door, pausing only to tuck the five pound note into an earthenware mug by the sink.

He looked around the little back garden and saw a rusting, ancient bicycle with a shabby leather saddle propped against the back wall of the cottage. Would it even run? he wondered.

A quick glance at the tyres showed they were reasonably well inflated and the rust seemed mostly on the surface. It would have to do.

He heard a heavy knocking on the front door of the cottage and froze. Keller and Sir John were just a few feet away from him, obscured only by the walls of the cottage. He heard voices; there was another sound as well. A metallic clinking of a chain and a patter of clawed feet, and then Sir John calling.

'Heel, Blucher!'

Sir John had brought his dog – the Doberman – with him. That must have been why he had left Keller to keep watch, he assumed. An icy current of fear coursed through his limbs. He realised must leave immediately, before the animal caught his scent.

He stepped forward to the bicycle and stopped suddenly as he realised the little garden was not turfed, but laid with gravel. Just one step had made a sound that seemed as loud as the snare-drum in a dance band. Had it been heard?

He paused and waited, listening to the voices at the front door. His forehead wrinkled in confusion as he heard Clelland speak, but the man sounded as if he were talking gibberish.

'*Feasgar math*,' said Clelland.

'What's that?' asked Keller.

'*Ciamar a tha thu?*' replied the old man.

'Dammit man, what on earth are you saying?' said Keller.

'He's speaking Gaelic,' said Sir John. 'Some of the old folk still speak it around here. Do you speak English, my good man?'

'*Dè?*'

Despite his fear, Shaw could not help smiling. The old man was doing his best to forestall his pursuers. He wondered how long he had before he must make his move.

'Come along now,' said Sir John, more impatiently this time. 'I'm sure you do speak English, don't you?'

'*Dè?*'

'English. *Sassanach!*' exclaimed Sir John angrily. 'You can speak English I'm sure, damn you. Stop pretending you can't.'

There was a pause. Shaw could not possibly move while there was complete silence, and he hoped the old man would start talking again. He soon did.

'Oh, English is it?' said Clelland cheerily. 'Certainly, certainly. I'll be happy to oblige. Only I'm a wee bit deaf.'

'That is quite all right,' said Sir John loudly. 'I wonder if you can help us. We are looking for someone.'

'Out on a run?' said Clelland uncertainly.

'What?' asked Sir John.

'You're out on a run?' asked the old man. 'Only I'm a wee bit deaf.'

'We are looking for a man,' said Sir John loudly. 'A clergyman'.

Shaw grabbed the bicycle, trying to minimise the sound of crunching gravel, and wheeled it carefully to the back gate.

'What was that noise?' said Sir John.

'Nothing, just my dog oot the back,' said Clelland.

'I thought you were deaf,' said Keller.

'What did ye say?'

'I said I thought you were deaf!' shouted Keller.

'Aye, that I am,' replied Clelland.

'Then how did you hear that noise?' asked the surgeon suspiciously. 'It was very quiet.'

'I didnae hear anything,' said Clelland. 'It was you said there was a noise and I just assumed it was my dog. He's a big noisy brute, my dog. He'd be a match for anyone, yours as well. I mind one time, he fought off two men who came into the cottage, and…'

Shaw realised this was his moment; he hurled open the ancient wooden back gate and mounted the bicycle in one fluid movement. Within seconds he was bumping and swaying over the stony track which led upwards to the woods.

He heard a shout and the furious barking of the dog behind him, and from the corner of his eye saw Keller and Sir John emerge from the front of the house. He pedalled harder and then looked back; Keller raised his rifle a fraction but Sir John discreetly pushed it down and let the dog off its lead.

Within seconds the animal was behind him; Shaw pushed desperately on the pedals and the rusting chain of the bicycle squealed in protest; the steep uphill climb would have been difficult at the best of times, but with his legs still aching from his previous escape, it was sheer torture.

He dared not look round but felt the snapping of the dog's jaws at his ankles; the woodland and the brow of the hill were only yards away and he somehow found a final reserve of energy sufficient to make it into the darkness of the trees. Almost immediately he felt the bicycle swerve and then surge forward; ahead was a steep incline carpeted with dead pine needles; the bicycle slalomed for a moment and then he righted it.

He heard a frantic skittering and then the barking of the dog retreating into the distance. Risking a look behind, he saw the animal's paws trying to find purchase on the slippery forest floor. Then there was a repeated whistling from somewhere in the distance. Shaw looked again and the dog had turned tail and run in the opposite direction.

He breathed a short sigh of relief and concentrated on keeping the bicycle upright. After a few moments he emerged out into the sunlight and saw the stony track reappear; it soon joined with a metalled road; he assumed it was the one that Clelland had said would lead to the public telephone box. As the smoother surface of the road enabled him to maintain his balance more easily, he looked around, but could see no sign of his pursuers. He pedalled harder, hoping against hope that he could make it to the box before they did.

'Why did you stop me firing?' said Keller angrily as the two men hurried towards the Bentley. 'I had him in my sights. And why did you call off the dog?'

'Don't be a damned fool,' said Sir John, as he bundled Blucher into the back of the car. 'That old man in the cottage thinks we're looking for a friend. Do you really think he'll expect us to let a dog savage him? Besides, there could be other people in that wood and we don't want witnesses to my dog mauling someone to death.'

'But he's getting away,' said Keller petulantly, as they sat down in the vehicle. Sir John started the engine noisily and the car moved off. He watched as the old man tugged his forelock, grinned and turned back inside the house.

'That old fool knows something,' said Sir John, 'but I doubt Shaw told him the full story.'

'We can deal with him later,' said Keller.

'Don't be absurd,' said Sir John. 'We're not going to just kill anyone who might suspect what we're up to. It's that sort of behaviour from your associates that's caused all this. Shaw doesn't know this country but he seemed to have a pretty good idea of where he was going. My guess is that man told him about the telephone box up the road. It's about a mile away if I remember rightly.'

'My God,' exclaimed Keller. 'We have to stop him.'

'We will,' said Sir John firmly.

'But what of the police?' asked the surgeon. 'You said

they were asking questions, that they wished to meet with us.'

'Indeed they do,' said Sir John as the car bumped off the track on to the metalled road which led around the side of the woodland, in the direction that Shaw was cycling. 'But I've bought us some time. An hour, maybe two. I sent them in the wrong direction. It's vital that we stop Shaw before he has a chance to talk to the police.'

'But what if he told everything to that old man?'

'I doubt he did. Shaw's the sentimental type who won't want others to come to harm. He probably thinks we would have put the old fool to torture.'

'Perhaps we might have to,' murmured Keller.

'You're developing a taste for killing, old chap,' chuckled Sir John. 'Not healthy. Stick to the floozies instead, is my advice. Far safer.'

Keller folded his arms and glared at the passing countryside. 'I see no sign of him. What if he has got away?'

'There's nowhere for him to get away to,' said Sir John. 'This godforsaken moorland goes on and on, with impassable hills on either side, for at least five miles, all the way to Aviemore. There's only one proper road good enough for a bicycle – this one. We'll see him in a moment.'

'How on earth will we get close enough to inject him?' said Keller, fumbling in his medical bag.

'We don't,' said Sir John, his eyes scanning both sides of the road as the car passed by the side of the little wood through which Shaw had escaped. 'We get him with this.' He patted the hunting rifle held between Keller's legs.

'But he is unarmed,' protested Keller. 'What if the police make trouble…?'

'He'll be armed when they find him,' said Sir John.

He patted the weapon propped beside him by the driver's seat. 'With this shotgun. Remember I told the copper at the Colonel's house he'd gone out with a gun?' he continued. 'Poor chap refused to come quietly, fired at us, and regrettably we had to defend ourselves, etc etc.'

'I see, I see,' said Keller, a wolfish smile spreading across his face. 'Clever. But what of the injection, the one to make him appear mad? I have it made up in my bag.'

'We won't need it if we can shoot him first,' said Sir John. 'Only use that stuff if he manages to find other people and we can't firing. And do it *discreetly*.'

'Very well,' said Keller. 'I will have it ready in my pocket just in case. But wait…what about the Colonel's house? What if the police find…'

'Doesn't matter,' said Sir John. 'In fact it helps our cause. They think Shaw is a dangerous madman, well, turns out he killed three people before we bumped into him.'

'But will the police believe that?' asked Keller worriedly. 'Shouldn't we tell the police we saw him do it?'

'Too late for that, old man,' said Sir John. 'We didn't mention it to the bobbies when we met them and it would look awfully queer if we mentioned it afterwards. That sort of thing doesn't just slip one's mind. But there's no need to say we saw him kill anyone.'

'Why?'

'I took Lewin's pistol when we dashed out, remember? Well, once we've dealt with Shaw, I'll make certain his fingerprints are all over it and that it's found in his pocket. The police will draw the simplest conclusion. Satisfied?'

'I suppose so…' murmured Keller.

'Good man,' said Sir John, and the car increased in speed as he caught sight of a figure riding a bicycle on the road up ahead. 'Hello,' said Sir John. 'Here's our man. Put one up the spout, Keller.'

'Up the spout…?'

Sir John pressed on the accelerator; the large car responded with a low, bestial growl as it surged forward, like some jungle predator about to pounce on a helpless gazelle. He turned to Keller and smiled, but his eyes held nothing but malice.

'I mean load the rifle. Our interfering parson is about to meet his maker.'

Chapter Eleven

McKechnie drove his little car into the driveway of Auchentorrin Lodge and manoeuvred the vehicle behind the cover of some trees where it would be unseen from both the road and the house. He stopped the engine, then instructed his passenger to stay in the car out of sight, with the dog Campbell for company.

He walked up to the front door and hesitated. He knew he ought he to go to the police, especially after what the man in the car had told him, but if what he said was true, Shaw's life was in imminent danger. His first priority, he decided, was to try to find him before anything could happen to him – then there would be time to speak to the police.

His first stop, at Sir John's house, had proved unfruitful; the granite-faced butler had simply said repeatedly that there was nobody at home, and McKechnie had given up in disgust. Presumably the man had been instructed to stay quiet, which had made him all the more suspicious. He had decided to try Colonel Shaw's house as a last resort, and then if Shaw could not be found there, he would go to the police.

As he approached the front of the house, he immediately sensed that something was wrong. He noticed the gaping hole in the upper storey that had once held a window frame; and saw on the ground below small pieces of glass and wood lying around. Somebody, he thought, must have used considerable force to do that – had someone jumped – or been thrown out?

No answer came when he knocked on the door. He tried the handle – the door swung open.

'Is anybody here?' he called out.

No answer came.

There was something in the air, a hint of a smell, or smells, that he could not quite identify, but which unsettled him. Unslinging his rifle, he drove home the bolt of the weapon, then held it in front of him.

'I warn you, I'm armed,' he shouted.

Warily he investigated the rooms on the ground floor and, finding them empty, he climbed the stairs. As he reached the top, he realised what the smell was. Cordite from gunshots, mixed with vapourised blood.

It was something he remembered from the war when he had stumbled into a cramped German dug-out in which all the inhabitants had been killed a few moments before. He had never noticed it on the battlefield, but in a confined space, it was unmistakeable.

He pushed open the door to the small bedroom – the one he assumed had had its window broken, and then recoiled in horror at what he saw.

'Should we not have waited a bit longer, sir?' asked Nesbitt.

McLeish started the engine of the police car, which was parked by the side of the road at the meeting place which had been arranged with Sir John.

'They've had long enough,' he said.

He gazed out across the empty moorland stretching away on all sides. 'An hour and nobody come back – that suggests to me either they havenae found Shaw, or…'

Nesbitt swallowed. 'Or they have, and he's killed them.'

'Don't be so dramatic,' chided McLeish. 'More like they've cornered him and can't risk leaving him. Remember they're armed so they'll not be attacked easily.'

'I suppose so,' said Nesbitt. 'Best get help then?'

'Aye. We'll away to the local police house. No, wait – we'll stop off at Colonel Shaw's place first. It's on the way, and there's just a chance this minister's come back that way. There's mebbe also a telephone there, if we can get inside.'

The police car speeded up as McLeish steered it on to the road leading to Auchentorrin Lodge; Nesbitt tugged at his collar nervously. He was beginning to long for his comfortable, safe desk in Inverness, and to wish that he had never got involved in all this.

McKechnie forced himself to look in the small bedroom again. It was a scene of carnage the like he had not witnessed since the war, and had no wish to witness again. He realised something terrible must have happened in the room – somebody, perhaps, had tried to escape out of the window and been shot in the process. There were clear signs of struggle. Had it been Shaw they were after? His mind raced as he tried to decide what to do. He realised he must now call the police, as soon as possible.

He turned to go but then heard a faint sound from the floor; a low, keening sound, almost like an injured animal. Cautiously he stepped into the room and realised it was coming from one of the bodies on the floor.

It was a woman, and she was barely alive. He propped his rifle against the bed and knelt down. She stared at him, her breath coming in short gasps. He could tell from one glance that she had only moments to live. It was hopeless to attempt to help her.

'Listen to me,' said McKechnie, gently but firmly. 'Where's Reverend Shaw?'

The woman looked at him blankly.

'Shaw. The minister. The priest. *Quickly.* You've not long to live.'

'He...jumped,' croaked the woman.

'And then where did he go?'

'*...a alerget pe deal...*'

'English, please. Say it in English.'

'He ran...*deal*...up the hill...to where there is...*o cabană*...a small house.'

'You're sure?'

'I saw...through the window...when the others left. I try...to get help, but nobody comes.'

'Where did the others go?'

'I think...they follow him...'

'Very well. Try to be still now. Say a prayer if you can.'

McKechnie took her hand and leaned close to her.

'Do you repent of your sins?'

The woman tried to speak but then her eyes glazed over.

'Make a sign,' urged McKechnie.

He felt a faint pressure from the woman's hand, and he hurriedly pronounced the absolution from the Book of Common Order which he knew from memory. The woman's grip relaxed and her face took on the waxy pallor of death.

He sighed, then stood up and looked out of the window. Beyond the large hedgerow on the boundary of the house, he could see a little track which led up the hill; in the distance there was a tiny wisp of smoke. He knew the house…what was the man's name…Clelland. Perhaps Shaw had sought refuge there? If so, his life could be in danger at this very moment.

McKechnie bounded down the stairs and within a few moments his little car was bumping and swaying its way along the track which led up the hillside.

A mile or so away, Shaw was still pedalling frantically along the road to Aviemore; he could hear the roar of Sir John's Bentley coming ever closer. Escape was impossible; the ground rose up about 18 inches on either side of the road, and the land all around was tussocky, damp peat bog.

If he tried to leave the road he would become a sitting target. The only thing he could do, he realised, was to keep moving in the hope he could somehow evade his pursuers. But how?

He looked round and the Bentley was upon him; it seemed impossibly near, the large headlamps staring blankly at him like the eyes of a killer shark. Shaw swerved to the left, the wheels of the bicycle skimming the bank at the side of the road.

The car fell back, then tried to ram him; he felt the mudguard brush his leg and he braced himself for an impact. Then he heard the wheels squeal in protest as they touched the side of the road and the car momentarily lost balance.

No further approach came, but he dared not look round. Then the engine roared once more and from the corner of his eye he saw the car on his right hand side; Keller was leaning out and trying to aim a rifle at him.

'Keep level!' shouted the surgeon to Sir John.

While Keller inexpertly fumbled with the bolt of the rifle, Shaw realised he had just one chance; if he failed he would be left for dead by the roadside. As Keller aimed, he swerved his bicycle towards the car and with his right hand, shoved the barrel of the rifle backwards into the vehicle.

Keller fired, and a hole appeared in the canvas roof of the car. Sir John then tried to ram him; Shaw lost his balance and felt the bicycle give way underneath him as the front wheel made contact with the wire rim of the Bentley's nearside wheel.

He knew from experience of cycling on country roads in winter to let himself go limp before his body made contact with the road; he hit it on his flank and rolled over. Before he could get up, the Bentley swerved into a ditch at the side of the road and slid to a halt. He lay on the road, dazed, and heard muffled shouts and the grinding sound of a starter motor.

He picked himself up and glanced briefly at the bicycle; its front wheel was buckled and it would be impossible to ride it again. He began a limping run along the road. He zigzagged as he ran, expecting Keller to start shooting, but no firing came. For a moment he could not think why; surely he was a clear target?

Then he realised why. Up ahead on the road about a quarter a mile away was a group of men on bicycles; they slowed and turned off the road at a junction. Sir John, he assumed, would not risk firing with witnesses that close by.

Shaw then heard a strange sound, and wondered if his hearing had been affected by the fall. It was a rising and falling sound, like the sound of waves on the seashore, but melodic, with a call and response. It was singing! He squinted and realised there was a low stone building on the brow of the hill ahead.

It must be, he realised, the chapel that Clelland had mentioned. He was almost there – almost at the telephone. The thought spurred him on and he picked up his pace, his lungs aching.

Then he heard the sound of the Bentley behind him and he steeled himself for an impact, but none came. The car raced past him and disappeared over the brow of the hill.

Puzzled, Shaw slowed down to a brisk walking pace. Had they gone? Or were they about to unleash some new fiendish plan?

He did not have to wait long to find out. As he approached the chapel he saw the telephone box nearby, with its white walls and 'OPEN ALWAYS' sign on its red-painted window frame.

Sir John's car was parked by the box; and the baronet stood outside it. In one hand he held a loose cable protruding from the back of the kiosk; in the other he held a pair of pliers. He waggled both hands at Shaw, and smiled.

Shaw tried to think. He could not summon help and could not possibly hope to outrun them. He heard the strange, rising and falling singing from the nearby chapel. Whilst he was near there, he realised Sir John and Keller would not dare fire; it would attract too much attention.

The only way they could stop him would be if they could get close enough to inject him with some form of drug which would send him mad. He looked at the two men, who were walking slowly toward him, and then at the chapel.

He heard again the strange rising and falling sound of unaccompanied voices singing; he suddenly recognised it; it was the hymn *All people that on earth do dwell,* sung to the tune known as the Old Hundredth. As the singing drifted across the moorland on the breeze he could even make out some of the words:

> O enter then His gates with praise
> Approach with joy His courts unto…

Some instinct within him spoke suddenly; 'go there'. He needed no further encouragement, and sprinted towards the squat, grey building. What on earth, he wondered as he ran, would he do when he got there?

If he told the congregation what was going on, Keller and Sir John would step in and with the aid of drugs and their no doubt convincing arguments, he would be made to appear a madman.

He suspected also they would try to pin the blame for the deaths of Lewin, McVitie and Miss Petrescu on him; perhaps even the death of his own uncle. He shuddered; all he could do was play for time.

As he neared the chapel door he slowed down, trying to regain his breath. If he could stay in there long enough, they could not approach him; after the service ended, of course, they would still be there, but he would be able to at least rest and think a while before the next assault.

He looked round and saw that Sir John and Keller had returned to the car and were driving slowly alongside him to the chapel. They parked some distance away; Sir John remained in the car but Keller walked slowly from the vehicle to the chapel, stopping before he reached the door. He must have left his rifle in the car, and instead stood with his hands in his coat pockets, watching the entrance.

Shaw opened the door of the chapel which led into a little vestibule. Instantly a little man with a bald head and a drooping moustache, wearing an ill-fitting suit and a shirt with a large, old fashioned collar, jumped to his feet.

He looked Shaw up and down. 'Are ye the minister from England?' he asked in amazement.

Shaw was momentarily taken aback, and answered before he had time to even consider the question.

'Erm...yes!'

'The Lord be thanked,' said the bald man earnestly. He took Shaw's arm firmly and led him into the chapel. The little building, plain and whitewashed, was packed out with people, men and women and a few children, all soberly dressed as if for a funeral.

Some sort of official stood at the front waving his arms like a conductor as the congregation launched in to another *acapella* verse of the hymn Shaw had heard outside.

'My name's Lovat,' whispered the bald man. 'Elder of the congregation. We got word on the telephone outside that your train from Carlisle was delayed and you might not make it. But the Lord looks after his own, and is mightily to be praised!'

The man was leading Shaw gently but firmly down the aisle of the chapel; he saw heads turn and eyes peruse him over raised hymn books. Carlisle – of course!

Shaw remembered what McKechnie had said, that the chapel was having a special service led by a guest preacher from England. They thought it was him!

Before he could even think about explaining, Shaw was led into a little wooden pulpit at one end of the chapel, occupying the place where the altar was in Shaw's church. It was raised up and the only ornate thing in the whole building. Lovat smiled and shut the little gate in the side of the structure behind Shaw. The singing ended, and Lovat cleared his throat.

'Brothers and sisters, we have been blessed,' he announced. 'Contrary to my previous announcement, the sermon will go ahead as planned.' He smiled and nodded at Shaw, and sat down in the front pew. Shaw then looked down at the congregation staring up at him, his mind a blank.

Nesbitt staggered back from the doorway of the small bedroom at Auchentorrin Lodge, his handkerchief clutched to his mouth.

He took a deep breath and turned to face McLeish. 'I wasnae expecting anything like that.'

'No,' said McLeish, who was surveying the corpses in the room impassively. 'We came in looking for a telephone and this is what we found. Thoughts?'

'What do you mean, sir?'

'What do you think happened?'

'It must have been Shaw. Gone mad, like the doctor and Sir John said.'

'Mebbe something like that,' said McLeish. 'They may have been trying to subdue him and then he killed them and jumped out of the window.'

'Sir John said he came running from the house, or something like that,' said Nesbitt. 'But who are they?'

'Servants maybe,' said McLeish. 'The woman's dressed like some sort of nurse. But there's something else. Sir John said Shaw had a shotgun, but that's a pistol shot wound.'

He pointed at the prone body of the woman on the floor, and then gingerly lifted aside the curtain which partly covered the man lying by the window. His midriff was soaked in blood which was beginning to congeal.

'He's been shot with a pistol too, I'd say,' said McLeish.

'God's sake, Shaw's armed to the teeth,' said Nesbitt.

'Could be,' said McLeish. 'Right. There's nothing we can do here the now. Come on.'

'Where are we going?' asked Nesbitt as he hurried down the stairs after McLeish.

The Inspector reached the car and jumped in, followed by Nesbitt. He gunned the engine and the vehicle shot forward in a spray of gravel on to the road.

'We're away to the police house in the village,' said McLeish. 'Once we're there, you explain things to the bobby. See if he knows anyone wi' a shotgun in the area, and requisition it. Then get every man you can find in the streets to form a search party. Go into the pub if they've got one. If there's any grumbling, offer a shilling per man. I'll vouch for it.'

'Right,' said Nesbitt, the colour beginning to return to his face after the recent shock of seeing three corpses. 'And what'll ye be doing, sir?'

McLeish took a bend in the road at dangerously high speed, the wheels of the car briefly losing their grip on a patch of mud. He righted the wheel and turned momentarily to face Nesbitt.

'I'll be on the telephone to the Chief Constable to get every spare man from Inverness down here in motor cars and on the train. Armed as well. I'm going to recommend they take no chances and shoot to kill this man Shaw if they have to.'

Shaw could not remember a time when he had faced so many expectant faces in a church; there were seldom more than thirty people at most of his services in Lower Addenham. For a moment he thought of coming clean, but then heard the door at the rear of the church open; he looked up to see Keller enter.

The man looked around awkwardly. A steward by the door tapped him on the shoulder and pointed to his hat, which he removed self-consciously. He was then shown to a pew at the back of the church. Thank the Lord, thought Shaw. He cannot possibly hope to get near me. I am safe, if only for a brief time.

He then realised he had to say something. But what? His sermons were always carefully planned, with quite a lot of academic research and analysis of the text. Not only had he not prepared for this, but he did not even have a text.

There were one or two coughs and mutters from the congregation. He bowed his head and intoned his usual opening invocation.

'May the words of my mouth and the meditations of my heart be acceptable in Thy sight, O Lord our strength and our Redeemer. Amen.'

There were no corresponding 'amens' from the congregation. He looked up and noticed one or two glares from the watchers in the pews. Had he done something wrong? Perhaps the Old Covenanters had some other form of words before a sermon. He realised he knew very little about the Scottish churches and absolutely nothing about this particular denomination.

Frantically he wracked his brains for a text. Then his eyes landed on a board on the wall to his left; it listed the Ten Commandments and was painted in the style of the early nineteenth century. That must surely be safe ground, he thought, and took a deep breath.

'My sermon is taken from…' He paused. What on earth was the text? Exodus something…he looked down and noticed more glares this time, as one or two of the congregation turned and whispered to their neighbours.

'Exodus chapter twenty,' he suddenly said with confidence after noticing it in smaller print at the bottom of the board on the wall. '"And God spake all these words, saying…Thou shalt have no other gods before me."'

He detected a sense of relaxation in the congregation as he began to speak. It was if he was acting as a conduit for something else that spoke through him, rather than himself struggling to find the words.

'How many of us here can put his hand on his heart and truly say, "I have no other gods"?'

There was silence; he had their attention now. He wondered if, being a dissenting church, they might expect a little more enthusiasm in a sermon than was common in the Church of England.

It was vital, he realised, that he held their attention for as long as possible, so that he could find some means of getting away from Keller and Sir John.

He tentatively thumped his fist on the pulpit and raised his voice. '*How many?*'

He noticed some rapt expressions down in the pews; he decided to continue in the same vein. Before he spoke again, he banged the pulpit again, harder this time.

'How many of you can say they have kept all of the Ten Commandments; *look*, they are there on the wall next to me.'

He pointed dramatically at the board and then turned to the congregation. 'How many? Let me tell you…brethren and, erm, sisters… not one of you. *Not one!*'

He paused for a moment and risked a look at Keller, who glared at him and then raised his arm. He looked at his wrist-watch and then pointedly at Shaw as he crossed his arms.

'Why,' continued Shaw, 'even in this room there may be one of you who has committed the most vile act; the most heinous sin. The most dastardly breaking of the commandments, which all lead to the same end; that you worship other gods!'

Shaw smiled inwardly as he saw several members of the congregation look uncomfortably at the person next to them, and then back at him.

He looked directly at Keller. 'But there is a message for you, indeed, for all of us, miserable offenders,' he said, pointing with his index finger at the people in the pews.

He could scarcely believe that such a simplistic and improvised sermon was holding their attention, but it seemed to be working. He decided there was a chance, perhaps a very slim one, that he could prick the conscience of Keller.

He looked directly at the man and continued.

'Yes, my dear brothers and sisters. There is a message of hope and salvation to the vilest offender. Repent, and be forgiven. Fall down on your knees and beg His forgiveness, or face…erm…face His wrath at the, ah, the terrible day of judgement.'

Shaw paused and looked at Keller, but the man simply stared impassively at him; then Shaw saw his eyes flick to his right. Shaw followed his gaze and looked through the clear leaded window on his left.

Sir John was leaning against the bonnet of the Bentley with his arms folded. Shaw realised the man could see both the front and back of the chapel; escape would be impossible. He had to think!

'A moment of silence, brethren,' he said, 'while we reflect on my words…'

The congregation bowed their heads. Shaw thought frantically. There must be a way – but how? There were no other cars parked nearby, so he could not get away by begging for a lift. The congregation had presumably arrived on foot, or perhaps by bus.

If he tried to get away by either of those methods after the service, Keller and Sir John would surely have him. He looked at Sir John again, and then his gaze lighted on something leaning against the wall outside. It was a motorcycle.

Shaw raised his head and smiled. He continued for as long as he could with his improvised sermon, thumping the pulpit and raising his voice in the manner of some Methodist clergy he had seen; it seemed to go down well but after 25 minutes or so he realised he could play for time no longer; he had to act soon.

After a brief extempore prayer he stepped down from the pulpit; there was a final hymn and then a retiring collection. Without waiting to be asked, Shaw stepped into the little vestry at the rear of the church, closing the door behind him.

Lovat burst in to the little office a moment later, his arms laden down with velvet collection bags.

'Well done, Mr Fenwick, well done!' he exclaimed. 'By the looks of it we've had the best collection in years. Some of the congregation want to shake your hand – they're even asking if you'll be back to preach on the Sabbath. We're used to our sermons a wee bit dryer here, but they definitely liked it!'

'Thank you, but my name is not Fenwick,' said Shaw.

'But surely you are,' said Lovat in a confused voice. 'Mr Walter Fenwick, of the Free Dissenters Chapel in Carlisle. The English branch of our denomination. I have your letter here somewhere.'

Shaw shook his head. 'My name is Reverend Lucian Shaw.'

'Then what are you doing here?' asked Lovat.

'I was...sent here in his place,' replied Shaw.

'Aye well, at least someone *was* sent,' said Lovat with a shrug of his shoulders. 'You made quite the impression. Come and meet a few of the folk in a moment.'

'One moment, if I may,' said Shaw, moving to the door.

He opened the door of the vestry a crack and looked out. There was a hubbub of conversation as the congregation, in high spirits, milled around the central aisle of the chapel. His eyes widened in alarm as he saw Keller impatiently trying to move through the crowd towards him.

He closed the door and discretely turned the key in the lock while Lovat placed the collection bags in a cupboard in a corner of the room.

Through a small window partially obscured by a lace curtain, Shaw could see Sir John watching the people coming out of the chapel carefully, while drumming his fingers on the roof of his car.

'I would like to meet your congregation,' said Shaw, 'but I am afraid I am in rather a hurry. In fact, it is imperative that I leave this instant.'

'Oh?' replied Lovat, his moustache seeming to droop with disappointment. 'That's a pity. Have you another engagement?'

Shaw wondered momentarily whether to tell the whole truth to Lovat, but decided, as with Clelland, it was too much of a risk. Instead, he pointed out of the window.

'Do you know that man?' he asked Lovat.

The elder peered through the window. 'Him? Yes, I think so. He's the laird over at Inverbrodie, is he not?'

'That's right. Sir John Debayle-Bradley. I'm afraid he objects to my presence here.'

'Does he indeed?' asked Lovat suspiciously, turning away from the window. 'On what grounds, may I ask?'

'We have had a…disagreement on…moral matters. He has already tried to prevent me from preaching here and I should like to avoid him. If he approaches there is liable to be a scene.'

'Don't say any more, Mr Shaw,' said Lovat, raising his hands. 'I think I understand. And I'm not having it. We Scots don't take kindly to the gentry – especially not the English gentry, as I think he is – coming here and interfering in our religious freedoms. We didn't allow even King Charles the First to do that so we certainly won't allow the likes of Sir John High-and-Mighty to either.'

Shaw heard a rattle at the door; Lovat went to open it.

'Do not open it, please,' said Shaw quickly, trying to sound calm. 'That will be Sir John's assistant. I fear he may attempt to give me…something to permanently deprive me of my right to preach.'

'A writ of some sort, you mean?' said Lovat, angrily. 'I've heard of such things. This is disgraceful. This door's staying locked,' he added, more quietly. There was a murmur of conversation outside and the rattling stopped. 'What can I do to help?' asked Lovat.

'Could you kindly inform me,' said Shaw, 'who owns that rather splendid looking motorcycle outside. A Triumph Model H, I believe.'

'I can do that easily,' said Lovat. 'She's mine! I can see you know a bit about motor bicycles. Some of the other elders think it's sinful to ride such a machine, but I cannot see anything in scripture to forbid it. Can I offer you a lift?'

'That is most kind,' said Shaw, as he looked again out of the window cautiously. 'If you could take me to the next town – Aviemore, I believe, – to a telephone kiosk, I shall be able to…make some necessary arrangements.'

'There's a telephone box in the road outside,' said Lovat. 'Could you not use that?'

'I am afraid Sir John has disabled it.'

'Disgraceful,' said Lovat with disgust. 'Damaging government property as well? Right, it'll be an honour to take you to Aviemore.'

He went to the door leading into the church, removed the key from the lock and crouched down. He peeped through the keyhole then stood up and faced Shaw.

'Is the other party a well dressed gent, with eyeglasses?'

'That is he.'

'He's still waiting there. I don't like the look of him much. Saw him when he came in; he kept his hat on and looked like he'd never seen the inside of a kirk before.'

'Without wishing to sound uncharitable, he is a most disreputable person,' said Shaw.

'The last time anybody tried to stop a preacher in this kirk,' growled Lovat, 'was in 1847 when the elders of the New Covenanters tried to shut down the Old Covenanters. It's all written down in the Sessions books. Do you know what they did to them?'

'I dread to think,' said Shaw.

'They threw stools at their heads and ran them out o' the town,' said Lovat, quivering with anger. 'I'd like to do the same the now, but as the scripture says, "a soft answer turneth away wrath." Come out the back way with me and we'll get on the motorcycle.'

'Ah…I would prefer if you brought the machine round yourself,' said Shaw. 'If I come out with you, Sir John will see me and may…serve me…himself.'

'Of course,' said Lovat. 'Stupid of me. Wait here, Mr Shaw. Keep the back door locked. I'll start her up, bring her round and then you can jump on and we'll be away.'

He took a cloth cap from a peg by the door and then

looked at Shaw. 'Did you not have a hat and coat?' he asked.

'Ah...no,' replied Shaw. 'I was obliged to leave the presence of Sir John rather quickly and had no time to take them.'

'"If a man will contend with thee in judgement, and take away thy coat, let go thy cloak also unto him,"' quoted Lovat. 'You've certainly suffered for the faith. Will you take my hat and coat? You can send them back later by post.' He proffered the garments to Shaw.

'Thank you,' said Shaw, 'but I shall be quite well as I am. It is perfectly warm outside. Please hurry.'

Lovat frowned. 'Very well,' he said, and stepped out of the back door. Shaw breathed a sigh of relief as the door shut behind him. He turned the key in the lock and looked out of the window to see Lovat mount the motorcycle and put on a pair of goggles. Sir John eyed him with moderate interest, but then directed his attention to a group of men walking out closely together from the chapel.

After speaking briefly to a member of the congregation who passed by, Lovat mounted the motorcycle. There was a dry click and then a rattling roar as he kick-started the engine into life, and tip-toed the machine slowly round the side of the chapel to the back door. When Shaw judged the moment was right, he hurled open the door, and jumped on the pillion, gripping Lovat's waist.

He felt his body thrown backwards as the motorcycle set off with alarming speed, turning in a tight loop and passing within inches of Sir John's feet. Shaw managed to regain his balance and risked a look behind him; the Bentley was already in motion, with Keller desperately hopping on and off the running board trying to open the passenger door like some malevolent comedian in a cinema comedy.

Chapter Twelve

Shaw had ridden pillion on a motorcycle before but had never particularly enjoyed the experience. He knew the model of Lovat's machine as he had once considered buying one for his parish visiting; in the end he dismissed the idea.

Motorcycles, he had decided, were too noisy and fast; the pedal bicycle, by contrast, allowed for peaceful contemplation and had the additional advantages of being cheaper and good for one's health.

Now, however, Shaw was grateful for the speed of the powerful machine he was sitting on and the staccato roar of its four-horsepower engine. For a moment he enjoyed the sensation of flying along the long, straight road with the endless moorland on either side; the sun was low in the sky now and darkness could not be far away. If he could get to Aviemore and find a telephone without being seen by his pursuers, all might be well.

Shaw's hopes were confounded when he looked round briefly and saw Sir John's Bentley bearing down on them, travelling at high speed.

He steeled himself for another fall in the road; this time, he thought grimly, such a collision might well prove fatal. But no impact came; the large motor car surged forward and overtook them. A few moments later Shaw realised why.

Lovat turned his head momentarily and shouted. 'I see what he's doing. There's a narrow bridge over the burn up ahead. He's going to try to block us.'

Shaw squinted through the rushing wind and saw that the Bentley had stopped a few hundred yards ahead, where the road rose slightly above the moorland on a stone bridge.

'Don't worry, Mr Shaw,' shouted Lovat merrily. 'There's a little short cut I know that a motor car cannot travel on. But a motorcycle can. It's a drover's track that'll take us over to the old military road on the other side of the valley. That'll put half a mile between him and us.'

The motorcycle slowed down; Shaw looked ahead and saw that the two men had stepped out of the Bentley; both were holding firearms. He swallowed, apprehensively, but Lovat did not seem to notice as he slowed the Triumph down almost to walking pace.

'Here it is,' said Lovat. Shaw was jostled and bumped as the motorcycle left the road; the track was so badly maintained that Lovat could travel only at the speed of a trotting horse. Shaw noticed that the track bent slightly round ahead, so that it was within two hundred yards or so of the road bridge. Horrified, he saw Sir John raise his hunting rifle.

It was all over very quickly. The first shot punctured the front tyre of the motorcycle; Lovat fought with the handlebars, managing to retain control as he brought the machine quickly to a skidding halt, then pushed it back on to its stand.

'A puncture!' exclaimed Lovat without looking round. 'That's all we need!' Then came the second shot, which hit the engine of the motorcycle. Shaw felt a momentary stinging sensation on his shin, as if it had been touched by the very tip of a whip, and heard a sound which reminded him of a pellet gun hitting a metal target at the fairground. The engine cut out as the bullet shattered its workings, and suddenly there was an eerie silence.

Lovat looked down at the engine and then into the distance at the two men by the bridge.

'What in the Lord's name...' he began, but then was thrown backwards into Shaw's arms as a bullet hit him somewhere in the centre of his body. Shaw managed to roll out from under him and dive behind the motorcycle; he could see through the spokes of the rear wheel that Lovat was lying motionless, face down on the ground.

There was another shot; this one ricochetted off the fuel tank then hit a nearby rock with a high-pitched whine. Up ahead he could see Sir John with his dog on a leash, with Keller next to him putting cartridges into his shotgun. Shaw looked around desperately for cover. There was none nearby; all he could see was an area of crags and large boulders a hundred yards or so along the track.

That would have to do, he realised; once they came close enough to him to use a shotgun, it was unlikely they would miss. There was nothing he could do for Lovat, but if he could only elude them for half an hour or so, he thought, it would be dark and he might get away. Without further thought, Shaw sprinted towards the rocks.

Fear propelled him; all pain was momentarily gone from his legs as they pounded across the boggy, tussocky ground. He knew without looking back that Sir John's dog had been unleashed; he could hear the pattering of its feet across the stones. He realised he had one chance – to get on top of the smooth, rounded crags a few yards ahead of him, and hope that the dog could not follow.

A bullet shattered a nearby rock, sending splinters up dangerously close to his eyes, but he ran on; with the last of his strength he was able to jump forwards and hurl himself at the largest of the crags, seizing hold of the top. Pushing with his legs like a rope-climber, he slithered up the crag and rolled on to its concave top, which afforded him a few inches of shallow cover.

Another bullet pinged off the rocks and he slithered round to face his pursuers. The dog, mercifully, was not able to get any purchase on the rock and began jumping up on its hind legs, barking and slavering; with a trembling hand Shaw wiped flecks of the animal's saliva from his face. The sun was now almost obscured behind the distant hills; if he could only hold them off until dark!

He heard a whistle and the dog skittered away; then he lifted his head up slightly and peered over the edge of the rock; out of the gloom came Sir John and Keller. He heard the baronet shout to the dog as he tied its lead to a gorse stump. Then he called out across the moor.

'It's over, Shaw. You can't get away.'

Shaw stayed silent, his head down. He prayed fervently, then looked around for some kind of weapon; anything that might be of use; but the top of the crag offered only a few small stones. He smiled grimly as he thought of the Biblical story of David slaying the giant Goliath with a pebble; somehow he doubted he could improvise a sling with his handkerchief.

'Come down, old chap, there's a good man,' said Sir John amiably. 'Let's discuss it like gentlemen.'

Shaw raised his eyebrows in surprise. Why did Sir John wish to discuss anything now, when he had been quite happy for him to have been killed earlier? Perhaps, he thought, the man was becoming worried and this was a trick to get him out in the open and kill him. Was there a possibility that others were on their way, or was he simply concerned that, as darkness fell, Shaw might escape more easily?

He adjusted his position slightly and saw that Keller was creeping around the other side of the crag, presumably to cut off any escape. All he had left was his power of speech, and he decided to use it to delay as long as possible.

'Why should I trust you?' he called out. 'You wanted me dead earlier.'

'You led us a merry dance, Shaw,' replied Sir John. 'I see you have considerable skill and resourcefulness, not to mention courage under fire. That could be useful to us.'

'Us?'

'There are more of us, you know, in addition to Keller and myself. Men with vision, and the means to carry it out. You could join us.'

There was complete silence, apart from the faint stirring of the gorse bushes in the breeze; then came the sound of Keller's boots squeaking slightly as he crept around the rock. Shaw swallowed. It could not be long before the man was able to climb up one of the nearby crags and fire at him.

'How could you let me join you, with what I know?' Shaw called out.

'You don't know as much as you think you do,' replied Sir John. 'And if you decided to tell anyone that, well, Keller here can always have you committed at any time. Just remember that. But if you do as you are told, well, you could have the world at your feet. You could have anything.'

'If you mean money, I have no need of it,' said Shaw.

'Of course not! I would not insult you with such a proposition. I mean something of…spiritual use. A bishopric. An *arch*bishopric, even. I have connections in the church, you know. Think of the *good* you could do.'

Shaw suddenly saw a passage of scripture in his mind's eye, laid out in large, clear type as if it were in the Bible on the lectern of his own church. The text seemed to be illuminated in the warm glow of the setting sun. It was from the Gospel of St Luke, concerning the temptation of Christ in the Wilderness.

> 'And the devil, taking him up into an high mountain, showed unto him all the kingdoms of the world in a moment of time. And the devil said unto him, all this power will I give thee, and the glory of them…if thou wilt worship me, all shall be thine. And Jesus answered and said unto him, get thee behind me Satan, for it is written, thou shalt worship the Lord thy God, and only him shalt thou serve.'

Shaw blinked and the vision disappeared, the illusory Bible and its lines of print returning to the slab of rock dotted with black moss in front of him.

'I can't hear anything, Shaw,' shouted Sir John. 'This is your last chance. Come down and you can have whatever you want. Stay there, and Keller will shoot you like a dog.'

Shaw looked round to see Keller standing a few feet away on a nearby crag, his shotgun pointed straight at him. The man could not fail to hit him at such a close range.

Slowly, Shaw pulled himself to his feet and raised his hands.

'I should like to answer your proposal,' he said.

'Good man,' called out Sir John, who was now standing just a few feet away at the foot of the crag. 'I knew you'd see sense.'

'Oh, I have seen more than sense,' said Shaw. 'I have seen a vision. But not the type of vision I think you have in mind.'

'I am open to offers,' said Sir John. 'Within reason.'

'I decline your offer,' said Shaw simply. 'I do however ask that you administer the *coup de grace* rather than Mr Keller. I fear he is not much of a shot.'

Sir John's eyebrows were raised briefly in surprise, but then his face became impassive again; he uttered a low chuckle. Somehow, it was the most sinister sound Shaw had ever heard.

'You're a damned fool, Shaw. Martyring yourself for a non-existent cause.'

'One day we shall both know if what you say is true,' said Shaw, calmly.

'Oh, spare me that rot! You're a throwback, Shaw. A Victorian irrelevance. Even a century ago your church was dying. Your god's had his day. Now it's the time for mine.'

Sir John stepped closer and raised his rifle; Shaw looked him in the face, and noticed a twitch of unease in the man's eyes. He wondered if he had it in him to kill in cold blood.

'And who is your god, may I ask?' said Shaw. 'Money, I suppose. Or power.'

'I'm my own man, Shaw. I don't need idols, like your sort do.'

Shaw could not help smiling. 'At least tell me why. What was it all for? The murders, the deception?'

'If you're going to be up before the pearly gates,' said Sir John, 'then no doubt you'll hear all about it there so I won't waste time telling you. Get on your knees,' he ordered. 'Your head's too far away from up there.'

There was the sound of a dog barking from fifty yards or so away, and Sir John turned. 'Quiet Blucher!' he shouted, and the animal fell silent. 'Damned dog,' he said under his breath, and then looked up at Shaw again.

Shaw was about to comply but something made him look round slightly. Keller was no longer covering him but lay slumped face down on the crag, the shotgun lying next to him, its barrel broken open to reveal two empty chambers.

'What the devil…?' said Sir John, swinging to his left.

Without thinking, Shaw aimed a kick at the man's head, but he was too far away, and the tip of his shoe only clipped the side of Sir John's ear. The blow was sufficient, however, to knock the man off balance and he staggered backwards several feet, still holding his rifle. Then there was a loud report to Shaw's right, and he looked down to see a man pointing a smoking rifle at Sir John.

It was McKechnie.

'Up on your feet,' he barked, 'and drop your weapon.'

A low, guttural laugh came from Sir John's throat as he stood up; a small rosette of black blood had begun spreading from his ear where Shaw had kicked him. Shaw shivered; it was as if the sound came from the very depths of hell itself.

'I said drop your weapon,' roared McKechnie.

'I…shall do no such thing…' said Sir John, catching his breath as his laughter subsided. He raised his rifle and pointed it at McKechnie's midriff.

'Don't think I won't shoot you down like the mad dog you are,' said McKechnie.

'Indeed?' said Sir John. 'I take it you've killed Keller already.'

'No. But he won't be any use to you for a wee while.'

'I don't think you're going to kill me either. I don't think you've got it in you. What sort of man of God would that make you?'

'I've killed men before' replied McKechnie impassively. 'Braver ones than you, and men that were fighting for the love of their country, not to fill their own pockets.'

'Perhaps,' said Sir John. 'But you'll find it rather hard to do that with a rifle you haven't loaded.'

'What are you talking about?' demanded McKechnie.

'A good bluff, but I do know about guns, old chap,' said Sir John, gesturing with his rifle.

'You've just discharged that weapon without reloading it,' he continued. 'By the time you've worked the bolt again, I shall have sent you to the same place I shall send Shaw a moment later. Cheerio.'

Sir John raised his rifle and McKechnie's hand moved to the bolt of his own weapon, but it was too late to stop him. Sir John fired, but in the moment he did so, a black shape launched itself at the baronet, forcing the man to the ground. His limbs flailed as he dropped his rifle.

In the gathering gloom Shaw could not see clearly what the black shadow was that had fallen upon him, but then a bony white fist was raised and plunged down into Sir John's face.

Sir John reeled, but then threw the figure aside and leaped to his feet, pulling an automatic pistol from his pocket. In that instant, McKechnie rammed home the bolt of his rifle, took aim and fired.

Sir John was thrown backwards, the pistol dropping from his hand, and then he fell to the ground and moved no more. The dark figure got to his feet and faced them.

Shaw's eyes flitted from the man to the moorland, where he saw a line of figures walking slowly towards them; he realised they were policemen. They were led by a man in a raincoat and trilby hat. A whistle was blown and the man's voice rang out clearly in the still air.

'Police. Everybody stay exactly where you are.'

Shaw did not recognise the man's face, but knew him by his voice; it was Inspector McLeish, the one who had called at Auchentorrin Lodge.

McKechnie looked at the policemen and then back at the figure who had lunged at Sir John.

'For the Lord's sake, man,' said McKechnie angrily, 'I told you to stay in the car.'

Shaw blinked and looked again at the figure.

Incredulously, he spoke the man's name slowly.
'Uncle James!'

'There's still so much I don't understand,' said Shaw, as he sat in his uncle's drawing room with a large glass of whisky.

The police had finally departed. The last few hours had been a blur; what seemed like hundreds of men with cars, horses and dogs approaching them over the moors with lighted torches.

Then had followed relentless questioning from McLeish as well as various other policemen, lots of note-taking and even threats of imprisonment before some semblance of the truth could be established to the satisfaction of all parties.

Once the bodies had been removed from the bedroom of Auchentorrin Lodge, Shaw, his uncle and McKechnie had finally been left alone, albeit with the promise of further interviews the following day.

'It's hardly surprising,' said the Colonel. 'This is the first chance we've had of a proper chat. Are they all gone?'

'The police, you mean?' said McKechnie, who stared gloomily into the flickering fire, turning a glass of whisky in his hands. 'Aye, that's the last of them gone ten minutes back.'

'I was a fool not to have suspected Sir John earlier,' mused Shaw gloomily. 'He even told me when we first met that he was due to meet someone on the train from London – that, presumably, was Lewin, but the man never showed up because he must have had to leave the train after murdering Moffat. I think he let that slip because he did not realise who I was. Or perhaps he did, and was simply toying with me.'

'He was clever, my boy, clever, said the Colonel. 'But I expect the first thing you wish to know is why I am still alive.'

'I did wonder,' said Shaw. 'I was led to assume you were at the bottom of a peat bog.'

The Colonel laughed. 'The old Boer trick worked then.'

'Old Boer trick?' asked McKechnie.

'Heard about it when I was out in South Africa,' said the Colonel. 'Never tried it; not much chance when I spent most of my time behind a staff desk in Mafeking.' He tapped his leg at the knee. 'This game leg made sure of that.'

'What did you do?' asked Shaw.

'I managed to get away from the house, and did my best to run to the station. That Keller fellow and Sir John had been staying up half the night drinking at my house, and so came after me with that hell-hound of a dog in tow.'

'Go on,' said Shaw.

'I got to the bottom of the hill and realised I was never going to make it to the station. But then I thought of something. What they didn't know was that I had an old bird hide down there.'

'A what?' exclaimed Shaw.

'A bird hide,' said the Colonel, smiling. 'Built it years ago so I could watch the birds on the moor without being observed. Completely hidden in the crags. I keeled over and must have passed out for a moment – that probably saved my life as they couldn't see me to shoot at – and when I came to, I remembered it was nearby.

'I practically had to drag myself along the ground, but managed to get in it without being seen. Just before I did,

I carried out the old Boer trick of throwing my hat and shoes on the bog, to make them think I'd drowned in it. The dog nearly got me but in the end he gave up because he couldn't see me.'

'Of course,' exclaimed McKechnie. 'I remember you mentioned you had a place for watching birds down there. I should have remembered.'

'No reason why you should have, old boy,' said the Colonel. 'Wouldn't have done any good anyway. I didn't stay there long after Keller and Sir John left anyway.'

'What happened then?' asked Shaw.

'I managed to fish out my hat and shoes and walked in the bally damp things two miles over the valley to my little cottage, a shack, really. It's up in the hills, near another bird watching spot. What they call a but-and-ben.'

'I'm aware of the expression,' said Shaw. 'But why did you not go straight to the police?'

'How could I?' asked the Colonel. 'I had no real evidence of what they were planning, and I knew with one jab from one of Keller's filthy needles they could turn me into a gibbering wretch and have me committed to an asylum. That's exactly what they would have wanted – for me to bring the police round and then get that poison into me when nobody was looking.'

Shaw nodded. 'That tallies with what they told me about their methods. But why did they not simply inject you with the drugs and then have you committed?'

'I would have been no use to them, dear boy. You cannot commit someone and then have free rein over his financial affairs. Courts have to be involved and so on. You can only do it if you have power of attorney, and I refused to grant it to them.'

'What happened after you got to the but-and-ben?' asked McKechnie.

'I stayed up there for a day or so and tried to get in touch with Moffat, the man I'd employed to find out a bit more about Lewin and his crowd.'

'But you could not get in touch, because Moffat was dead,' said Shaw.

'Yes, I know that now,' said the Colonel sadly. 'I only found out when I managed to telephone his landlady from the telephone box near the cottage. I was in something of a funk for a day or so, wondering what to do. We old chaps get like that. I would have made a firm decision when I was in the army and had a company of men behind me, but now…well, I don't seem to have the resolve I used to. And I don't mind admitting, Lucian, I was scared stiff.'

'That is completely understandable, uncle,' said Shaw.

'It was then I decided the only chance I had was to get McKechnie's help,' said the Colonel. 'I had to go to his house like the proverbial thief in the night, in case the place was being watched. He nearly shot me as a burglar.'

'Nonsense,' scoffed McKechnie. 'You were never in any danger.'

'How did you find me?' asked Shaw.

McKechnie took a sip of his whisky and poked the fire. 'When your uncle told me what was going on, I drove us as fast as I could to Sir John's house. But his butler must have been told to keep quiet because he said Sir John was out. So we drove to the Colonel's house and that's when we found the bodies.'

'That, alas, was my fault,' said Shaw. 'They turned on each other. I suspect partly due to my attempts to sow mistrust amongst them.'

'Don't be ridiculous,' chided McKechnie. 'It wasn't your fault they decided to kill each other. You did what you had to do. You're just lucky that old window was rotten.'

'But how did you know where I had gone?' asked Shaw.

'The woman – what was her name now?' said McKechnie.

'Miss Petrescu,' replied Shaw.

'Aye, her,' said McKechnie. 'She was still alive. Just. With her dying breath she told me you'd run away up the hill to Clelland's cottage.'

'Perhaps she repented, at the last,' mused Shaw.

'I think she did,' confirmed McKechnie. 'Clelland told me what had happened, and that you were on the way to the telephone box up the valley. After that we asked at the Covenanter's kirk, and one of the elders said you were away to Aviemore on a motorcycle.'

'Of course,' said Shaw. 'Lovat – the man on the motorcycle – must have mentioned that to the other elder before we left. Such a shame. I left him for dead.'

'You had no choice,' said McKechnie. 'Those two would have killed you *and* him if you'd stayed to help. Anyway, the doctor who tended to him thinks he'll pull through, the Lord be thanked.'

'Amen,' replied Shaw. 'I shall insist on paying for his motorcycle also. At least I left a deposit for Mr Clelland's ruined bicycle – I must not forget to thank him!'

'All in good time, Mr Shaw, all in good time,' said McKechnie. 'Anyway, after that, we spotted you up ahead on the moor, with those two devils after you. I knew it would be fatal to approach directly, so I took the old military road across the valley and parked behind one of the crags. I've had a wee bit of experience in the war of crossing enemy territory unseen, and dealing with armed men without firing a shot.'

'So have I, but you wouldn't let me leave the car,' grumbled the Colonel.

'Och man,' chided McKechnie good humouredly. 'In your day they wore red coats with white hats, and walked slowly towards the enemy like they were going in to bat at Lord's. What would you know about modern warfare?'

'It's a damned good job I *did* get out of that car,' replied the Colonel gruffly.

'Point taken,' said McKechnie. 'I dealt with Keller – knocked him out and disarmed him – and was going to stop Sir John as well when I got interrupted.'

'Interrupted!' barked the Colonel. 'I like that. I saved your skin, padre, and don't you forget it. You owe me a drink or two at the Benmurie for that.'

'I just wish it had not been necessary to kill Sir John,' said Shaw.

'It'll be on my conscience, right enough,' said McKechnie, 'but I trust to the Lord to forgive me. I had no choice.'

'I agree,' said Shaw. 'But now we will never really know what all this was about. If Sir John had stood trial…'

'Keller's pouring his heart out to the authorities, from what I could tell when we were taken to the police house,' said McKechnie. 'We'll get the full story eventually. He was jabbering away to that Inspector McLeish faster than the man could take notes.'

'Trying to save his own skin, the damned wretch,' said the Colonel. 'He'll hang though, you mark my words.'

He then went to the sideboard and fetched a dusty crystal decanter, refreshed the men's glasses with whisky and sat back in his armchair, staring into the fire.

'That gang is responsible for the deaths of at least two people, that we know of,' he said sadly. 'Moffat on the train, and that poor devil of an actor that you told me of, Lucian, who was used as my double. I don't even know his name. I doubt they were the only ones they killed.

'I suspect they have a trail of corpses behind them, from what I heard them talking about. Keller will hang for sure, when it all comes out, which it will.'

'I still don't understand what it was all about,' said Shaw. 'How on earth did you become involved with these people?'

The Colonel sighed and took a large sip of whisky.

'It all started when I got some chaps from Edinburgh University to do some digging on my land. There were some changes to the soil I didn't like the look of. After I received a report from them, I had a knock on the door from that man Lewin and his henchman, McVitie.'

'What did he want?' asked Shaw.

'Wanted to buy my land. Claimed he would give me a good price for it. I said I wasn't interested and shut the door on him. But then the next day he came back, this time with Sir John in tow. It all sounded very generous, but there was something I didn't like about them. That Lewin in particular. Reminded me of the sort of chaps one used to meet in Cape Town, running all sorts of shady deals for both the English and the Boers. I decided to have someone look into their organisation before I went any further.'

'That was Mr Moffat, the private investigator,' said Shaw.

'Correct,' replied the Colonel. 'He did some digging and his initial findings were not encouraging. I asked him to find out a bit more, but before he could reply, that cad Sir John and his minions came back. This time with Keller and Miss, whatshername, Petrescu in tow. Again, they were polite at first, but then it all got a bit heated. Sir John said if I didn't sell up, they'd use the law to get me off the land. Well, I wasn't having a pompous ass like him acting like the lord of the manor and I told them in no uncertain terms to leave.'

'But they came back?' asked McKechnie.

'Didn't need to,' said the Colonel. 'Without me knowing, they slipped something in my drink. I'd been silly enough to offer them all a dram when they came round, and Keller must have poisoned it. I was out like a light for several days and in the meantime, they got rid of Moira – that's my housekeeper – paid her to go and stay with her sister in Glasgow for a week, would you believe it, and started proceedings to take power of attorney over my affairs. They kept me in and out of consciousness for a while, and kept trying to get me to sign things. I signed every one of them "Charlie Chaplin" just to spoil their blasted papers.'

Shaw could not help smiling, despite being horrified at his uncle's treatment. The old man continued talking.

'After a while I realised they'd had enough, and were planning to kill me,' he said in a matter of fact way.

'This old house has all sorts of little quirks and one of them is being able to hear what's going on in other rooms quite clearly in certain spots. So I did a bunk out of the window and ran off. It's only because of the girl – woman, I should say, that I managed it.'

'Miss Petrescu?' asked Shaw.

'That's the one,' replied his uncle. 'She was the only one of them with half an ounce of decency. I didn't get the full picture but I got the impression she wasn't happy about having me bumped off. She didn't have the courage to go to the police but at least I managed to persuade her to get McKechnie here to send you a telegram saying I was at death's door.'

'But was that not taking a big risk?' asked McKechnie. 'What if they'd realised she'd done it?'

'I knew I couldn't risk getting her to send a message saying I was about to be killed,' said the Colonel. 'Besides, she wouldn't have done it anyway. This way if they found out, I could just say I wanted my next of kin near me.'

'With the idea that you would be able to inform me of the criminals' plan when I arrived?' asked Shaw.

'Precisely, dear boy, precisely. I knew you wouldn't let me down, and you didn't.'

'And yet,' said Shaw, 'Miss Petrescu made no attempt to inform me of what was going on.'

'I imagine she never had a chance,' said the Colonel. 'Either Keller or Sir John were always hanging around. I got the impression they did not fully trust her.'

'But why not just ask for me?' demanded McKechnie. 'Why get your nephew all the way up from England when I'm staying only a mile away?'

'Didn't want to trouble you, old boy,' said the Colonel sheepishly. 'I thought you'd think I'd taken leave of my senses. And I thought it might be better if I could get my next of kin here, as he'd have more legal rights.'

'If you knew that I had been summoned, why did you try to escape?' asked Shaw.

'They brought the plan forward. I'd heard them talking, you see. I didn't have time to wait, so I managed to persuade Miss, er, Petrescu, to leave the bedroom window unlocked – they always locked the door and the window, you see. Managed to get some clothes over my pyjamas and I was off.'

The Colonel turned to Shaw. 'So that's my story, but how on earth did you piece together what was going on, dear boy?'

'From what I could gather myself, and what I learned this evening while being interviewed by the police,' said Shaw, 'Moffat had worked out from the names on a letter he had found at Lewin's London office, that Lewin's people – McVitie and Petrescu – were part of a known gang involved in fraudulent land deals. It is quite probable they have killed people before to the same ends. Quite how Keller and Sir John got in with them, we do not know. Sir John claimed to have considerable influence in society.'

'He would have,' said the Colonel. 'The blighter liked to show off about it – typical upstart behaviour – and bragged to me while I was doped about how he and various pals of his were going to have a lot more power in the future. I think he only told me because he had already decided to kill me. Seems he was the type with no loyalty to king or country, or anyone except himself, flitting about the world from one country to the next in the same way you or I move from one room to another in a house.'

'Of course,' said McKechnie. 'He was standing for Parliament. Trying to get more power here, maybe?'

'And that was presumably why they had to bring the plan forward,' said Shaw. 'The General Election is next week.'

'Correct again,' said the Colonel. 'As I understand it – though my mind was a bit foggy at the time – getting my land was all part of the plan – he had to have it before the election in order to make an announcement that he knew would get him elected. Seems he wasn't as sure of his popularity with the voters as he made out.'

'But what announcement?' asked Shaw emphatically. 'Why in the Lord's name was he so keen to get his hands on your land?'

'Aye, I'd like to know that too,' said McKechnie. 'What use would a few boggy acres be to the likes of Sir John?'

The Colonel smiled gently and stood up. He walked to the French windows at the other side of the room. Shaw realised with surprise that it was almost dawn; they had been talking for hours.

'Come outside, Lucian. You as well, McKechnie. I'll show you something.'

Shaw felt terribly tired as they stepped out into the garden, but he knew sleep would be impossible after the events of the previous day. It was chilly, the air damper than before, with the promise of winter in it.

The first light of dawn was tingeing the valley and there was barely any wind, giving the scenery an artificial appearance, as if it were a stage set. There was no movement either, not even a bird or a waving tree. Down in the valley, he saw the first rays of sunlight illuminate the railway line and the distant expanse of Loch Nairn.

'All this down to the railway, and about half a mile on either side of us,' said the Colonel, 'is my land. When I bought it, they were more or less giving it away.'

He opened the ancient, moss-dappled gate at the bottom of the garden and they trudged through to the moorland, their shoes squelching in the peaty mud. Shaw noticed that strange smell once more, and he struggled to place it. For some reason it reminded him of the little garage and blacksmith's shop on the outskirts of his own village of Lower Addenham.

'I first noticed something wasn't right when the habits of the birds changed,' said the Colonel. 'They seemed reluctant to land, as if the place was tainted in some way. That's when I got in touch with a chap I know at Edinburgh University who's a keen bird watcher like me. He got on to the boffins – geologists or what have you – and they had a look and what do you think they found?'

There was a moment of silence, and then McKechnie spoke, his eyes widening.

'For the Lord's sake, of course…it's oil!'

'That explains the smell,' said Shaw. 'I knew I recognised it, but it seemed out of place here.'

The Colonel took a deep breath of air and then chuckled.

'I expect like me you thought oil only came out of the ground in Persia,' he said. 'It seems we have it in Scotland as well, and rather a lot of it.'

'Why was it never noticed before?' asked McKechnie in disbelief.

'No idea,' replied the Colonel. 'The geologists think it might have been some sort of, what do you call it, tectonic movement, that brought it up. They think it's a sort of mother-lode that runs all the way out to sea.'

'And it's all under your land?' said McKechnie.

'Not all of it, but the only bit they can drill into. Enough to make whoever owns it the next Rockefeller.'

'Then why did you not sell?' said McKechnie incredulously.

'Heavens, Padre,' scoffed the Colonel. 'I'm nearly eighty years of age. I've no wife nor children. What on earth would I want it for? To build myself a pyramid like King Tut?'

'I assume Sir John Debayle-Bradley heard of the discovery, and that is when the trouble began,' said Shaw.

'Indeed,' replied the Colonel. 'I had no intention of selling the land and seeing it turned into some blasted hellscape with furnaces and pipes as far as the eye could see,' he said. 'I held fire on the scientists' report, wondering what to do about it, but Sir John must have got wind of it somehow.'

'Keller is connected with Edinburgh University,' said Shaw. 'Perhaps he somehow heard…'

'Something of that sort, I imagine,' said the Colonel, who began tamping tobacco into an ancient, blackened pipe. He lit it and inhaled the smoke hungrily.

'Good Lord, that's good,' he said, between puffs. 'I thought I'd had my last taste of tobacco when those devils got hold of me. Now, where was I?'

'Sir John found out about the oil,' prompted Shaw.

'That's right,' said the Colonel. 'Made me a generous offer. I told him I wasn't interested and liked the land as it was. He got progressively more unpleasant and that just made me dig my heels in more. That's when they drugged me and hatched the plan to force me to sign over the land.'

'But they told me that they had power of attorney over you,' said Shaw. 'Why did they need to force you?'

'Power of attorney, my eye,' said the Colonel. 'That was a ruse to get rid of you. They were planning to get it but didn't have it. I hopped out of the window and they thought I'd drowned in the bog.

'That put them in a tricky position, so they must have come up with the idea of getting that actor chappie you mentioned to impersonate me instead. Then along you came, and fortunately you saw through him.'

'I must confess I was taken in at first,' said Shaw. 'But then it has been some time since I last saw you…'

'No need to apologise, Lucian, dear boy,' said the Colonel, removing his pipe from his mouth and pointing the stem at his nephew.

'These fellows were damned clever, and ruthless with it. The Inspector seems to think Lewin's mob – that Glaswegian guttersnipe and the foreign woman – had been mixed up in this sort of thing before, and that's why poor Moffat had to be killed.'

'All this for money,' said McKechnie, shaking his head.

'Not only money,' replied the Colonel. 'Power. Why do you think Sir John wanted the whole thing signed over to him so quickly?'

'Of course,' said Shaw. 'The General Election. Presumably, a large scale oil pumping operation would create many new jobs. He wanted to announce that before the voting. Good Lord, he even mentioned something important was soon to be announced in the newspapers. He said it to the porter at the station when I arrived.'

'It would turn Inverbrodie into a boom town, like California in the Gold Rush,' said the Colonel. 'Fortunes would be made overnight, jobs for anyone who wanted them. New shops, hotels, all the rest of it. Not just for the town, but the whole county. Imagine the appeal of that to the voters in a slump. He would have been swept in to power without contest.'

'That reminds me of something Sir John said out on the moors yesterday,' said Shaw. 'Do you remember? He said there were more like him. Men with vision, and the means to carry it out.'

'Yes, I heard that,' said the Colonel, his lip curling in disgust. 'When he thought he was going to finish me off and get the land, he subjected me to some of his ideas while I was helpless in bed. I could see the man loved the sound of his own voice and wanted an audience for it. That's why getting elected was just as important to him as the money from the oil.'

'Strange,' said McKechnie. 'I had him down as an English country squire. Interested in shooting and fishing, and not much else.'

'Not him,' replied the Colonel, shaking his head. 'He had no love for this land, nor its people and traditions. The sort of cove who's more comfortable in Monte Carlo than the Moray Firth. It's men like him who are the real power-mad ones, you know. Not these bally fools in Germany and Italy strutting around in flashy uniforms. Because it's men like him who *finance* them, you see. Without the Sir Johns and their filthy lucre, who pays for the uniforms, and the guns, and the tanks?'

Shaw thought for a moment, and recited a quotation he had once read in a newspaper article on finance.

'"I care not what puppet sits on the throne of the British Empire; he who controls money, controls the world."'

'Who said that?' asked the Colonel.

'I've no idea,' replied Shaw. 'Some great banking scion, I assume. It does, sadly, seem rather apposite.'

'I dread to think what Sir John's "vision" for the world was,' mused McKechnie.

The three men fell silent, all thinking on what had been said. The sun was now up, and the wraiths of early morning mist had begun to disappear. McKechnie took his leave, anxious to get back to his wife, leaving Shaw and his uncle to trudge back to the house. Before they reached the back door, Shaw stopped and looked out across the moors.

'I suppose the oil will just continue to ooze from the ground, keeping the birds away,' he said sadly.

'Not a bit of it!' exclaimed the Colonel. 'I've been thinking about that. The geologists said most of the oil could be drained back into the ground, with a just a little taken out from a small pumping station that wouldn't spoil the landscape. In years to come, they think the technology will exist to pump it up from beneath the sea bed, where it won't bother anyone. This way we can dry the land out for the birds, and produce a bit of income too.'

'I thought you said you did not want money,' said Shaw.

'I don't want it for myself, but I do want it for the land,' replied the Colonel, his face glowing with a youthful enthusiasm that had been absent up until now. 'I've a mind to set up a sort of trust. For youngsters, you know, to come camping and watch birds. It'll create a bit of work for the locals too. It will be my legacy.'

'A splendid idea, uncle,' said Shaw.

'Glad you think so. Now, how about a spot of breakfast, before the onslaught of officialdom begins. I imagine the newspaper wallahs will be here on the first train.'

'Yes, thank you,' said Shaw, as they turned to go into the house. Then Shaw paused at the threshold.

'Something troubling you, my boy?' asked the Colonel.

After a pause, Shaw replied slowly.

'Sir John said I was a throwback, and the church was dying. I can't help thinking he had a point.'

'Nonsense, dear boy,' said the Colonel. 'People have been saying the dear old C of E is on its last legs for as long as I can remember, but somehow it still soldiers on.'

'But can it much longer? Can it survive – in a world ruled by the likes of Sir John Debayle-Bradley?' said Shaw doubtfully.

'Listen, Lucian,' replied the Colonel emphatically. 'There are men like you and McKechnie in every town and village up and down the land, across the Empire too, quietly working for good, week in week out. It might sometimes seem as if nobody's listening, but they are, even if it's only once a year at Christmas.

'You're making a difference. There are thousands of you, perhaps hundreds of thousands, and only a few men like Sir John in the world, of any importance. They may be in positions of power – so they think – but power's a drug that addles the brain; they don't have the ear, and the trust, of the people – the ordinary, decent people – in the way chaps like you do.

'All they've got to show for their lives is money – trinkets and baubles, nothing real. In the end it's the common man who wins out against the tyrants. He always does. But he needs encouragement. So keep on, my boy. Keep on.'

Before they entered the house, Shaw took a last look across the valley. A wisp of steam rose in the distance, and he saw a tiny illuminated sliver move closer. It was the night train from London. He felt comforted by the knowledge he would soon be on a similar train, going in the opposite direction, back to a gentler, smaller landscape and the reassurance of home.

Other **Reverend Shaw** books by Hugh Morrison

A Third Class Murder (Reverend Shaw's first case)
An antiques dealer is found robbed and murdered in a third class train compartment on a remote Suffolk branch line. Reverend Shaw is concerned that the police have arrested the wrong man, and begins his own investigation.

The King is Dead
An exiled Balkan king is shot dead in his secluded mansion. Reverend Shaw believes that the culprit is closer than the police think, and before long is on the trail of a desperate killer who will stop at nothing to evade capture.

The Wooden Witness
After finding the battered corpse of a spiritualist medium at an archaeological site on the Suffolk coast, Reverend Shaw is thrust into a dark and deadly mystery involving ancient texts and modern technology.

Murder in Act Three
When village gossip Joan Hexham is killed during an amateur dramatics performance, everyone assumes it is an unfortunate accident – except Reverend Shaw. But can he prove it was murder, before the killer strikes again?

Murder at Evensong
A notorious radical cleric – 'the most hated parson in England' according to the newspapers – falls to his death in Midchester Cathedral. Reverend Shaw is determined to find the assassin, but at what cost to himself?

Published by Montpelier Publishing
Order from Amazon or your local bookshop

Printed in Great Britain
by Amazon